ONE MORE NIGHT

"May I please come in?" Matt asked.

Dorinda stepped out of his way, but didn't move away from the door. He closed it behind him, then faced her.

"I am sorry for letting you walk out of my life ten years ago. When I said I missed you, I really meant it. We grew up together. We were part of each other. I thought it would always be that way. I didn't know what I was giving up and I didn't have the faintest idea how much I was going to miss you."

She felt her anger and tension start to slip away with the sincere apology. This was what she'd been waiting for. Hoping for. "I did," Dorinda said softly. She looked into his eyes. They grew dark as comprehension dawned.

She didn't know who moved in first, but an instant later his arms were around her, and hers were wrapped around his waist. She remembered every time they'd touched like this. Then his lips descended on hers. The feel of his mouth over hers was so familiar. They were a part of each other. They belonged together.

The kiss turned deep and urgent. One of his hands slid up her back to grasp her nape, but she pulled her head back, out of reach of his mouth.

"Matt, you're kissing me as though this will be the last time you'll ever see, touch or taste my lips again."

BOOK YOUR PLACE ON OUR WEBSITE AND MAKE THE ARABESQUE ROMANCE CONNECTION!

We've created a customized website just for our very special Arabesque readers, where you can get the inside scoop on everything that's going on with Arabesque romance novels.

When you come online, you'll have the exciting opportunity to:

- View covers of upcoming books

- Learn about our future publishing schedule (listed by publication month and author)

- Find out when your favorite authors will be visiting a city near you.
- Search for and order backlist books from our line catalog

- Check out author bios and background information

- Send e-mail to your favorite authors

- Join us in weekly chats with authors, readers and other guests

- Get writing guidelines

- AND MUCH MORE!

Visit our website at
http://www.arabesquebooks.com

SOMETHING OLD, SOMETHING NEW

ROBERTA GAYLE

ARABESQUE

BET
BOOKS

BET Publications, LLC
www.msbet.com
www.arabesquebooks.com

ARABESQUE BOOKS are published by

BET Publications, LLC
c/o BET BOOKS
One BET Plaza
1900 W Place NE
Washington, D.C. 20018-1211

First Printing: June, 1999
10 9 8 7 6 5 4 3 2 1

Printed in the United States of America

My thanks to my 'crew,'
Karen O., Laura, Edith,
Bhamati, Kathy, Sammy, Rich,
Eoin

and especially Karyn J.—who inspires me
with her strength and her joy in life.

And let me not forget Kendall—
whose knowledge of professional b-ball was invaluable,
since she went out on a limb and let me document which
teams she picked for the 1999 finals.
Go Knicks!

> Bride, n. A woman with a fine prospect of happiness behind her.
>
> > Ambrose Pierce. *The Devil's Dictionary.*

1.

"Stop worrying, Drin," Gwendolyn ordered. "You're chewing your lipstick off." Dorinda obediently stopped chewing her upper lip and tried to quell the nervousness that gnawed at the pit of her stomach. She looked into her sister's eyes in the mirror and saw herself, with the few tiny differences that only their mother could see. They *looked* exactly alike, from the curve of their eyebrows to their golden brown skin and curly shoulder-length red-brown hair. But there all resemblance ended. Gwen was high spirited, impulsive and gregarious, while Drin knew herself to be cautious and controlled. If this had been Dorinda's wedding day, Gwen would not have had to force a smile as two identical pairs of eyes met in the mirror.

No. But it was Gwen who was getting married. Dorinda tried to relax.

"Mom and Dad promised they'd be good," Gwen said reassuringly.

Dorinda wanted this day to be absolutely perfect for her twin sister, but she had no idea what her parents might be doing in the chapel, and she couldn't help being anxious. They had been known to act inappropriately in this church before. For example, both their pro-choice rally and their gay rights rally had offended much of the congregation. The church board, too, had been somewhat annoyed, since they had voted down both events, unanimously, when Earl and Janine had originally proposed them.

Her cousin, Jo Ann, who was without a doubt the sweetest woman in the world, gave Dorinda a hug. "They're here, aren't they?"

"That's what worries me," Drin said dryly.

Jo Ann gave up on her and turned to Gwendolyn. "They're nice to Herbie," she said. Aunt Josephine, her mother, never approved of any of her boyfriends, so Jo Ann could truly appreciate that kind of tolerance. Gwendolyn gave her cousin a one-armed hug, so she would not wrinkle the creation she was wearing.

"And they look nice," Jo Ann added, looking from Gwen to Dorinda, obviously hoping to apply a little more balm to Drin's troubled spirit.

Earl and Janine had actually dressed for the wedding, to Dorinda's amazement. They didn't wear the typical formal attire, of course. Even Gwendolyn Fay couldn't work miracles—but the father of the bride looked quite presentable in his new grey suit. Herbie bought it for him, and it was an expensive Japanese design, and was loose and comfortable, as well as elegant. Janine had worn a navy blue tuxedo dress. The tuxedo was her idea, but the dress was for her daughter. The thought of their compromise didn't really make Dorinda feel any better. It was too easy a gesture for them to make.

Jo's sister, Jeanine, offered her own brand of comfort. "I'll go take a look out there. I'll make sure they're being good." She went out through the huge oak door, but was back in less than a minute. "Here comes Butterfly McQueen," she announced disdainfully.

The diminutive Rachel, Gwen's college roommate, came

in almost on her heels. "Your mother said no thanks," she reported in her breathiest little girl voice.

"Have you ever known our mother to wear a smidgen of makeup, or seen my dad in a three–piece suit? I don't think so," Dorinda replied.

"And you won't today. They just don't believe in it. And there wasn't anything like enough time to convince them." Gwen shrugged fatalistically.

Rachel ignored them. "Sit down, Gwennie. I'll finish your face now."

Rachel was a wonderful beautician. Her make–up brought out their best features, especially Gwendolyn's. And, therefore, of course, Drin's as well. She and her twin shared the same high foreheads and cheekbones, inherited from a great–grandmother who was Cherokee. Straight noses with only a slight flare to indicate their African heritage gave their faces strength while their mouths were ultra feminine—the bottom lip fuller than the top. Today they even wore the same shade of dark red lipstick.

Dorinda hated wearing the stuff. As flattering as it was, it got on everything, and she was definitely a no–muss, no–fuss girl. But today was her twin's wedding day and as her maid of honor, she had let Rachel do her face in the same tones as her sister, so they looked more alike than ever. Their large almond–shaped eyes gave them a trusting, open look that misled strangers into believing they were easily led, although Gwendolyn was far too headstrong to be at all malleable, and Dorinda knew herself to be too self-protective.

Their appearance, though, gave everyone the impression that they were both sweet and sexy. The latter was the result of their shapely figures, which neither Drin's jeans nor Gwen's power suits could hide. Drin found it annoying to look like a sex kitten when she felt like a nerd. Even Gwendolyn had to admit that it was difficult to get people to take her seriously as a business owner. It was even worse when people saw them together. Most thought identical twins were 'too cute'.

Dorinda remembered the last time she had been here with Gwen, both of them dressed as angels. In those days, cute had been a compliment they accepted gratefully. They'd admired themselves then in the same floor-to-ceiling mirror in front of which Gwen now stood, looking absolutely stunning in her wedding dress. It was a long old fashioned white satin princess design with hundreds of tiny pearl buttons and yards of lace in the train and the veil.

"You look so beautiful," Jo Ann enthused, their cousin's eyes welling with tears as she looked at Gwendolyn. "Just beautiful."

Jeannie caught Drin's eye and raised an eyebrow. "She's crying again." She pressed a tissue into Jo's hand. "Anyone would think you were the bride," she taunted her sister.

"That should do it," Rachel said as she put the finishing touches on Gwen's makeup. She stood back to admire her handiwork. Gwendolyn examined herself critically in the mirror, then she smiled her approval at her old friend, who was also currently her part-time employee at The Beauty Spot, Gwen's salon.

"I love it," she said. "Thank you, Rachel. I look good."

Drin had to agree. Gwendolyn had insisted on having her sister, her two favorite cousins, Jeannie and Jo Ann, and her oldest friend, Rachel, as bridesmaids, and all of the women, Dorinda included, had dropped everything to find and buy the four matching dresses which complemented the wedding dress the bride had accepted as a gift from her mother-in-law.

The decision to dress the bridesmaids in white too had been the subject of a huge fashion debate, but Dorinda had to admit that the effect was incredible. Her sister's ornate gown stood out against the simple A-line sheaths that the other four women wore, and the shiny white fabric brought out the golden tones in her and her sister's skin, and complimented the skin tones of the other three women, which ranged from Jo Ann's creamy tan to Rachel's chestnut hue.

Rachel retouched her lip color, clucking at Drin like a mother hen. "It's going to be a fantastic wedding," she said sweetly.

"And a great party!" Jo Ann added, giving Gwen's shoulders a little squeeze in lieu of the exuberant hug it was clear she was dying to give her, but which might have wrinkled her dress. Rachel got the hug instead, and she returned it enthusiastically.

"I wish your mother had let me do her face, too," Rachel said as she finished with Gwennie's hair, which, as well as the baby's breath, had a spray of miniature white roses tucked into the braids piled high on her head.

"Be grateful they're not handing out pamphlets out there," Gwen said.

Janine and Earl Fay distributed flyers almost every week, urging the churchgoers to write to their elected officials concerning topics from Governor Pataki's cutting spending on relief agencies to Disney's treatment of their workers in Haiti. Half the congregation was probably here hoping to see some kind of fireworks. The Fay children had grown up in this neighborhood and had attended Sunday School at this church. Amazingly enough, her mother and father had talked the pastor into performing the ceremony at St. Francis Church, and with virtually no notice. But Earl had told Gwennie that it didn't mean he condoned the marriage.

To say Janine and Earl Fay were non-conformists was putting it mildly. They had never believed in following the rules, and in Dorinda's considered opinion, her parents were lunatics. Gwen had taken the precaution of having the preacher delete the portion of the wedding vows which involved objections from the audience. Janine and Earl married only after their children were old enough to talk them into it. Since they didn't approve of marriage as an institution, it was anyone's guess as to how her parents might decide to comport themselves at the ceremony. Gwendolyn, as usual, didn't let it bother her. Dorinda crossed her fingers and said a small prayer . . . every five minutes.

"I love your parents," Rachel enthused, "I wish mine were more like them."

"No you don't," Gwen and Drin responded simultaneously. They caught each other's eyes in the mirror and started laughing.

"Don't you love these dresses?" Rachel changed the subject as she arranged sprigs of baby's breath artistically in the hair of each of the bridesmaids.

"I love mine," Jo Ann gushed.

"For once, I have to agree with you," Jeannie said. "I'll actually be able to wear this again. It won't just sit in a closet forever like the other bridesmaid dresses I've had to buy over the years." As the oldest of the group, she had been even more anxious than Dorinda about the costume they'd had only one afternoon to shop for. But even Jeannie had been pleased with the dresses they had found.

Jo Ann surveyed herself happily in the mirror as she put the finishing touches on her own makeup. The deceptively simple dress accentuated the length of the older woman's trim legs, while the tailored waist hid the slight swell of her abdomen. The tailored bodice accentuated the bust, which Drin didn't need, but which was a boon to Rachel, Jeannie, and Jo Ann's less buxom figures. Gwendolyn had done it. The dresses were truly flattering to all four women.

"It's a little, umm, short though," Jo Ann said. Jeannie's younger sister gave Dorinda a demonstrative glimpse of how awkward and uncomfortable she herself must look, as she tried to pull her dress down further over her thighs. Jeannie slapped her sister's hands away. Dorinda made a resolution not to fuss with her hemline anymore. As exposed as she might feel, the style was chic and perfectly acceptable, and pulling at the skirt was not only pointless, it was also less than attractive.

"All set," Rachel announced. "And we do look good, if I do say so myself." Dorinda looked at their reflection in the mirror and was impressed again with the miracle her sister had wrought. Gwennie looked magnificent, of course.

Dorinda marvelled at her sister's ability to plow through the obstacles inherent in organizing a formal wedding in less than a month's time, especially with her parents constantly harassing her. But the wedding would be beautiful, if everything went as planned. Dorinda was hopeful . . . but she wasn't holding her breath.

"What was Janine doing?" she asked Rachel.

"Talking to my mom. Don't worry, everything's going to be fine," she finished, as though that took care of everything.

"Every time someone says 'don't worry,' I get more worried," Drin said perversely.

"That's why I never need to worry about anything," Gwen said. "You take care of that for all of us."

They had never been the kind of twins who knew each other's thoughts, nor did they do everything together. Within the family they each played very different roles, and they each had their own lives, and their own circle of close friends. Dorinda would have given anything to have her crew in the church today. They would have known about, and understood, the confusing mix of emotions she was feeling: love for her sister, hope for Gwen's happiness, anxiety at the prospect of walking down the aisle, and fear that her unconventional family would turn this event into a circus. The wedding had been planned so quickly, though, that her friends had been unable to attend. Drin missed the girls and the support they would have given her, but she knew perfectly well that this was Gwen's day, and the only important thing was that it was her sister's friends who bustled about the small room around them.

Gwen was the epitome of the iron hand in the velvet glove, and she always got her way. Their father had chased away three caterers and two florists with his need to lecture them on the evils of matrimony. Janine said she had meditated on the possibility of a wedding, and had completely adjusted to the idea of seeing her daughter marry, but Dorinda wasn't sure she was going to be able to deal with the reality. But Gwendolyn Fay never brooded over anything. It wasn't her nature. Dorinda was the only cautious one in the family. Her mother had nicknamed her the Worry Wart when she'd been five or six.

"You just don't appreciate them because you're their daughters," Jeannie said.

"So they don't approve of marriage, so what?" Jo Ann defended them.

"I know quite a few women who wouldn't mind their attitude—in fact, they'd welcome it," Rachel interjected. "It's better than being pushed to get married every day of your life, which is what most of us suffer."

"I think it's sweet," Jo finished.

"It's not helpful on your wedding day, though," Gwen said reasonably.

"Believe me," Jeannie said with conviction. "You guys are lucky to have Aunt Nina and Uncle Earl. They've always been there for all of us."

"I know that," Drin said impatiently. Gwen nodded. "But—"

"But nothing," Jeannie said emphatically. "I remember coming to your house after school and having a ball with Aunt Nina. At our house, we always had to play dress up. I think my mom's got pictures of all of us in her wedding dress. But your mother always had some cool project for us to do."

"That's not the way I remember it. I remember you always wanted to eat dinner at your house. And watch television. Which we didn't have."

"I loved the TV," Gwen said.

"But your parents were right. I wouldn't let my kids watch it—if I had kids," Jo Ann said.

"I loved Aunt Jo's soaps," Dorinda tried to explain. "Just like you liked coming to my house, I liked going to your house after school."

"We'll never agree," Gwendolyn said. "This is one of those cases where the grass looks greener on the other side of the fence."

But Jeannie was shaking her head. "Do you remember when my dad died?"

Drin sobered. "Yes." Uncle Stan had been the first person she loved who had died. He'd been in his mid-thirties, and a blood clot in his brain killed him instantly. Jeannie had been nine, Jo Ann only six.

"Aunt Nina was amazing. She was the only grownup who seemed to understand."

"That's because she did," Drin said, nodding agreement.

"Remember the shaving cream?" Jeannie asked, smiling fondly. "Jo Ann and I were smelling Dad's shaving cream—trying to remember him—and your mother came into our room and started a shaving cream fight."

Dorinda remembered. It was during the wake. She'd enjoyed it, but she'd been thoroughly embarrassed afterwards when her mother stood in the doorway, saying goodbye to their guests, with wisps of dried foam floating from her hair, skin and her black dress and wafting out the door. Jeannie was misty-eyed, and Jo Ann was nodding. Thinking back on it now, Drin realized her mother's eccentricity had served a wonderful purpose. Though Drin had been ashamed of her then, on reflection Jannie had made two sad little girls forget that they were supposed to be in mourning, if only for a few minutes. Drin loved her mother for that.

"It's not that we don't share many of her convictions, but does she have to be such a kook?" Dorinda complained. "There are people who are making a difference right now, and many of them weren't even born in the sixties. My mother and father could join them—instead of having to stand on their own.''

''They're not joiners,'' Jeannie said simply.

''If they're happy, why don't you just let them be,'' Jo Ann suggested. ''If it ain't broke, don't fix it,'' she said philosophically.

''That's the big question, though, isn't it?'' Drin asked rhetorically. ''Is it broke? For example, we really don't need a repeat of the graduation incident.''

''No chance,'' Gwen replied. ''They swore they would behave themselves.''

Gwendolyn occupied the unique position of being the only force on earth that could channel the Fays' unbounded energy in a productive direction. That talent had come in handy over the past month.

Aunt Willie was the only one who paid any heed to Drin's misgivings about whether Mr. Wright was indeed Mr. Right.

''If you can keep your head around you are losing theirs, it's just possible you don't understand the situation. Jean Kerr,'' she said flippantly. She added seriously, ''Gwen's making her own bed, and she's the one who will have to sleep in it.'' Aunt Willie had a platitude for every occasion. ''At least,'' she had added, *''She* doesn't have her head buried in the sand like some people I know.'' There could be no doubt that Willie was referring to Dorinda's decision not to date since her last unsuccessful relationship. But Aunt Willie had chosen the wrong idiom this time.

''That's exactly what I'm afraid of. If anyone is burying their head in the sand, it's her, not me. I have carefully considered and reconsidered the consequences of my actions. *Gwendolyn* is rushing into this marriage and just ignoring Herbie's faults.''

''You make what seems a simple choice: a man, or a job, or a neighborhood—and what you have chosen is not a man, or a job, or a neighborhood, but a life. Jessamyn West,'' Aunt Willie declared.

"That's my point," Drin said, frustrated. "This is a big deal, and Gwen's not using her head."

Of course, Willie had a comeback for that one. "I don't think all this angst is about her choice, it's about you. Sisters hold up a mirror to ourselves and show us what we can be. At least she's grabbing for that brass ring. You should try it."

Dorinda had to admit that Gwendolyn looked happy. She was radiant. This room had been used by countless mothers to make last minute adjustments to their children's costumes before the Christmas pageant, and to straighten the lace on little girls' frilly white dresses. But Drin couldn't imagine there had ever been anyone in this room who was as beautiful as Gwendolyn Fay was at this moment.

Her brother, Rodney, yelled through the door, "I hope you're ready ladies. It's time."

They all took one last look in the mirror at their reflections. They were a quintet of beautiful black women, all looking their best.

For generations, dark-robed, dark-skinned men had paused in this antechamber to adjust their collars before striding down the wide center aisle of the church, through their congregations, and up to the pulpit. Dorinda was sure none of them could have been as nervous as she felt at that moment.

The wedding march began and Dorinda took her place in line. She marched slowly down the aisle, feeling, despite herself, a deep appreciation for the beauty and the sanctity of her surroundings. The pews were decorated with ribbons and flowers, and pedestals arranged about the church held white and pink roses.

Herbie looked better than he usually did, Dorinda thought, as she marched up toward him. The tuxedo gave him a kind of elegance, though it couldn't hide his bulging frog eyes and over thin, almost skeletal frame. His appearance, combined with his work as a mortician, had led

Dorinda to christen him Jack, the Pumpkin King, and as she came to know him better, the nickname seemed more and more apt. He seemed an odd foil for her sister, the Fairy Princess.

But Gwendolyn had fallen for Herbie from the moment she met him—at a funeral of all places—and she was convinced he was The One. When she'd announced they were going to be married, Dorinda had taken her out to dinner and tried to express some of her feelings about the engagement . . . as diplomatically as possible. She should have known from past experience that nothing she could say would change the course of events her stubborn, impulsive sister had set in motion. Gwendolyn steamrolled over her reservations without a moment's hesitation.

Of course, no one else in the family had shared Dorinda's concern. The Fays were notorious for following their hearts and Gwen and Drin's parents had only insisted Gwendolyn and Herbie should start a family first, and wait until they had been together for ten or fifteen years before taking an irretrievable step like marriage. After all, that was what they had done.

Her brothers' complaints had to do with having to wear suits. But Gwen had even convinced her brothers to stand up on the groom's side to even out the numbers as, unlike his bride, Herbie Wright could not find four men willing to stand up for him at a moment's notice. A co-worker from the mortuary had agreed to escort Rachel down the aisle, while Rodney and Terrence would walk arm in arm with their cousins, Jeannie and Jo Ann.

Ronald Clarke had agreed to be the best man, but as he was Gwen's partner, Dorinda suspected the tall, cool, handsome man was more her twin's choice than the groom's. In fact, Herbie and his best man had only recently been introduced when Ronald had broken up with his high school sweetheart. Gwen had recruited Drin, Herbie, and various other friends to help her in her mission to rescue her business partner. Caught in the throes of first love herself, she couldn't bear to see him go off to lick his wounds in private. She had insisted he socialize with her and her large circle of friends and Dorinda had been one of the party one night during his enforced "recovery". She'd even tried to protect him from her sister's well-meant interference. But Gwen had been determined to help him forget about his ex and find a nice, new girl.

It hadn't seemed to Dorinda that night that he and Herbie had much in common. Ronald was charming, self-possessed and smooth-spoken and Dorinda thought Gwen was right about one thing: he was too good to let go to waste. Herbie, on the other hand, was a bumbling, clumsy fool who told awful jokes and always laughed at the wrong time.

Dorinda couldn't imagine what Gwen saw in him. But it was too late to worry about it now. Not that that would stop her. Amazingly, the butterflies in Drin's stomach quieted as Ronald Clarke smiled at her and took her arm. As the best man, he was her escort down the aisle. It was small consolation, but at least she knew they looked good together.

But even that small comfort was denied to her.

As they walked slowly toward the altar at the front of the church, Aunt Josephine could clearly be heard to say, "Wow! Who's that hunk with Dorinda?"

Aunt Willie's response was inaudible, but Jo's next question resounded through the chapel. "Are they dating?" She probably couldn't hear the echo of her voice bouncing off the high rafters above.

People nearby were whispering to each other and Drin felt their amused stares burning into her back. The altar seemed a million miles away. Drin turned to glare at her aunts and saw Willie lean down to whisper into her sister's good ear. Dorinda caught Aunt Josephine's eye, smiled and nodded.

Jo nodded back, but it didn't stop her from wondering, aloud, "How could she come to her sister's wedding without a date?"

Family is just accident . . . They don't mean to
get on your nerves, they don't mean to be family. They just are.

Marsha Norman. *'night Mother*.

2.

It was no more than Dorinda should have expected. It
was amazing that the ceremony had gone as smoothly as
it had. No Fay family gathering was complete without an
incident that was, at the least, unusual. Sometimes her
relatives' actions were downright bizarre. Dorinda supposed she should be grateful that no one had tripped
going down the aisle, or said something awful about the
bride or groom. Given the choice between being humili-
ated in public and having her sister's big day ruined, Dorinda would gladly lay down her pride at her sister's feet.

But when she got married, if she ever married, she was
definitely going to elope.

Dorinda's mind emptied of all her plans and schemes
as she watched Gwendolyn and Herbert Wright exchange
vows. It was fascinating—like watching a hideous accident
in slow motion. She could barely tear her eyes away from
her twin's beaming face to take in Herbie's proud, satisfied
smile.

The bride and groom turned to face their eager audience. Dorinda and the rest of the bridesmaids and

groomsmen followed suit and gazed out at tearstained cheeks and congratulatory smiles.

"I now present to you, Mr. Herbert Wright and Mrs. Gwendolyn Wright," the pastor said, ending the ceremony. For all their protestations, her parent's smiles were wide, and she caught a glimpse of a tearstain on her father's cheek.

There was a rousing wave of applause which followed the wedding party back down the aisle and out into the sunny churchyard. Everyone started hugging and kissing everyone else. Relief that it was over was prevalent among the highly charged emotions finding release in the warm, early summer air.

The bridesmaids and groomsmen all congratulated each other. Dorinda was passed from one brother to the next, and then she found herself face to face with Ronald Clarke again. He held open his arms and she walked into them, the earlier awkwardness, if not forgotten, at least momentarily pushed to the back of her mind.

"We did it," he said, as proudly as if he'd arranged the whole thing, marriage, wedding and all.

"We made it," Dorinda agreed.

"With our dignity virtually intact!" Jeannie said wryly, "I'm sorry about my mother." Jeannie and Jo Ann, at 41 and 38 respectively, had long ago learned to ignore their mother's eccentricities.

"It's okay," Dorinda shrugged.

"It could just as easily have been me." In all honesty, Jeannie had long since decided that marriage was not for her. "I didn't bring a date either."

"Me, neither," Ronald said.

"Even if I had, that wouldn't necessarily mean Mom would have been happy. You should hear what she thinks of Jo Ann's latest," Jeannie added. But Dorinda didn't want to discuss Aunt Josephine's opinion of her younger daughter's latest boyfriend. She'd heard it all before. Jo Ann, hard as she tried, never quite managed to get all of the components lined up. If she loved the guy, her mother hated him. If he liked her, Aunt Josephine couldn't stand him. She was caught in a pattern of meeting, dating, and moving on, from which there did not appear to be any escape.

Dorinda understood about patterns like that. Her own love life followed a similar repetitive theme. She was a magnet for jerks who hid their lack of sincerity below a layer of ruthless charm. It had to be her personality. Her identical twin was besieged by one Prince Charming after another, with the exception of Herbie, of course.

It was probably Gwendolyn's inexperience with immature, self–indulgent fools that blinded her to Herbie's true nature. Dorinda had recognized him as a pretty serious loser immediately. She'd had years of practice. Even men who had a history of being decent, honest, truly honorable guys displayed none of those traits when they were with her. Dorinda could actually kiss a prince and transform him into a toad. Hence, her lack of a date for this affair. She had purposely chosen to attend the wedding alone, rather than add a "date" to the stressful family gathering.

Aunt Jo would never understand. She thought people were meant to live as couples. Dorinda had hoped to avoid her father's older sister as much as possible. In fact, she'd planned to steer clear of her family altogether and play hostess to Gwen's friends since her sister would probably be too busy to attend to her guests.

As those same guests started to filter out of the church, Dorinda remembered that in order for her plan to work, she had to send those attending the reception directly to the hotel. The family would be taking pictures for the next half hour or so, and she didn't need outsiders witnessing the madness.

Once all the guests had gone on to the hotel that had been booked for the reception, Dorinda felt—almost—content. She could never completely relax around her family but moments like these were too precious to waste them on wishing for perfection.

Gwendolyn was in luck, as usual. She couldn't have chosen a more beautiful day for her wedding. The sun shone in a nearly cloudless blue sky. A light breeze kept it from being too warm. The muggy heat that would make Brooklyn sizzle in less than a month hadn't descended on the city yet.

The two newly united families spilled over the church courtyard. Herbert had no brothers or sisters, but his aunt and uncle and their mates had stayed and were talking with his parents and hers. The older couples were as vibrant as any of the younger crowd, excited and pleased with the day's events.

Dorinda admired her mother and father from a distance. They looked much younger than their fifty-six years, their round faces unlined and healthy looking. They might have been related by blood rather than marriage, so perfectly matched as they were with their almost identical golden brown skin, big brown eyes and kinky black Afros streaked with grey. Old pictures she had of them showed her father in an Afro picked out three or four inches from his head, her mother sporting wigs ranging from bright red curls to a smooth black Cleopatra style, but, over time—as her father liked to say—they'd come to resemble each other.

Herbie's parents were very typical of their age. His mama's hair had been curled, set and blown dry in a flattering wavy style, while his father's close–cropped newly grey hair was very Schwarzkopf. Mrs. Wright was a tiny woman, with a light tan skin tone and the keen features white magazines held up as the epitome of black beauty. Her husband was dark, his skin turning a shade grey as it sometimes did in men his age, but his strong physique, big bright eyes and wide smile, and his booming basso voice gave the overwhelming impression that he, too, was some years younger than Dorinda knew him to be.

The groomsmen, Alfie from the mortuary, and her

brothers Rodney and Terrence, like their counterpart bridesmaids Rachel, Jo Ann and Jeannie, varied in stature and build. Her brothers, Rodney and Terrence, shared her parents' complexion and both were slim and tall. Rodney, at twenty two, had their father's features, his deepset eyes and broader nose—on a younger scale. Terrence looked more like mother, a more roman nose and rounder chin and jaw. Alfie was a little older and thicker around the middle, but he looked good in his tuxedo. Trying to see them all as a stranger might, Dorinda couldn't help but conclude that Ronald Clarke stood out as the best looking man in the group—He had those West African good looks; with a neat natural hair cut, exotic black eyes, and well defined cheek bones above sensual lips.

When Gwendolyn waved her over, Dorinda motioned to Ronnie that he should join her, thinking it was time to have their pictures taken. She was definitely going to get one of herself and Ronnie in his tux for her crew to drool over.

But Gwen had something to tell her. "I meant to mention this before," she said. "I thought, in case he called you or something, I should mention that Matt was here today. At the wedding."

"Matt was here?" Dorinda echoed, in shock. Ronnie politely faded away. She barely noticed.

"I didn't think you'd mind," Gwendolyn said, too casually. She was lying. Dorinda could always tell.

"*Matt* is here?" Dorinda repeated.

"Didn't you see him?"

"No," Dorinda said, still in shock.

"He was sitting near the aisle, in the back row. But he'd be hard to miss. That is one beautiful man."

Dorinda's amazement was beginning to wear off, to be replaced by anger. "How could you invite him, Gwen?"

"His parents are some of our parents' closest friends. They had to be on the guest list, so . . . I had to invite him, Dori. Besides, you two dated in junior high. How long has it been? Ten years?'' Gwen still didn't get it. Matthew Cooper had broken her heart. Ten years hadn't served to put it completely together again.

"More,'' Dorinda said. "I mean, we broke up when I was 16, almost 12 years ago. We were still friends after that, though. But I haven't seen him since I went away to college. *That* was about 10 years ago,'' she clarified, as though the recitation of these trivial details would bring a change to Gwen's heedless attitude. It didn't.

"So you should be over him by now,'' her twin said in an offhand manner.

"Over *him?*'' She caught Gwen's eye and realized how petulant she sounded. "Sure, of course. I'm over him, I just . . . you could have given me some warning.''

"That's why I thought I would tell you he's going to be at the reception.''

"How could you spring this on me now? You should have said something sooner!''

"Honey!'' Herbie called out. Gwen's head snapped around toward his voice and Dorinda knew she'd lost her.

"I just did,'' Gwen said and hurried to Herbie's side.

Dorinda wondered why Gwen had bothered to omit the word "obey'' from the wedding vows. "It was probably Herbie's idea,'' she muttered under her breath.

"Herbie had an idea?'' Aunt Willie materialized beside her. At seventy years of age, and five feet, ten inches tall, she was an imposing and attractive woman. "Some people take more care to hide their wisdom than their folly. Jonathan Swift,'' she said, as if that explained everything.

"What?'' Sometimes her Aunt's maxims, while infinite in number, didn't quite fit the situation.

"Herbie's not exactly the brightest penny, is he?'' Willie clarified her oblique comment.

"It doesn't matter what I think,'' Dorinda said. "Gwendolyn married him. It's her opinion that counts.''

"That's true. And according to Jane Austen, it is better to know as little as possible of the defects of the person with whom you are to pass your life. Perhaps that's why love is blind." Willie's lined face creased even further as she smiled wryly.

"Aunt Willie, I am going to do my best to make this the perfect wedding day for Gwennie. And so should you. And the whole family," Dorinda said fervently.

She stood tall, straight-backed, and indomitable, unbowed by age and certainly unfazed by Drin's lecture. "Are you suggesting we may better join the foolish crowd then cling to wisdom, lonely though unbowed."

"Be a part of the crowd for once. Please. So Gwen can remember this as the best day of her life."

"Boring isn't memorable," Willie admonished.

"Gwen just got married, took the plunge, promised to love Herbie forever. I think that's excitement enough for one day," Dorinda said.

"I'm not so sure." Willie looked down at her, her expression one of doubt. "Being married isn't nearly as exciting as getting married. George Eliot."

"Then do it for me. I beg of you. *I* have definitely had enough excitement today. Thanks to you." Even though Aunt Josephine had actually made the announcement, Dorinda held Aunt Willie responsible for informing her sister that she was dateless today, in the middle of the ceremony. Willie should have known better.

"Oh, that." Her aunt had the good grace to blush. "I didn't know she'd shout it out like that."

"You know what your sister is. She's a lunatic on this subject." Dorinda knew Jo would never feel a moment's guilt for the pain and embarrassment she'd inflicted on her niece. She had tried many times to explain to Aunt Josephine that women of the nineties didn't need a husband to be happy and fulfilled. But the elderly woman wasn't buying it. She'd never been happy with her brother Earl's decision to wait years to marry Dorinda's mother, Janine. And only the knowledge that Willie's first love died in combat during WWII reconciled her to her own sister's spinsterhood.

She might not be able to rein in her outspoken sister, but Willie could be blamed for giving her sensitive information at such a critical moment in the day's events.

"You want your pound of flesh." Willie sighed. "Go ahead, I'll be your sacrificial lamb."

Dorinda ignored her dramatics. "You did it on purpose," she accused. Willie knew as well as anyone that Aunt Jo was convinced human beings were designed for marriage. Her own husband had died prematurely in his early forties and had since been granted sainthood. "You knew perfectly well that Josephine was going to say something at some point today about it. She does it at every wedding. All she can talk about is Uncle Stan this and my husband that . . ." Jo had conveniently forgotten all but the rosy parts of her marriage.

"I know," Willie said, her cherubic face wrinkling further as she considered her misdeeds.

"Even if I were dating Ronnie Clark, she'd have found something wrong with him by the time we reached the end of the aisle."

"No man can live up to Stan's memory," Aunt Willie admitted. "But my sister is not the only one around here with a selective memory."

"What's that supposed to mean?" Dorinda asked.

"You're just like her, Drin, except she only remembers the good times, and you focus on the bad parts. Love doesn't always have to end in death or disaster."

"Everything ends with death," Dorinda stated. "As for disaster, do you by any chance remember the humiliating, degrading way my last few relationships ended?"

"Why is betrayal the only truth that sticks?" Willie said philosophically. "Arthur Miller."

Dorinda stopped her aunt before she could warm up to the subject. "Okay, okay." Ex-loves and broken hearts were a popular subject among authors, and Dorinda had heard the litany of quotations from every scribe and orator ever published.

"It wasn't love's going that hurt your days, but that it went in little ways. Edna St. Vincent Millay."

Dorinda tried again to divert her aunt's attention back to the day's main event—the wedding. "This isn't the time or place—" she started.

"We could not learn to be brave and patient, if there were only joy in the world. Helen Keller," Aunt Willie pontificated. "Nothing comforts like sunshine after rain."

Rodney must have heard her as he approached them. "William Shakespeare," he and Drin said simultaneously. The quote was one of their aunt's favorites. "What's she talking about now?"

Drin shrugged. "Don't ask."

"We're discussing Dorinda's social life, or the lack thereof. You can't give up on love just because a couple of jerks didn't know it when they had a good thing. As James Thurber said, Don't let that chip on your shoulder be your only reason for walking erect."

"Hey!" Thankfully, her older brother Terrence joined them. "Rod, you were supposed to bring them over to get their pictures taken."

"Let's go!" Dorinda exclaimed, grateful for the diversion. Arm in arm, they strolled across the lawn.

Terrence leaned down to whisper in her ear. "Don't tell me. How many ways are there to say 'dateless' anyway?"

"We hadn't gotten to that yet," Dorinda told him, giving him an evil glare.

The photographer separated them. She wanted all kinds of photos of both the bride and groom's families, separate and together. She shot Dorinda and Gwendolyn and Herbie with the boys and her, then his parents, then both. There were bridesmaids alone, with the groomsmen, with the bride and groom, and with their families. It went on and on until finally the woman said, "I think I've got enough."

"I hope so!" Rodney slipped his fingers inside his collar to try and loosen it.

"You must be happy. They look so . . . conventional," Aunt Willie said. She followed Dorinda as everyone shuffled toward the cars waiting to take them to the reception. The sun was starting to set, turning the tender young leaves of the maple trees into flickering gold. "Am I forgiven?"

She looked truly repentant, and Dorinda didn't have the energy to stay angry with her aunt. "Sure. You want to ride with me?"

"Definitely."

Once inside the car, Dorinda couldn't help thinking, *I can't believe Matt's going to be there.*

She must have said it aloud, because Aunt Willie said, "Matt's a sweetheart."

"I know." Dorinda wasn't disputing the fact. She had grown up with Matt, and the whole family had always loved him—herself included. It had made the breakup that much harder to bear. She always pictured herself meeting him again, years later. But in her imagination, when that fateful day occurred, she'd planned to look fantastic, have a great husband and beautiful children, and perhaps be the CEO of an internationally respected company. "At least it could have been *my* wedding, or—"

"You should have brought a date," Aunt Willie pointed out.

"I guess," Dorinda agreed reluctantly. She had been about to say the same thing, so she couldn't very well argue. He must have heard Aunt Josephine . . . although, if he was sitting at the back of the church . . .

"What about Damon?" Willie said.

"Damon? Damon Brown?" A vague suspicion formed in Dorinda's mind, and slowly started to grow. "What does he have to do with this?"

"He was there, too."

That was just what she needed. Another old boyfriend to witness her humiliation.

Revenge is a dish best served cold.

William Shakespeare

3.

Damon Brown was not the worst of it. Meeting Matt and Damon again, in the same hour and place, would have been difficult enough, but when she checked the register, which the guests had signed upon entering the reception, she found that two other exboyfriends had also signed in. The relationships she had with Tom Grayson and Jeff Hubble could not compare with the catastrophic experiences she'd had with Matt and Damon. However, each of the four men had, in his own way, taught her the depths to which her heart could lead her.

The two worst, though, were her first boyfriend, Matt, who had unknowingly trampled her heart into the dirt, and Damon, his successor, who, with his graceful lies, had set her on the disastrous path she'd followed for the rest of her short, sad romantic life. She had given each of the four men if not her whole heart, than her body, and a part of her soul.

Dorinda could only brace herself for the torturous evening ahead. They'd all be waiting to show off their latest conquests to their former lover. She could hardly blame them since that was exactly what she would have done.

A large, hairy, male arm came around her waist, which she recognized immediately. Drin leaned into her father's hard body.

"Hey, baby," he said. "How are ya doing?"

"Wonderful," she said dryly, then more sincerely, "How about you?"

"I can't wait to dance with all these beautiful young girls," he joked. He loved to play the part of an old lech, but for all of her father's faults, his devotion to her mother had never wavered. Her parent's passion for each other still burned bright and strong after thirty–odd years together. They were a living example of what a relationship could be. He was watching his wife greet their other guests even as he made the off–color remark.

"Save a Lindy for me," Dorinda said, giving the hand at her waist a gentle pat before she moved away.

"Will do," Earl promised.

Another woman might have found reassurance in approaching her old boyfriends surrounded by her nearest and dearest, but Dorinda prayed her family didn't realize what was going on. Her parents and her brothers were as likely to tease her about this embarrassing situation as they were to try and brawl with any man whom they felt was annoying her. She could never guess how they would react, and tonight was not the time to find out. Dorinda would never forgive herself if Gwendolyn's reception was ruined by a brawl.

The reception was being held at the Prospect Park Hall, housed in an unprepossessing stone building. The stolid exterior of the building did not match its elegant interior. Dorinda felt like royalty as she walked through marble pillars onto a plush red carpet. Glittering crystal chandeliers caught the eye a moment before the grand staircase with its double balustrade. Red and white textured wallpaper covered the walls and gold accents throughout the entrance hall caught the light and shone on her as she passed through the grand hall.

She walked up the stairs slowly, and into the rented hall, pasting a broad smile on her face. The ballroom had been decorated in Gwen's wedding colors. White and pink blooms adorned not only the tables, but also had been placed around the room in huge golden urns. The three hundred guests were all different ages, sizes, shapes and shades of color. The crowd shifted and flowed about the room, at tables, at the bar, on the dance floor, and near the bandstand where a quintet played; the five black women wellknown locally for their ability to play everything from classical to jazz to rock and roll music.

The first of the encounters she dreaded was not long in coming. Jeff Hubble spotted her right away. He came straight toward her, towing his date along by her slender arm. "Dori, honey, how are you?" He was medium height, with skin the color of a cardboard box, and bright white teeth.

"Fine, thanks, and you?" Jeff had been a pretty decent guy, but for one small flaw in his character. He had to be the most calculating person she'd ever met.

"Great. I'd like to introduce my date, Chloe. Sweetie, this is Dorinda Fay."

"Hi," Chloe said, her southern accent so strong it was evident in the one small word. She was a pretty girl, with an open, trusting expression that made Dorinda ache to warn her about the man who was her escort.

"Hi, Chloe, I hope you're enjoying the party," Dorinda said sincerely.

"I love weddings," she said. Dorinda wondered if Jeff was still using the same old routine to pick up women.

"So does Jeff," Dorinda couldn't resist mentioning. He was still very attractive. He made sure of that; keeping his body fit, his hair slick, and his smile perfect. She remembered his daily exercise regimen, the weekly trip to the barber, and the quarterly visits to the dentist. He'd even gotten his teeth capped when they'd been together.

"I know. We met at one." She couldn't believe it. He was still at it. He was wearing an Armani suit she hadn't seen before. Jeff had an extensive collection of formal wear, since his favorite setting for picking up women required it.

"Isn't that funny? We met at a wedding, too," Dorinda said sweetly. "Jeff, honey, you must be sure to tell Chloe all about it." Jeff sent her a warning look, but Dorinda had suddenly realized that there was a way to warn this sweet young girl about what was to come. "It was so romantic," she gushed. "We danced until dawn."

Chloe was looking a little confused, but she still hadn't gotten it. Dorinda knew she shouldn't get involved, but only she could save Chloe from suffering as she had. Jeff had had her convinced that it was something lacking in her that changed him from a perfectly nice man, looking desperately for a commitment, to a man who fled, as if the idea of marriage with her was unthinkable. "Then we went to another wedding. It was our one–month anniversary, and after we danced all night *again,* he talked one of the limo drivers into taking us to the beach and we drank a bottle of vintage champagne that Jeff bought to celebrate the occasion and ... well, I won't bore you with the details."

Chloe's chagrined expression told Dorinda all she needed to know. Jeff must have already mentioned or perhaps already opened the Dom Perignon. "He's the only man I know who understands how women feel about weddings. He's sort of made a study of it." Chloe's surprise had turned into thinly disguised anger. For once, Jeff Hubble's romantic courtship would be seen for the lie that it was, before the damage had been done.

Dorinda hadn't found out that Jeff's constant proposals were an act for a long time. Even after he dumped her unceremoniously when she had started making wedding plans of her own, she had thought that it was her fault he didn't want to marry her. But soon she discovered he only liked to attend other people's weddings. They were his favorite background for seduction. When she set out to warn Chloe, she had hoped that she was giving the girl a chance to see Jeff for what he was *before* she started to believe his veiled suggestions that the next wedding they attended might be their own. It hadn't occurred to her that she might be nipping his plans for this evening's seduction in the bud. She walked away feeling pretty good about the unexpected outcome of her good deed. It had turned out even better than she might have hoped. It could even be called revenge, of a sort.

Dorinda was dancing with Ronnie when she finally saw Matt. He was threading his way through the tables with two plates of food from the buffet. She watched as he sat next to a woman with cascading black curls flowing over her shoulders and down her back. She examined the woman's head, trying to detect whether all that beautiful hair was a weave. It was petty of her, but if she was to be compared to his date, Dorinda needed some ammunition to bolster her ego so she could combat the feelings of inferiority which already threatened to overwhelm her. The woman was flawless. Her hourglass figure was perfect. She didn't even need to wear high heels to show off her long, shapely legs, her flats complimented her flowing silken dress perfectly.

Dorinda was sure her face would be as beautiful as her body. And it was. She avoided the beautiful couple for as long as she could, but Matt must have been keeping an eye out for her.

He waylaid her twenty minutes later as she came off the dance floor with the exhausted best man. "Francie, I'd like you to meet Dorinda Fay. Drin, Francie Stone."

"Francie, this is Ronald Clarke. Ronald, this is Matt Cooper and Francie Stone," Dorinda said. Ronnie stared admiringly at Matt's date. Although he'd been nothing but nice to her, at that moment she wanted to hurt the man.

"Dorinda, Ronald, it's nice to meet you," Francie said sweetly, offering her slender hand. "It was a lovely ceremony." Of course, she had to be nice, too, Dorinda thought, as she held out her own short, stubby fingers for Francie's firm, warm, handshake. Ronald didn't let go until Dorinda put her hand on his arm.

"It's been a long time, Drin," Matt said. When he broke up with her, he'd been honest, direct, apologetic. They had been best friends from childhood, and then became boyfriend and girlfriend in junior high school. Dorinda loved Matt for as long as she could remember. He loved her, too. Until he met Joan Tyler. Joan was beautiful, popular, and self-assured. She was everything he was not. She made him feel like he was those things, too. At least that's what he told Drin. What he didn't say, but she could guess, was that she, herself, was a constant reminder of Matt's early years as the tall, skinny, smart kid who spoke his mind no matter how uncool he sounded, and therefore had been relegated to nerd status by most of their class.

Joan elevated Matt's standing in their high school, while Dorinda stayed just where she had always been, and Matt, still technically her best friend, had left her behind. She had hated Joan Tyler, and that had eaten away at their friendship until it ceased to exist.

"It's good to see you again," Matt said. He had always looked good to her. Ten years had done nothing to change that. He was a little over six feet tall and had a nice solid build. Unlike Jeff, he didn't need to work at it. Genetics had provided a nice frame, and he kept in shape because he was intelligent enough to eat right. He had deep–set, almost black eyes behind his wire rimmed glasses, a strong nose, full lips and a square jaw. He still wore his hair in a natural style, and his chocolatey neck looked just as tasty as ever. Just the sight of him was enough to make her insides melt.

She could feel a half smile forming on her lips. "Hey, Matt."

His answering smile sent a shiver straight through her. "I've been meaning to get in touch with you."

"You should have," Dorinda said. "I missed you." Her voice was a caress. She had almost, but not quite, forgotten the lovely Francie, who cleared her throat and awakened Dorinda from the spell she seemed to have fallen under in Matt's presence. He could still make her feel like they were the only two people in the world. However, Ms. Stone was not, apparently, the type of woman who stayed in the background for long.

Recalled to the woman's presence, Drin joked. "So I guess Joan is history?"

Matt laughed. "From way back," he said. "Your parents must have told you. My mother certainly keeps me up to date on your life."

Her parents had stopped reporting to her about him years before, but she nodded. "They didn't mention you'd be here, though."

"I figured it would be a chance to see you again. Finally," he said.

"Oh, really?" She lowered her eyes, then forced them up again.

"I miss you, too, Drin."

She couldn't look at him, so she turned to Francie, who was chatting with Ronnie apparently unconcerned about her date's conversation with his ex. Drin must have been mistaken earlier when she got the impression Francie wasn't pleased by their reunion. She had probably never entertained a doubt about him, or any other man.

Why should she? Dorinda thought. *What man would look at any other woman when she was in the room?* Ronnie was clearly entranced.

"May I borrow your date for a moment?" Francie asked. Dorinda nodded, dumbstruck. She had assumed Matt and

Francie had heard Aunt Josephine's comment, but apparently they hadn't.

"Would you like to dance?" she asked Ronnie.

What does she need another man for, when she's got the best one in the place? Maybe she isn't so nice after all, Dorinda thought, as she watched them saunter on to the dance floor.

Drin was dancing with Matt when Damon Brown cut in. She tried not to let her annoyance show. Jeff Hubble might be a cold, calculating user, but Damon was a heartless dog. He didn't even pretend to be a nice guy. Dorinda didn't have that excuse to fall back on. He had always been a self-indulgent bastard, but at least he was honest about it. She remembered the first time he asked her out.

"My date's a drag," he said. "Let's go have some fun." She'd been shocked that he'd chosen her, and flattered, so she ignored her conscience and left the party with him. He had looked athletic, and acted as though he had tremendous self-esteem. He was a handsome man with a bronze complexion and a gleaming bald head but she had been incredibly attracted to him largely because he was none of the things Matt had been. Where her first boyfriend had been tall, he was under six feet. His extremely muscular arms, torso and legs had been a direct contrast to Matt's long, lithe body. And his round, jovial face did not remind her of Matt's thin, intelligent visage at all. He'd also differed in that he had cold eyes and a tight little mouth, but she'd ignored those telltale signs.

Despite all the evidence to the contrary, she had convinced herself that he wasn't really the pig he seemed, and spent almost a year trying to understand him, and, when that proved impossible, to change him. Damon didn't appreciate her efforts. He put up with her, for a while, and then dumped her with the same consideration and compassion he'd shown the date whom he'd deserted at the party on the night they met.

"How did you end up here?" she asked him.

"Surprised to see me?" he asked with a smirk that made her wish she could drive her heel through his shoe and into his foot.

"No, Aunt Willie saw you at the wedding. She thought you might be here."

"Oh. Well, a friend of mine asked me to bring her. What could I say?"

"Oh and are you actually telling people these days that we were an item?" When they had gone out together, he would never admit they were a couple. Whenever asked, he insisted they were just friends, even to her family when she brought him to meet them.

"Dorindalyn, you haven't changed a bit. An item? What a charming, old–fashioned name for two people who happened to sleep together, once or twice."

"So why did you come?" she asked through gritted teeth. "You always said marriage was a joke in this day and age. A holdover from the Stone Ages."

"I couldn't resist seeing you and your sister together again, Dorinda." Throughout their relationship, Damon had hinted that he was interested in seeing her twin sister and her at the same time. Perhaps even on the same night. It had repulsed her then, it made her feel physically ill now.

"I'm tired of dancing. Let's stop, shall we?" she suggested.

"A lot of men fantasize about having identical twins, Dorinda. I'm sure I'm not the first to suggest it," he said softly, for her ears alone.

"Get away from me, Damon," she hissed.

Luckily, Ronnie was nearby, speaking with Herbie and Gwendolyn, and she practically ran to him as they came off the dance floor. Like almost everyone else, he'd had a little too much to drink, both before and since the wedding, and when she brushed against him, he nearly fell. But they caught each other, and held on.

It must have looked to Damon as if they were together,

because he raised an eyebrow and said, "So Aunt Willie was wrong about you two?"

Ronald didn't seem to understand the question, and Dorinda was not about to enlighten him. "As you can see," she answered Damon.

The song had ended, and Matt brought Damon's date back to him. "Thank you for the dance, Roxy," he said to the woman, who had already coiled herself around Damon's arm. Roxy's white–blonde dyed hair was cropped close to her head. Her blue–black skin was pulled so tight, it was clear she'd had a face lift, which made it hard to guess her age, and she was so heavily made up that Dorinda was sure she was in her forties or perhaps even older. She supposed it took someone that desperate to put up with Damon's shit. She might have felt sorry for the woman, but Roxy's venomous glare in her direction made her skin crawl.

"Aren't you going to introduce us, honey?" Roxy asked in an airy little–girl voice that was about as natural as her Anglican nose and slightly slanted eyes.

"Roxy, this is Dorinda. Dorinda, Roxy." At a little nudge from her clawlike hand, he added, "My wife."

From Matt's horrified expression, and what she could see of the couple, she guessed they were made for each other. She'd wondered why Roxy had been invited to the wedding. She didn't have to wait long to find out.

Herbie looked over at them and smiled at Roxy. "Hi, Rox. How are you?" Amazingly enough, Gwendolyn examined Roxy jealously.

"Herbie! Thanks for the invite. I can't believe you actually tied the knot." She held up her hand, pointing at her own wedding ring with her thumb. She didn't miss Gwennie's hand tightening possessively on Herbie's. "Don't worry, honey. Herbie and I are history. He's yours now. You are Mrs. Wright, right?" Roxy laughed at her own tasteless joke.

"And you are Mrs. Brown," Dorinda jumped in. "Gwendolyn, you remember Damon Brown, don't you? He and I dated in college," she explained to the others. "He was that one who had the thing for identical twins. Remember?" Dorinda forced a laugh. It sounded real enough, to her ears. Matt looked surprised, and Ronnie confused.

Gwendolyn caught on instantly. "Oh, yes. Hello." She turned to her soulmate. "Herbie, meet Damon. I can't tell you how *bad* he was back then. I guess he's straightened up, though. Now that he's married."

"I didn't think any woman would ever tame you," Dorinda added, for good measure.

Roxy looked from Gwendolyn to Damon to Dorinda, and then turned on her heel with a muttered command to Damon, "It's time to go!" Damon hesitated, then followed.

Gwendolyn turned to Herbie, "You were involved with *her?*"

"It was a few years ago," he excused himself. Gwendolyn looked at him as if he were mad. "She didn't . . . she looked . . ." he stuttered. "I never would have recognized her." Gwendolyn appeared to be mollified, and Herbie changed the subject. But Dorinda couldn't help thinking that he had recognized her right away. The woman couldn't have changed that much.

"Herbie's a lucky man," Matt whispered in her ear.

"I was just thinking the same thing," she said softly. She could still feel the heat of his breath against her neck, and she turned to face him. And saw Francie approaching.

"Your date is looking a little neglected," she said, trying not to sound too pleased.

"Francie," he said, turning to greet her. "Would you like to dance?"

"I've been dancing," she pouted. "Without you."

Dorinda decided she really wasn't a nice woman after all. Matt had only missed two dances. She didn't need to make him feel guilty about it.

"I'm sorry," Matt apologized, promptly. "Are you tired?

Would you like a drink instead?" Francie rewarded him with a smile.

"It's a slow one; I think I can manage," Francie said, smiling impishly. Matt led her on to the dance floor.

"You want to try again?" Ronnie asked.

"What?" She was still watching Matt and Francie, who fit together like two pieces of a jigsaw puzzle.

"A dance?" he prompted.

"Sure," Dorinda agreed.

"Maybe this time we can make it through a whole one without one of your ex-boyfriends cutting in." Drin laughed, absurdly flattered at his envious tone. She saw him in a new light; he was very handsome, and clever, and he'd been in two long–term committed relationships that she knew of—ten years with his high school sweetheart, and four as her sister's business partner. Too bad he wasn't her date, she thought suddenly. That would have shown them.

An instant later, Drin felt terrible for even thinking something so malicious. Here was a perfectly nice guy, being wonderful and charming to her, and all she could think of was using him to get back at her exes. She was filled with remorse for the wayward thought, and for the way she'd been acting. But the fourth and final of her exes was out on the dance floor, apparently waiting for her.

As soon as Thomas Grayson saw her and Ronnie take the floor, he waltzed his partner over to them. "Hi, Drin," he said happily.

Dorinda had never tried to talk to someone other than her partner while waltzing before. It worked about as well as trying to thread a needle while wearing mittens. "Hey, Tom." She lost her balance, but Ronnie caught her.

"This is Maureen." Her fourth ex introduced his date.

"Nice to meet you," Dorinda said wryly. "This is Ronnie Clarke," she said proprietarily. To hell with scruples. Ronnie didn't seem to have noticed anything amiss. "Ronnie, this is Tom Grayson, and Maureen."

"Hi, Maureen, Tom," Ronnie said.

"I wanted Maureen to meet you," Tom said to her. "We just got engaged."

"You're kidding!" Dorinda exclaimed.

"No, really," Maureen said. "He just asked me."

"And she just said yes." Tom's grin was contagious.

"Well, congratulations," Dorinda said, with heartfelt sincerity. Thomas had always been a good guy, and Maureen looked just as sweet.

"Yes, congratulations, Tom," Ronnie echoed.

"I think this calls for a toast!" Dorinda suggested. Ronnie nodded, and they all walked off the dance floor, where they'd only been blocking the other couples anyway as they tried to dance and talk at the same time.

"Champagne, Sir," Dorinda demanded of the bartender, when they reached the bar. "For all of us."

"Not for me," Maureen said. "I'll have ginger ale."

"In a flute," Dorinda told the bartender, without missing a beat.

"To Maureen and Tom," Ronnie toasted the happy couple.

"To us," Tom and Maureen chorused. They seemed very happy. If, as Dorinda suspected, she was pregnant, they both appeared to be excited about it.

"To weddings," Dorinda said, the words escaping her mouth before she realized what she was saying. After dreading this day for weeks, and after all that had happened at the wedding and at the reception, she was surprised to find she hoped she'd be invited to Tom and Maureen's wedding. "Well," she mused under her breath, "I guess I'm an optimist, after all."

Ronnie heard her. "Aren't we all," he said. And he held up his glass.

She clinked her flute against his with a fatalistic shrug, and drank. "Shall we dance?" she asked.

Of all sad words of tongue or pen, the saddest
are these; what might have been!
John Greenleaf Whittier

4.

Ronald Clarke was a nice man, but he drank too much.
At least, he did at the wedding. Which was why Dorinda
found herself sitting alone at two in the morning, rubbing
her feet under the table, and trying to figure out how she
was going to get home. She could take a taxi, of course.
But the hotel they had chosen for the reception was all
the way out in Park Slope, and the closest main drag on
which she might find a taxi at this hour was a good fifteen–
minute walk away. Her feet hurt too much for that.

Unfortunately, all of the people whom she knew who
had come to the reception in their own cars were long
gone. She supposed the designated drivers hadn't enjoyed
the drunken revelry of the early morning, post-wedding
crowd enough to stick around. The cars that had been
hired had all been released long ago. They had driven
home those members of the families of the bride and
groom who had wanted to leave, as well as Rachel and Jo
Ann and their dates. That was what they had been hired
to do. It had been planned that Dorinda would accompany
either her family or the bridesmaids, but it hadn't worked

out that way. She'd still been celebrating when the chauffeurs had reached the end of their wait.

"Hey, beautiful," said a familiar voice. She looked up into Matt's eyes. Francie stood slightly behind him and to the right, and didn't look too pleased to be there. "Need a ride?" he asked.

Dorinda didn't hesitate. "Sure. Just to Empire Boulevard. I can get a taxi there." She slipped her feet back into her white satin heels.

"Don't be silly," Matt said. "You only live a couple of blocks from my place. We can take you home." He helped her up in his gentlemanly way, and she remembered again what a sweet boy he'd been.

"How do you know where I live?" she asked.

"I told you my parents keep me informed."

"I don't want to take you out of your way," Dorinda made one last-ditch effort not to intrude on his new life.

He offered an arm each to her and Francie. "I am going home with the two most beautiful women here. I'm a lucky man." He tugged them gently toward the door.

"Yes, you are," Francie said. She smiled around him at Dorinda; she smiled but it lacked sincerity. "Most men would be satisfied with one."

"I'm not most men," Matt joked.

"No, I guess you're not," she said, grimly. Dorinda could almost hear her asking herself why she was putting up with this nonsense. She looked Matt up and down. He waited for her to finish her quick appraisal, a confident expression on his face. This was not the shy boy whose self-esteem Dorinda had constantly bolstered in grade school and junior high, the boy who was seduced by Joan Tyler's popularity.

Francie gave Matt an approving smile, and he grinned back at her. Dorinda looked away.

"Shall we," he said, opening the door for them to pass through.

"Thanks," she muttered, waiting for Francie to echo

the sentiment. When she heard nothing from that corner, she glanced sideways up at the woman. As Francie stepped through the door, she inclined her head, as if she were a queen and Matt some kind of doorman. In Francie's case, apparently, love meant never having to say thank you.

Matt's car was a new Lexus with an automatic locking system. He pressed a button as they approached, and the lights, both within and without, suddenly illuminated the almost deserted parking lot. It was a nice, cool—early summer night, just before dawn, and the light threw leafy trees and bushes into heavy contrast. On the black cement, white lines glowed in the moonlight. It might have been romantic; the crickets chirping, stars glinting down, except for the fact that they were three, not two. Dorinda felt more like a third wheel than she could ever have imagined. The love of her life, or ex-love of her life, was escorting his current lady home, and she was tagging along for the ride. How pathetic did that make her? Her crew was going to love hearing this, she realized.

"Go on, it's open," he suggested, as her hand reached automatically for the door handle. Francie didn't even lift a finger. Matt jogged around and opened the door for her before striding back to the driver's side of the car. Dorinda and Francie were already in the car when he slid in.

"Nice wedding," Matt said, obviously trying to make conversation.

"We'll talk about that later," Francie said. "Right now, I'd like to hear about you two."

Dorinda choked. "You tell it, Matt. Men have such a different perspective, don't you think?" She looked from Francie to Matt. There was a little tension between them, but neither seemed as uncomfortable as she felt. She supposed, to Matt, it was just a single incident of ancient history. Still it seemed to her an odd request for his current girlfriend to make of his ex.

Francie focussed on Matt, regarding him curiously.

And I'd love to hear this, Dorinda thought.

He tried to get away with telling the short version. "We've been friends forever. Then in junior high school we started dating," he offered. "We broke up after the first year in high school."

Francie wasn't about to let him get away with that. "What happened?" she asked.

"Nothing," Matt said. "We should have just stayed friends, I guess."

That gave Dorinda a jolt. To her, it had seemed so right when they had begun to go out, the natural next step in their relationship. They had loved each other deeply. She'd realized later that it had been a mistake, but at the time it had seemed perfect. She supposed it had not meant as much to him. Apparently, he'd written it off as a youthful indiscretion, and gotten on with his life.

"No, really. What happened?" Francie probed.

"It was so long ago. Why do you want to know?" he challenged her.

Dorinda looked out the window at the streets of Park Slope. As its name implied, in Drin's neighborhood small parks and large abounded, as did trendy shops and older, family–owned ones, and well–maintained brownstones and townhouses. They even passed the occasional garden being cultivated in a small patch of lawn. The area had grown more prosperous—yuppies and buppies took advantage of the rising property values—but the newcomers couldn't ruin it for her. It was the area where she had grown up . . . with Matt.

"I want to know all about your checkered past," Francie said coyly.

When Drin spoke up, she surprised even herself. "We weren't in love, we just loved each other. In a way, I guess Matt was right. We never should have gone out. We got hormone activity mixed up with passion. Then Matt fell in love with someone else," Dorinda explained.

"Oh." Francie was apparently satisfied. "Matt and I were set up. On a blind date. A friend of mine thought we would hit it off, but I didn't think I'd have anything in common with a computer engineer from Brooklyn."

"Where do you live?"

"Manhattan," Francie responded, as if that explained everything.

"What do you do?"

"I'm a model."

"Really?" That did explain a lot. "I don't think I know any models. Are you studying acting or something?"

"No. I enjoy my work. I don't have time for much else."

"That's unusual. I mean, in New York City everyone seems to want to be something else. Usually when I see models interviewed on television, they're trying to act, or design clothes or something." Dorinda didn't realize how insulting that might sound until after the words had left her mouth and bounced around the silent interior of the car for a moment. She hadn't meant to be offensive; she had just said what she was thinking, as she usually did. The habit often got her into trouble. She would have apologized, but was afraid that would just make it worse.

Francie went on the offensive. "That's just age," she said. "Older models. And some who are not sure their 'look' will remain in fashion."

Meow! Dorinda nearly said it aloud. She was also dying to ask Francie how old she was, but she restrained herself.

"Which building is it?" Matt asked.

Dorinda looked out the window and saw they'd turned on to her street. "The third one up, the red brick." He coasted slowly to a stop in front of her building.

"It was very nice to meet you," Francie said, dismissing her.

"Thanks for the ride." Dorinda directed the comment at the back of their heads. Suddenly she couldn't get out of there fast enough.

"I'll watch 'til you get inside," Matt called out as she closed the car door with slightly more force than was necessary.

She went quickly into the building, then turned and watched his taillights disappear up the street before going up to her place. It was a relief to walk into her apartment and immediately remove the dress that had confined her for so many hours. She put on a pair of sweats, and stretched, hoping to release some of the frustrated tension which the events of the evening had created.

After she'd eased her tense muscles, Drin sat on her big, comfy couch, on the afghan that Aunt Josephine had crocheted for her, and drank in the peace and quiet of her second floor apartment. She had thoroughly cleaned the whole place in a vain attempt to calm herself before the wedding. At the time it had seemed a futile exercise, but she was glad she'd done it now. The lack of clutter, the clean straight lines of the recently repainted walls, the simple, comfortable chairs in the living room and dining area, and the rest of the white melamine furniture that comprised her haven were as comforting to her as was sitting with her things about her—her computer and other equipment, her books, her photographs. She had a nice life, and she thought she had made peace with her past. The evening had been quite a revelation.

It was late, but Drin knew that, despite her weariness, she wouldn't be able to sleep if she went to bed. Her mind was whirling. With everything that had happened, she felt as though she'd run the complete gamut of emotions; fear, panic, sorrow, excitement, even some joy.

She smiled as she remembered Damon's face as he trailed off after his angry wife. It might not have been the most honorable thing she and Gwen had ever done, but it had certainly been satisfying. The curious thing about it was, if she'd been asked before she'd been reunited with her ex-boyfriend, Dorinda would have said she'd put her resentment of Damon Brown behind her. For that matter, her relationships with Jeffrey and Tom were ancient history as well. And other than an occasional pang when she looked through her scrapbooks, she didn't often think of her first love, Matt Cooper, now that her parents didn't mention him anymore.

She had a fulfilling career, a loving—if bizarre—family, and a busy social life. She didn't miss having men in it—especially not the ones she'd seen this evening. Now that time had passed, she realized that these men, whom her memory had captured and filed away as good examples of their sex, were actually not that special after all.

I'm not denyin' the women are foolish, God made 'em that way to match the men.

George Eliot

5.

"Work is hell," Dorinda proclaimed, as she slid onto her favorite bar stool next to her best friend, Daria. They met Claire and Tamika almost every Monday night at the No Name Bar and Grill on Willoughby Street.

"I thought weddings were hell," Daria said.

"That was Friday, this is Monday." They worked together, but as office manager, Daria had more regular hours and had arrived earlier to stake out their usual spot at the long wooden bar. The pub was a grubby old Irish alehouse which had stood in this spot since early in the century—when it had been much more popular. It hadn't been remodeled, or even renovated, since those early days but the old tin roof was an historical treasure, and the long wooden bar had easily stood the test of time, built, as it had been, to withstand the brawls and commotion of those hearty Irish immigrants.

"Where are Claire and Tamika?" Dorinda asked.

"Bathroom run. So how did the wedding go?" Daria leaned toward her conspiratorially.

"You don't want to know." Gerry, her regular bartender

looked in her direction. "Seabreeze, please," Dorinda told him.

"I do. Bad pun. Forget it. Is that why you avoided me all morning?" Dorinda had been out of the office all afternoon, fine–tuning a client's locked computer system.

"I wasn't avoiding you. I read the e-mail from Bob, which did not put me in a better mood, and then I had to go to Applebaum's."

"Did your mother behave herself?"

"Except for that one crying jag around midnight, she was fine. Dad, too. Aunt Jo was her usual self."

"I thought you weren't going to talk to her."

"I didn't. In the middle of the ceremony, while I was walking down the aisle, she *announced* that I was dateless."

"You're kidding," Daria said, but she was smiling.

"It's not funny. Four—count 'em, four!—of my ex-boyfriends showed up."

"Anyone I know?" Daria taunted. She was a throwback to the forties, in her appearance at least. She would have been called a handsome woman then, and she attracted men like honeybees, now. Her face was a perfect oval, and her eyes were the same shape. Her brows arched high on her forehead, which gave her a permanently curious expression, and she tended to purse her lips when intrigued, which was often.

"They're from before your time. But I told you about Matt."

"Matt, the perfect man?"

"He still is. And he was with the perfect woman." Dorinda was still unsure about Francie. "Maybe."

"Who else? Tom?"

"That's right, you met Tom, didn't you?" Drin remembered. "Well, he got engaged. At the wedding."

"Right in front of you?"

"Pretty much."

Daria sucked wind until her cheeks caved in. "Ouch."

"No big deal. Damon was there with his *wife.*"

"Damon? Am I remembering this right? That's Damon from college, whose shopping and cooking and laundry and typing you did, even though he told his friends you were just a friend and they could go out with you if you wanted? Who dumped you for no reason at all."

"That's Damon."

"So what do you care if he got married? I feel sorry for his wife."

"Don't bother. She's as bad as he is."

"Perfect. You should be thrilled. It sounds like he got what he deserved."

Claire and Tamika came back from the bathroom. They had been best friends since kindergarten and did most everything together.

"Hey! You're here! So how was the wedding?" Claire asked.

"I don't want to think about it," Dorinda said, taking a long slug of her drink.

"Four of her exes were there. Including Matt and Damon," Daria volunteered.

Claire and Tamika were friends from the neighborhood, unlike Daria, whom Dorinda had met after college. They knew Matt.

"Matt was there?" Tamika asked. "How is he?"

"Apparently he's dating the perfect woman," Daria told them.

"Too bad," sympathized Claire. She was a short, plump girl, with a face like a black madonna. Her round cheeks and big brown eyes were unadorned. Like Drin, she didn't wear any cosmetics. She was a natural woman, the earth mother type both inside and out.

"He's not bald or anything?" Tamika asked. Unlike her best friend, Claire, she was tall and thin and wore dramatic makeup and the trendiest clothes she could find. Every emotion showed on her expressive café-au-lait face.

"No, remember I told you I saw him that time on the

IRT," Claire said. "He looked good. He's improved with age."

Dorinda put her head down in her arms on the bar. "Can we talk about something else?"

"Wait. Just give me the highlights. Who is this woman Matt was with? And has Damon matured at all? And who were the other two exes?" Claire asked.

"The woman was named Francie something, and she's a model," Dorinda informed them. "Damon is worse, if anything, and he's married to a total witch."

"I hope you were nasty to him," Tamika said wickedly.

"Well, not nasty exactly, but I did manage to mention his favorite sex fantasy, about doing it with twins, in front of the wife."

"Good for you, girl," Daria congratulated her.

"I wouldn't have thought of it, but he brought it up."

"Ugh," Tamika and Claire said simultaneously. They had never met Damon, but they hated him for Dorinda's sake.

"The other two were Tom Grayson and Jeff Hubble."

"Jeff who?" Claire asked.

"He was the prince I hooked up with after Damon dumped me. He likes to pick girls up at weddings, then talk about getting married a lot."

"Oh, yeah. You told us about him," Tamika said.

"Every guy has his quirks, but you have dated some strange ones," Daria said.

"And you had a little retrospective showing at your sister's wedding. How did they all end up there?" Claire asked.

"Matt's parents are good friends with my parents, and Jeff gets himself invited to most weddings in this neighborhood. Damon's wife used to date Herbie. I don't know why Tom was there."

"He's from Brooklyn, too, isn't he?" Claire realized.

"After Matt, I knew I should only date men who lived outside the state," Dorinda said, completely serious.

"With your luck, they would have shown up anyway. Girl, what are the chances that Herbie's ex could end up marrying your ex?" Daria shook her head. "And that Tom guy. I can't believe he proposed to his girlfriend right there at your sister's wedding."

"What?!" Tamika shouted.

"He didn't," Claire exclaimed.

"Another drink for my friend," Daria said to Gerry as the bartender strolled by.

"You read my mind," Dorinda said gratefully.

"You two are starting to sound like Claire and me," Tamika said.

"We'll be like two old married couples, meeting here at the bar every week and ordering for each other. You'll be finishing each other's sentences any minute now." Claire continued painting the scenario.

Daria ignored them. "Tell me more. I can't believe I missed this. What a scene it must have been."

"I'm serious now. I don't want to talk about this anymore," She begged as Gerry set Drin's second drink down on the bar in front of her.

"Just tell me one more thing," Daria said. "You didn't stand around looking pathetic, did you?"

"No, I danced with Ronnie Clarke. The best man. You met him at that party I had, remember? He's my sister's business partner."

"The ebony prince? That is the Best Man I've seen lately."

"The one whose fiance ran out on him?" Claire remembered.

"He was a life saver." Drin held her glass up in honor of her rescuer, and then drank to him.

The chorus died down, and three pairs of brown eyes gazed at her expectantly. "A life saver, huh?" Daria said.

"What?" Dorinda asked.

"So? Do you think he was interested? In you?" Claire asked, straight out.

"What difference does it make?" Drin said impatiently, knowing what was coming.

"He was, wasn't he?" Tamika crowed.

"Look, if I hadn't been convinced before, this wedding decided it. I'm taking a vow of celibacy," Dorinda stated with certainty.

"Oh come on, Dorinda. This is too good to pass up."

"He's gorgeous. I wouldn't throw him out of bed for eating Oreos," Tamika said.

"No. No. No," Dorinda said, her voice rising. "I'm not going to talk about this. I have real problems to worry about. *We* have real problems to worry about. How's your mother doing, Claire?" The only subject that this crew cared more about than her disinterest in dating was Claire's mother's divorce settlement.

"She found my stepfather's hidden assets. He bought a boat. A big one. I think they call a boat a yacht when it's longer than thirty–five feet. This thing is like Trump's boat."

"Really?" She didn't have to feign her interest in this subject. The ongoing story of Mrs. Wheeler's divorce fascinated her. Especially pleased to have diverted the others' attention away from herself, Dorinda settled back into her chair to listen to the latest chapter in the saga.

"Donny had created some kind of corporation and put the boat in the company name, but the lawyers said the judge wasn't going to buy it. He did it three days after Mom kicked him out."

"So she's got him now, huh?" Daria said.

Tamika answered for her. "The judge may seize the boat, or just tell Donny to sell it and give her the money." Back when Dorinda spent all her time with Matt, she knew the two girls because they lived on the same block and attended the same schools she did, but she didn't spend any time with them. When Matt and she broke up, Tamika and Claire adopted her, and their friendship replaced his until she left for college. They had the kind of relationship

Dorinda thought she and Gwendolyn should have. They were like twins—much more so than she and her sister were. They finished each other's sentences, and had lived together since they moved out of their parents' homes. She couldn't imagine one of them without the other.

She hadn't had a friend like that since Matt, but Daria was close.

"How's work?" Dorinda asked when they had finished discussing Claire's mother and Tamika's boyfriend's ex-wife.

"My boss is driving me crazy, as usual," Tamika said.

"Join the club," Dorinda muttered under her breath.

"I heard that," said Tamika. "But we're talking about me, now."

"Fine," Dorinda agreed. "What has Roger done now?" Tamika worked for an art gallery in the city, and had dreams of someday opening her own gallery. Until then, she had to put up with Roger, an annoying character who thought of himself as a true connoisseur, but who was actually just an egomaniac.

"Roger thinks we should repaint, again, and this time he wants to hire some thugs who have been advertising on telephone poles all around the East Village. Our neighborhood has some true native artists, but these guys ain't them," she complained. "He wants to let them go wild, just do their thing, but I don't think he's going to be real happy with the results. And I'm the one who has to clean up the mess."

"So get the real thing," Daria suggested. "Between us, we could find some underappreciated artist who could do something really cool with the gallery walls."

Tamika looked at Daria with admiration. "That could work. It really . . . that's an idea worth considering. Daria, you're a genius."

"So, now, figure out how to make my boss disappear," Dorinda said.

"All right, tell us," Claire said, resigned.

"He's completely lost it," Dorinda took a long swig of her drink and Daria took up the tale. "Bob says the company needs an overhaul if we want to play with the big boys, and he actually expects the computer geeks who work for him, *including Drin*, to buy into this power trip. He wants the men in the office to wear suits, and the women to start dressing more 'professionally,' he says. The women, besides me, are Drin and Donna, the receptionist. And what he wants is for them to wear those short skirt suits like the ones on *Ally McBeal.*"

"He wants the receptionist to answer the phone with the firm's initials, instead of our names. Worst of all, he wants to meet our clients, and press the flesh, as he calls it," Dorinda added.

"What do you care? It's not your company." Tamika shrugged.

"Half the reason I went to work for Bob was because the position offered a regular paycheck, *and* complete autonomy. I never planned to get into the corporate scene. We're computer geeks. No one cares what we wear to work. I wear what I want. They don't even see us."

"I have news for you, little sister: you're already a part of Corporate America. You think you can work for one of the biggest banks in the country and not be a part of the system. What kind of bullshit is that?" Claire asked, in her direct way.

"I know I work for them, but I don't wear a skirt. Or a suit. That makes me invisible to them. I like being invisible. Invisible but essential. They need me; they don't own me."

"I love you reformed hacker types. You're like ex-hippies. You always think you're so out there. Get with the program, baby. You're one of us now. You're just another social security number to them, waiting for your check like everybody else," Daria said.

"Maybe I am, but I don't need anyone shaking hands with the suits at Chase Manhattan, pretending he represents me, or my interests. They were my clients long before I went to work for Bobby boy,'' Dorinda said, frustrated.

"Well, then, leave the shit behind. You don't need Bob, shake him off,'' Tamika suggested.

"I'm thinking about it.'' All three women stared at her, shocked. "Well, you suggested it,'' she said to Tamika.

"Why doesn't Bob's new mandate bother you?'' Tamika asked Daria.

"His thing is all about image. Since I don't see clients, he doesn't bother me,'' she responded.

"That's one theory,'' Dorinda said. "But I think Bobby's afraid of her. He knows she won't put up with any of his bull.''

"I can't believe you're actually thinking about leaving,'' Daria's voice trailed off.

"Going out on my own? Why not? I freelanced before.''

"But that was before you bought the house, and the car, and the thousands of dollars' worth of computer stuff in the house,'' Daria continued. "Do you really think you could pay for all that on your own?''

"Why not? My commissions are paying for it, now.''

"True. But the company pays for your office, and all that equipment, and everything. You're the one who's always raving about this new software and that new whatever . . . Our business has kind of a high overhead.''

"Don't you think I can do it?''

Daria considered for a moment, then a smile dawned. "Go for it, Drin. If that's what you want.''

Claire was less optimistic. "But you're not real detail-oriented, are you? I mean, didn't you forget to pay your taxes last year?''

"I didn't forget to pay them,'' Dorinda argued. "I just forgot to save money to pay them. And I found the cash, in the end.''

"You can't do shit like that when you're running your own company,'' Claire advised.

"I know that. I'd have to hire some kind of bookkeeping

service. But they have them in New York. They have personal shoppers who buy birthday gifts for you; I think I can find a C.P.A. or something to take care of that stuff."

"I think it's a great idea," Daria said. "But the office will be lonely without you."

"You could come work with me," Dorinda offered.

"Nah, I like it there. Where else could I have a building full of guys who would compete to buy my lunch, or condense my hard disk?"

"Or drive you home, or wash your hair, or kiss your feet . . ."

"Jealous?" Daria teased.

"Ha!" Dorinda snorted. "I don't date computer geeks. I am one."

"Come on, they're not all total geeks."

"No, some of them are cool," she conceded. "But not for me. All we'd end up doing is talking about computers."

"It would be safe," Claire said.

"That's for sure. You can beat those guys up with one hand tied behind your back."

"Dorinda probably wants some big old hairy—" Claire began.

Dorinda interrupted. "I don't want anything," she protested. "You know my policy—"

Claire went on as if she hadn't said a word. "She wants a good-looking, funky brother."

"If it were just a matter of body hair, I'd have taken care of the problem very differently. It's not the hair, it's not the smile, it's not even the personality. It's the principle of the thing." Dorinda stopped short of admitting she would choose Ronnie, realizing that at the least it would be admitting she thought him attractive.

"You'd what?" Tamika asked.

"She would . . ." Daria thought about that one for a moment and came up with, ". . . go out with Ronnie Clarke." She knew her friend too well. "Hey, they don't call them Best Men for nothing."

"See, I told you they'd be finishing each other's sentences," Tamika crowed.

"She did not. I wasn't going to say that. And anyway, even if Daria did, I don't want to," Drin spluttered. "I wouldn't presume to know what's going on in *her* mind."

"Chicken?" Claire asked.

"Maybe it's the name . . . Ronald," Tamika suggested. "Maybe he needs to change it. In romance novels, the hero always has a name like Stone, or Devlin, or St. James," Tamika said. "Maybe that's what Dorinda needs. Women in those books never fall in love with guys named Dick or Harold."

"What about Fred? He's romantic, and he's got an ordinary name." Fred was Claire's honey, and he was the sweetest man—a big teddy bear of a guy.

"You did give him that nickname." Dorinda wasn't above giving back some of what she was getting.

"Oh yeah. What was the origin of Big Bougie, anyway. I always meant to ask you," Daria said.

"It's not because he's macho, or hairy, or anything like that. It's just because he makes me feel . . . special."

"Well, when someone makes me feel like that, I'll start dating again," Dorinda vowed.

"Maybe Ronnie could be that somebody, if you gave him a chance," Tamika suggested.

"Uh–uh," Dorinda said. "For me to date anyone, I'm going to have to feel the feeling first."

"Anyone with the guts to open her own company should be able to handle a little date with the Best Man," Daria taunted.

"Think of it as a challenge," Claire joined in.

Dorinda groaned. "That's just what I need, another challenge," she said.

"Don't pressure her," Tamika said to Claire, giving her a little shove. "Dorinda will call him when she's ready."

"I don't think so," Dorinda said firmly. "We've had this

conversation too many times before. I don't plan to date anyone but you girls for a long time to come."

Tamika continued to talk to Claire, ignoring her. "One of these days, she'll have those feelings again."

"Hmmm, yes, we've all had *those* feelings," Claire agreed, grinning.

They were laughing at her. "Shut up," Dorinda ordered. "All three of you are just horny little—" Dorinda began.

"Careful," Claire admonished.

"I was going to say . . . horny little toads," she said, but she felt a smile tug at the corners of her mouth, too.

"Sure you were," Daria said sarcastically.

"I was. Now will you get off my back about Ronnie? I think my career is slightly more important than my non-existent love life, don't you?"

"I thought we settled all that," Tamika said.

"I'm still just thinking about it," Dorinda said uncertainly.

"You just have to decide what you really want," Claire said.

"This is great. Tamika solves your problems, Claire solves Tamika's problem. Now all we need to do is solve Claire's problems and we're all set," Daria said.

"Now that Mom's okay, my only problems are my honeys' problems," Claire said. "What about you?" she asked Daria.

"Me, I don't have any problems. I like my job, I've got thirty computer nerds eager to do anything I ask, and I've got you three."

"Like the four musketeers," Tamika said.

"I thought we were like old married couples," Dorinda reminded her.

"I'd rather be a musketeer," Tamika replied, airily.

"You don't want me anymore?" Claire pouted.

"We've been together since the second grade. The passion is gone," Tamika said dismissively.

"I understand." Claire sighed, playing along. "You need more excitement."

"This isn't just for me. It will be good for you, too. Don't you feel our relationship's gotten a little stale?" Tamika was clearly enjoying playing her role of disenchanted spouse.

"Maybe a little," Claire said, with mock reluctance.

"It is time we stopped being so selfish. The power of our love should be used to serve all humanity, not just ourselves and our friends here. We cannot shirk our duty, when we could be out saving the world." Tamika was getting deeper and deeper into her role.

"I guess," Claire reluctantly agreed.

"Think of the glory and the honor that will be ours!" Tamika slammed her fist down on the bar.

Claire reined her in. "Whoa, we can't be doing this for fame. Our motives must be pure."

"Of course," Tamika agreed, suddenly sober.

"And I will always love you best, even when you don't belong to me alone anymore," Claire said.

"Me, too," Tamika said.

"Can't we just be married musketeers?" Claire asked.

"I don't think so."

"Nah," Daria said. "I think you have to choose one or the other. No one gets to have it all."

"Amen, sister," Drin agreed.

> Life seems to be a choice between two wrong
> answers.
>
> George Eliot

6.

"Dorinda, there's a Ronnie Clarke for you on line two,"
her secretary announced over the intercom soon after she
started work on Tuesday morning.

"Okay, thanks," she said. She was a little nervous, and
more than a little curious, about why he was calling her
as she picked up the headset. "Hi, Ronnie."

"Hello, Dorinda. How are you?" She could tell nothing
from his voice.

"Recovering," she offered. "How are you?"

"I'm fine, thanks." He didn't say anything more, until
she was about to ask why he'd called, and then he suddenly
blurted out, "I was hoping to see you again. Gwen told
me that you're not dating these days, so I understand if
you don't want to go, but we don't have to consider it a
date. We could just eat dinner together."

"Will I have to fight you for the check?" Dorinda asked,
not sure what answer she was hoping for.

"Ummm, I'll try to restrain my natural impulses. My
mama raised me to be a gentleman, but I wouldn't want
to scare you or anything."

She liked his sense of humor. She also liked his straight-forward approach. But she wasn't in the market for a man. Not now, probably not ever. "I don't think it would be a good idea, Ronnie. I know you say it wouldn't have to be a date, but here you are calling, being charming on the phone, making promises you probably won't be able to keep . . . it sounds like a date to me."

"Well," he paused. Dorinda listened, but she also started to check her phone logue at the same time. "I don't exactly know what to say, now."

"How about, 'it was nice talking to you,' " Dorinda suggested. "See you around."

"It *was* nice talking to you. That's why I'm trying to talk you into having dinner with me. I enjoy talking with you. You have to eat, right? And so do I. So let's eat together."

"I already explained," Dorinda said. "And I thought you said you'd understand if I said no."

"I understand. I do. I just . . . feel that we could be friends. That's all."

"That's how all my worst relationships started . . . and ended," Dorinda said.

"All right. I give up," he conceded defeat with good grace. "At least for now. I'd better get going."

The 'at least for now' made Dorinda feel tense, so she quickly said, "Good-bye." She didn't wait for him to respond, but just broke the connection.

She didn't want to tell the girls about this, but she knew they'd find out somehow. Her personal business never remained private for long. Her friends were more efficient than the Associated Press.

As it turned out, it was Daria who first got the news. Dorinda was eating a sandwich at her desk at lunchtime when her friend barged in and asked, "So what did he want?" She sprawled in the chair across from Dorinda.

"Who?" Dorinda asked, a sinking feeling in the pit of her stomach presaging Daria's answer.

"The best man. Ronnie Clarke's his name, right?"

"How did you know about—?" Dorinda asked stupidly.

"Donna told me."

"She just volunteered the info?"

"I was telling her the wedding was a bust, except for the best man hitting on you, and when I mentioned his name, she said he called."

"Why were you—" Dorinda started to ask why Daria was discussing her personal business with Donna, but she stopped herself, realizing any answer Daria gave her would be unsatisfactory. "Never mind." The intricacies of Daria's mind could not possibly be explained in one quick conversation, and Dorinda was hoping that that was all they were going to have.

"Did he ask you out?"

"Yes," Dorinda said shortly.

"And you said no," Daria said, disgusted.

"Maybe Tamika was right. You do know what I'm going to say before I say it."

Drin made a lame attempt to change the subject before she ended up arguing with her best friend. Daria wasn't interested.

"I'm telling," Daria taunted her, like a pre-schooler threatening the worst. There was no need to ask who—or what —she planned to tell.

"You guys cannot make me go out with him. Besides, I already said no."

"We'll make you wish you hadn't then, that's all," her best friend said airily.

She was as stubborn as they were, and she had right on her side. "You can't," Dorinda said smugly.

"We can, too."

Dorinda's confidence faded a little. Dorinda knew they cared about her, but wished they could just leave it alone. She had explained her reasons for not dating over and over again. Why couldn't they just accept her decision? Her friends would be merciless in pursuit of their goal. The question was, what would they do to her? "Do you get some sort of perverse thrill when you torture me like this?'' she asked. "Because if you keep working my nerves like this, I'm going to lose it.''

"You have to learn," Daria intoned as she stood. "When we give you advice, you'd better take it. We know what's best for you.''

Dorinda watched her walk out of the office, and sat, stewing. She wondered if perhaps it wouldn't be smarter to just call Ronnie now, rather than subject herself to her friends' endless badgering.

But she couldn't do it. Ronald Clarke was a nice guy; straightforward, honest and sweet, but she didn't want him. There was no chemistry between them, and if there had been, she'd have been running as fast as she could in the opposite direction. Her use of him as a buffer against Damon, Jeff, and even Tom had been unplanned and unintentional, but she couldn't do it again just to keep her friends off her back. Ronnie didn't even know he'd rescued her. But that had been an emergency, and this wasn't. This was just an assault by her well-meaning, if misguided, woman friends, who couldn't accept the fact that she did not need, or want, to date at this time in her life.

She just didn't have time for a relationship. Honestly, she didn't feel she lacked anything without one. She was happy. She was healthy. She had her friends, and work she loved. She had problems to solve at work and at home, but a man certainly couldn't help her with them. Dorinda didn't hate men. Far from it: sometimes she craved a man's touch. But she had devoted enough of her time to the pursuit of love to know that she wasn't very good at it. This constant debate was just a waste of time.

Once she had wanted what everyone wanted—someone to share her life with, to meet challenges with, to support her when things were going badly and celebrate with her when she triumphed. Someone to have and to hold, as the wedding vows promised. Matt had been her ideal man, her perfect mate and partner, and then he hadn't. It had been one long downhill slide from there. Her attitude had changed along the way. Dorinda had no desire to get on the rollercoaster again, even if the entire world thought that that was what human beings were meant to do. She would not conform, just for the sake of a little peace and quiet, because to go along, in this instance, would take just as much time and cause just as much trouble as standing her ground. She could pick her battles, though. Next Monday after work she'd have her weekly drinks date with the girls. That would be soon enough to fight this one out.

Tamika had bought a copy of The Rules to the No Name once, and Drin had skimmed through the first few chapters. It was a mix of commonsense and nonsense, and her crew and she had debated which advice was which at length that evening. Drin concluded that it was irrelevant, for her, since it dealt with dating techniques which would lead to a committed relationship, something she had absolutely no interest in. She could only marvel at the popularity of the book. She couldn't imagine any normal, intelligent woman of her generation following the steps the self–help book advised. On the other hand, how many normal, intelligent women were there, really? Jerry Springer did not seem to be able to find any. And even the coolest, most progressive black women on the Ricki Lake show seemed to be a little messed up when the subject of relationships reared its ugly head.

The dating thing was as much a dilemma for those who did it, as her no–dating policy was for her. The only difference was that she would have been fine if she could have separated herself completely from the whole dating scene, but those around her couldn't seem to leave her alone about her choice. Her decision not to date was attacked on a daily basis by her friends and family.

She tried to put the whole awkward situation out of her mind. Hopefully, she'd discouraged Ronnie so that he wouldn't call again. If he did, she would say no again. She had told him where she stood, and if he didn't understand that, she couldn't help him. She could only try and keep him away from her matchmaking friends, family, and interested observers so that he would not be put on the spot as she had been. Eventually, he'd go away. The eggheads she worked with had finally gotten the message. Getting through the gigabites of inappropriate social impulses and assorted virtual reality fantasies that crowded *their* brains was virtually impossible. After her experiences with them, getting through to a normal guy like Ronnie would be simple.

Drin was able to put aside thoughts of the wedding, the Best Man, the girls, and her exes when she went into her meeting with Bob. Her employer was a strange man, a rarity, actually. Bob Henderson was a computer geek who had come to computers later in life, and had previously been a successful businessman, though Dorinda couldn't understand why. The fifty–year–old, flabby, sallow-skinned man was born to be a hacker. He was the first black man she ever met who looked pale because of all the time he spent indoors at the computer console. He found normal conversation indescribably dull, and was only truly happy when discussing the intricacies of various program applications or upscaling networks.

This odd-looking man combined his knowledge of business and his understanding of computers so that he could explain the benefits of the machines to those not completely in tune with this new era of information processing. When he'd realized that his business acumen, connections, and computer literacy were something of a rarity he was inspired to start a new company, at which he employed the less socially adept keyboard cowboys with whom he shared his obsession.

He heard about Dorinda through a mutual friend on the Internet. He'd worked with her father years before, and recognized the name Fay right away, then made inquiries about her before contacting her. At the time, Drin was offering her services to friends, and friends of friends as an analyst and troubleshooter. Dorinda had never really descended to the depths of geekdom. She was attractive, articulate, and enjoyed a few of life's offerings that were completely unrelated to the computer. She had always had plenty of work, and could write about computers and programs, teach, troubleshoot, even sell computers. But she had found herself to be incompatible with Corporate America. She hated trying to fit herself in a slot, or a specific job, or define a career path in a relatively new industry that was constantly changing as it grew. Bob's offer had suited her perfectly, and she enjoyed working with him. However, his company seemed to be on the verge of a new incarnation—and she wasn't sure she wanted to be a part of it anymore.

"Thanks for coming in, Drin," Bob smiled at the rhyme, and motioned for her to sit across from him.

"Uh huh," Dorinda grunted. She'd asked for this meeting, so his gratitude was either just for form's sake or it signified something more devious—like an example he might expect her to follow.

"So, what did you want to speak with me about?" His formality did not bode well. Usually, Bob tried to pretend he was just one of the guys. His office, though, was a far cry from the tiny boxes she and her colleagues were housed in. It was huge, with a designer Italian desk as its centerpiece, and objets d'art arranged tastefully here and there.

"I want to talk about the e-mail you sent yesterday," Dorinda said, taking out the message she'd printed out onto company letterhead. "Your new office guidelines are called suggestions, not orders, but the conclusion indicates that if we are not comfortable following these guidelines, then our jobs will be at risk."

"Where did I say that?" he asked, offended.

"At the top of the last paragraph." She read aloud, "These suggested changes are not mandatory, but employees should be aware that if they are not willing to follow these guidelines, their positions within the company will be reevaluated."

"Reevaluated," Bob said. "Not at risk."

"What's the difference?" Dorinda asked. "And who will be reevaluating us? I don't know about anyone else, but I defined my position here when I arrived, and I brought in my own clients. Are you saying that if I won't wear your uniform, I should take my clients and go?" It was perhaps premature to make the ultimatum, but Dorinda had never been a very patient woman.

"I certainly didn't mean to imply that I wanted anyone to leave the company. We're all partners here." He stroked his greying hair, which was combed back into a boyish natural. It was a gesture he often made when he felt unsure of himself.

"Bobby, this is not a partnership. We may all have our names on the door, but we are not voting on anything. And I don't particularly want to get involved in deciding the secretary's salary, or how much stationery to order, or what color the walls of the offices should be. I don't want to think about stuff like that, much less vote on it. But in giving up control over those elements of my job, I didn't mean to risk my autonomy."

"This company is growing, and I think we should all—"

She interrupted. "I read the whole e-mail. I know what you think. I'm just telling you what I think. You guaranteed me complete autonomy when I came here. Are you changing the rules, now?"

Bob sighed. Then sat back. "You never have had that," he said. "There are a lot of rules you've just never noticed. You've probably become accustomed to them."

"Maybe," Dorinda conceded, grudgingly. "But they don't include these kinds of things. I feel like you'll be infringing on my client relationships by insisting on meeting them. Not to mention the few small clients whom you want to meet in order to push them to use us more, or else drop from our roster. That's out of the question. In the bigger companies, they'll probably love you, but I don't want them to feel someone is checking up on me, or that they can go over my head if they have a problem, or anything like that." She didn't want to sound like she was whining, or covering anything up, but she didn't want Bob coming between her and her clients. They were her bread and butter.

"First, I'm not sure I'll meet everyone's clients. It will depend. Now that I've heard your feelings on the matter, maybe we could arrange something that would suit us both. Secondly, you are thinking about this the wrong way. I know you have clients who are a pain to work with. I can help you with that. I can keep people off your back, if I know them and they know me." Dorinda had heard all this before, when he first proposed the idea. It wasn't bad reasoning, but it still didn't make her comfortable. As skilled as he was in business, she found Bobby maddening sometimes, and she didn't trust him to keep himself in check.

She couldn't very well say that, though, so she went on to her next objection. "As for the clothes I wear, I'm comfortable in them. When I have to, like when we attended that expo last fall, I'll dress up a little, but in general I don't need anyone to tell me how to dress. I finished with that, for good, when I left Catholic school. If you remember, it was one of the reasons I came to work here in the first place."

He was smiling, and nodding, and it irritated her. "I knew you were going to bring that up," he said smugly.

She wanted to wipe that all-knowing expression off his face, but she controlled the impulse. "I'm sure." Dorinda said dryly.

"This is something we can ease into, gradually. Just try it. Once you start wearing skirts and suits more often, I think you'll be surprised with how much better you'll feel about yourself."

"I don't think so, Bob," Dorinda said wearily. "You should be aware."

"Give it a chance," he urged.

She wanted to state flatly, "No." The way her luck was going lately, Dorinda decided not to get into an argument that was bound to be as pointless as it was childish. "How have the others responded to the e-mail?" she asked.

"I haven't heard from too many people, yet," he said, dodging her question. Some of the men who worked in the office were extremely non-conformist and very outspoken, and Dorinda knew he'd heard from them. She certainly had. A slew of e-mails had collected on the subject between Monday afternoon and this morning. Perhaps everyone would pull together and vote down Bob's latest initiative. "When I get a consensus, I'll let you and everyone else know," he declared, ending the interview.

Dorinda could take a hint. She stood, and took his out-stretched hand. He held hers in his for a moment. "This will all work out," he said.

"Um hmmm," she murmured. Dorinda quickly made her escape.

She dropped by Daria's office on her way back to her own, and told her about the frustrating session. All that her friend could do was make sympathetic noises and offer to take her out for a drink.

"And get another lecture on the joys of dating?" Dorinda said, ungratefully. "No thanks. I'm going to go home, eat some pizza, and watch an action flick. *Beverly Hills Cop* is usually good for releasing some pent–up aggression."

"Try something from this decade," Daria suggested. "Or Denzel."

"Ummm, that virtual reality movie he made was good. A little depressing, though. No black women at all."

"None of them have any black women in them. If you want black women in an action film, you have to get Stallone or Segal or something."

"Since when? There are no black women in those movies either."

"I wouldn't know, I don't watch them. I remember Rae Dawn Chong in one of the early Schwarzenegger films and some Bond film had Iman, so I thought maybe they were in films with white action stars. Like that movie with Samuel T. Jackson and Geena Davis."

"Like Samuel Jackson with Bruce Willis or Danny Glover and Mel Gibson? No women, just men. Black sidekicks are all the rage, and white women have always been good expendable sex objects, but black women . . . no way!"

"That's because real women don't watch those movies," Daria teased.

"I'm counting on Spike," Dorinda said. "He's got to realize there's a hole in the market, and only he can fill it."

"Oh yeah," Daria said. "I can just see Joie Lee now, kickboxing and shit."

"It could happen," Drin insisted.

"Are you planning to audition?" Daria asked, tongue-in-cheek. "That outfit you're wearing could probably land you a bit part in the Avengers sequel. Of course you'd need a different top."

"There's nothing wrong with my clothes." Drin looked down at herself. Black spandex pants molded her legs from ankle to thigh, but a loose sweatshirt covered the rest of her.

"You've got that madonna/whore look down. It could be sexy, I guess. To a psychopath," Daria teased.

"I'm not trying to be sexy. I'm going to the gym at lunchtime."

"If you're not interested in looking good, why do you spend so much time at the gym?" Daria asked.

"Ever hear of a little thing called keeping in shape for your health?"

"Sure. Somewhere," Daria replied. "But I'm not interested in any philosophy that has Richard Simmons as its main advocate."

Happy families are all alike, every unhappy family is unhappy in its own way.

> Leo Tolstoy, Anna Karenina.

7.

It was playoff time again and Dorinda went home to watch the championship basketball game on her father's huge television set. She usually went home about once a month to have dinner with her mother and father, and often Gwendolyn and her brothers and their significant others. The NBA playoffs were traditionally such a time so on Thursday night, Dorinda found herself seated between her father and her older brother on the couch in the living room.

Her parents lived in half a duplex, which had made for a tight squeeze when the four kids lived at home. She and her sister had shared one room, her brothers had shared another. Her parents had made a tiny bedroom out of a small room beside the kitchen. When 'the children' moved out, one of the bedrooms had become a guestroom, the other the master bedroom. The living room, which had served as an extension of her parents' room had been refurnished, too. Drin sat on the big overstuffed sofa, sandwiched between lanky Terrence, the doctor, and her bulked–up younger brother, Rodney, who had just moved up from the Yankees' farm team. Although the new television was huge, and the couch was gigantic, Drin felt she was reliving her youth in the crowded house because of her brothers' bulk.

"It's nice watching it on a big screen, isn't it. You can really see Reggie Miller," her father said.

"Sure, Pops. Seeing those drops of sweat on Jordan's face magnified to four times their actual size really makes me feel like I'm courtside," she teased to her old man.

Her mother laughed. "Earl, she's never going to give you the approval you want. You bought a forty-six-inch television set because that was what you wanted. Don't worry about what anyone else thinks," Janine said.

"But I bought it for the whole family," he whined.

"And we appreciate it, Dad," Terrence said.

Rodney added his approving endorsement. "All I need is a twelve-inch dog and a sixty-four-ounce soda and I'm there."

"The food!" her father said, jumping up out of his chair—a ragged old armchair which he refused to get rid of. Earl was the arbiter of this room's decor, so it was a comfortable hodgepodge of old furniture, sports paraphernalia, and favorite toys from their childhood. The little room that used to be their bedroom was Janine's purview. Just as cozy as the livingroom, it was more color coordinated, with reds and oranges as the primary colors in the furniture and curtains. Her upright piano sat against one wall, covered with family photos, and her small collection of African art occupied a specially made shelf against one wall.

Janine wore her favorite red and orange floor–length vest over a brown bodysuit the same hue, but a touch duller than her goldtinged skin. The material flowed around her firm, shapely body as her mother helped Earl bring dinner out from the kitchen while the game started. Both of her parents cooked and now that they were semi-retired they usually did it together, but for years her father had done most of the cooking during the playoffs. He was a maniac about the sport and had been known to plan his annual vacation around the event.

Dorinda and her siblings were the only people her age who knew the entire history and all of the stats on the men who'd played in the American league during its short life. Julius Irving was her hero to this day. Even in his "Don't Blame the Cook" apron, Earl looked very masculine and dear—his wide, white smile creasing his round cheeks. The whistle blew for the tip–off, and before they had all even been served, the score was twenty to eighteen.

"Thanks, Dad," Terrence said, examining his hot dog closely before taking a big bite with obvious enjoyment.

"Looks good," Rodney said, then turned his attention back to the game. A second later, with his mouth full, he shouted, "Hey! Did you see that! He fouled him."

"He didn't foul him," Terrence said. "He hit his arm after he made the shot."

Rodney twisted a bite off his hotdog like he had the ref's head in his hands. "That basketball would have gone in the net if he had."

"Hey, guys, the refs are right there and they didn't call it," Earl said soothingly.

"So it didn't happen?" Rodney said, indignant.

"Whether it did or didn't is irrelevant. Look how mad Rodman is," Terrence said. They watched in awe as the Bears' hottest hothead drove the ball down the court with fury and finesse.

"Oh my God! Did you see that!" Tension was released for them all by the satisfying swoosh of the basketball going through the net. Tensions ran high during these games. That was half the fun of watching them.

Aunt Willie wandered into the room during the halftime break. She and Aunt Josephine lived together in the other half of the duplex, right next door. They were very close to their brother and his wife, and their children had been raised together, but each woman had her own full and busy life. Usually Willie didn't care for basketball. She said it moved too fast to really follow it. Janine had tried to convert her sister-in-law but it had been a vain effort as Willie was devoted to baseball, and considered interest in most other sports disloyal. She followed soccer a little because, she said, it was the most popular sport in the world, and two billion people couldn't all be wrong, but other than that she only watched sports she played—golf, tennis, swimming—and the Olympics. The only possible explanation for her foray into the living room on a playoff night was her desire to nag Dorinda.

Almost immediately, she asked, "Dorinda, how's work?"

"It's okay, I guess. I'm actually thinking of making a change."

"You are?" Terrence said, dragging his attention away from the cheerleaders. He had always wanted her to go back to school and never missed an opportunity to push his opinion on her. "What are you thinking of doing?" he asked innocently.

"I'm *not* going to get a master's degree. I'm thinking of freelancing again."

"You could do that AND get your degree," he said.

Janine was nodding. "Computers are everywhere, in every field. You could get some specialized degree and combine it with your knowledge of computers and do anything you want."

"I am already doing what I love," Dorinda said to her mother, shaking her head. Her entire family, despite her efforts, was virtually illiterate in her favorite medium—the computer. They could not understand what she did.

"But instead of programming or whatever you call it, you could design those computer games, or that . . . that thing, what do they call that, making designs on the computer?" Janine snapped her fingers as though the action would unblock her tongue.

"Graphics," Dorinda answered.

"Forget games, Drin could probably do some killer reference desk kind of thing. She likes sports—she could create an interactive sports directory where you could hear the announcer calling plays and games, and see the game on the television and look up the stats and strategy on the computer screen all at once," Rodney threw in. He had his own uses for her talents.

"Or you could teach," her older brother chipped in.

"Matthew is teaching at New York Tech and he seems happy," Earl said.

"I'm not a teacher. I mean, that doesn't come naturally to me, as you all know. I've tried to teach you guys enough. I have to do it as part of my job, but it's not my favorite thing, and if I design or write anything, I'd have to sell it, so I wouldn't be doing what I want; I'd be doing what my buyers wanted."

"It would be creative," Janine said.

"So is programming." Dorinda sighed. They'd never get it.

Aunt Willie had been quiet up until that moment, but she commented, "You could just start dating again and then you wouldn't have to pour so much of yourself into your work."

"I don't think dating is the answer to my problems. My boss is trying to re-create the company—and mold all of us into his image. I've either got to stop him, or I will have to leave."

"That doesn't sound like Bob," Earl said, shaking his head. Just then the whistle blew and he was lost in the game again as was everyone else but Dorinda and Aunt Willie, who was watching her speculatively.

Dorinda didn't want to have another discussion about her love life and was desperately trying to think of some way to avoid hearing the lecture she knew her meddlesome aunt was about to deliver without being completely rude.

Rodney saved the day. "I'd love to be able to work for myself," he said.

"I would enjoy that part," Dorinda replied. "I'm just

worried about whether any clients will come with me. The big ones, especially, loved it when I went to work for Bob. They got off on those monogrammed bills he sends them."

"It's called business stationery, or letterhead, and you could print it up yourself," Terrence threw over his shoulder. "You should know, you got me the program that my secretary uses to generate my letterhead."

"I know, but the old boy network loves their offset printing and it's not cost effective for a one–woman operation."

"I still say you're just using work to avoid a serious commitment to having a man in your life," Willie said. "There is no fear in love but perfect love casteth out fear."

Dorinda retorted with a quote of her own. "It takes two to make a love affair and a man's meat is often a woman's poison."

"Well if you're just going to make fun of me," Willie said, disgruntled. "Whatever happened to the concept of respecting one's elders." She toddled away and Dorinda was able to enjoy the rest of the game in peace, except that the thought of her situation at work kept intruding.

When she got home that evening there was a message from Matt Cooper on her answering machine asking her to call him if she had the chance. It took about an hour for her curiosity to get the better of her. It was an hour of remembering daydreams—fantasies, really, which had begun when she saw him at the wedding. She'd played them out in her mind before over the years.

She didn't know any woman who didn't occasionally think of her first love and wonder "what if." What if they'd stayed together? What if he'd chosen her? They were so young when they were in love it probably couldn't have worked out, even if he hadn't fallen in love with someone else. They might have grown apart, discovered that they wanted different things. But what if they'd met when they were older? What if they had just stayed best friends back in junior high school and were just coming together now, older, more mature, wiser than they were then.

They were pipe dreams. They were an absolutely impossible reconfiguration of a past that was over and done with. But they were seductive.

Finally, she had to know. What did he want?

For ten years, not a peep, and suddenly twice in one week he was going out of his way to reestablish contact. There had to be a reason, she figured.

"Hi, Drin," he said when she called him just as if it had not been ten years since her last phonecall to him.

"Hi, Matt. I got your message. What's up?" she asked.

"It was so good to see you, I thought we could have lunch or something." His voice gave nothing away. Perhaps this was a casual attempt at repairing their friendship, maybe it was something else.

Dorinda suddenly found she didn't care. "Why not?" she said. "When?"

"Whenever. Whatever's good for you," he answered.

"Saturday?"

"Sure."

They were off the phone again before she thought to ask him if he had some specific reason for calling. She figured she'd know soon enough.

Forty–eight hours later, she found herself sitting across from him at the No Name Bar. "I can't believe you're here," she said. He sat opposite her, sipping his drink. "It's funny seeing you again so soon after so long."

"I know. It's strange, but I've been thinking about you ever since last weekend. It was so amazing to see you again. I can't tell you how often I've thought of you."

"Really?" Dorinda was doubtful. He would have gotten in touch long before this, if he'd wanted to. Obviously he hadn't.

"I always hoped you'd call, or I'd bump into you somewhere."

"Like a wedding?" she said facetiously.

"I don't know about that." He smiled uncomfortably.

"Maybe in the market or the subway. I didn't think I should bug you, but I always wondered . . ." his voice trailed off.

"What?" Dorinda prompted, curious in spite of herself.

"I wondered if you had forgiven me for being so . . ." He stopped speaking again, apparently at a loss for words.

She didn't know him, couldn't begin to fathom his thoughts, but she could finish *that* sentence. In her own way.

"Stupid? Shallow?" she offered spitefully. The accusation lacked venom. He had not meant to betray her. She'd seen his infatuation with Joan Tyler, seen how he'd been lured away from her by the promise of a new girl and a different kind of romance.

She understood, but that hadn't made his ultimate rejection of her any less painful.

"I guess stupid just about sums it up," he said with a wry grin.

"I see you still go for the same type," she said. "Francie is very attractive. How old is she, anyway?"

"Twenty–four," he answered.

"She looks younger. That must be an advantage in her line of work."

"I suppose so. I don't know much about it," he said, resettling himself in his chair.

Dorinda wanted to watch him squirm even more. "You don't appear to have a lot in common," she commented. It wasn't revenge or a simple pound of flesh that she wanted. She hoped that seeing Matt again would allow her to exorcise her old demons. Her memory of him had been so rosy, with one slight aberration. He'd been her other half until he'd shown himself to have feet of clay. To this day, she'd blamed herself for not being what he wanted, for not being the one he picked. Dorinda needed to break open the old wounds, like a doctor rebreaking a bone that hadn't set, in order to let it heal properly. She didn't know exactly what she hoped to hear him say, perhaps only that he'd been a fool when he chose Joan over her. She wanted him to admit it had been his shortcomings, not hers, that had caused their breakup.

He just sat there, smiling ruefully at her.

"Is that all?" Dorinda asked, pleased to find her voice steady, and not at all as uneven as she felt.

"I was an idiot, what more is there to say," he said. "I'm hoping we can start again, become friends again. I missed your friendship."

"So did I," she admitted, but it was a half truth. Dorinda didn't tell him that she missed their old, easy camaraderie, but not his friendship from the time after they broke up. That had been a hard year. They'd been together, just like always, talking every day at school, going to dinner at each other's houses because their parents were such good friends. It had devastated Dorinda to watch him with the perfect new girlfriend. She had sometimes even thought she could come to hate him.

And without Matt, she'd felt so alone, at home as well as at school. He'd been the one person in her life who had made her feel she belonged somewhere. Even though they'd still been friends, she'd lost that.

Matt and she had had a meeting of the minds first, a dependence on each other, and trust. The passion had probably been inspired more by their hormones than anything else. Their deep and abiding love for each other had changed one day into something more and they'd lost their virginity together. It had been scary, but had lacked the adrenaline rush of that first kiss from a virtual stranger, that unknown quantity that piqued the excitement.

She couldn't stop thinking about Damon Brown. That was probably because she had always blamed Matt for sending her into his arms. It had been the differences between the two men that had made her choose Damon as her first lover after their breakup. Matt was tall and thin and intellectual, Damon athletic and crazy about sports. Damon worked out for hours every day. He'd drop to the floor in the middle of the night and do one or two hundred pushups. Dorinda had usually been able to beat Matt in a game of one–on–one.

Matt treated her like a princess. Damon treated her like a doormat. He hadn't exactly enhanced her college experience. As boyfriends went, he'd been one whom it was better not to remember. But the worst of it had been that she'd stayed with him for so long. Almost a year of her life had gone by before he dumped her. Luckily, when she wasn't with him, she was devoted to her studies, and she'd ended up with the best standing in her class, and won a scholarship as a result. As her Aunt Willie would have said, for every storm cloud, there's always a silver lining.

Unfortunately, since she met him the first week of school, her relationship with Damon had effectively nullified her chances of developing friendships with her own classmen. She had been much too busy trying to make herself indispensable to him to participate in any of the traditional freshmen rituals. After Damon, she had spent a long time recovering, pulling in on herself, and barely noticing the people around her. She was completely alone. She had lost her best friend, and, it seemed, her ability to make friends. She recognized her own role in creating the situation, but that didn't stop her from blaming Matt for most of it.

When she began to emerge from her depression, her favorite professor was also her closest friend, and since they didn't socialize with each other outside of the classroom, all Dorinda did was study and work. She attended a college an hour from her home, but most of her classmates from high–school had gone away to school, so she didn't have anyone to play with there, either. Because of her dedication to her studies, she graduated in three years instead of four so her academic career had been short, and rewarding in its own way, but it had been a solitary time, during which she'd grown very self-protective.

It had taken Daria's direct, no–nonsense approach to

pull Dorinda out of her shell. She had been the first real friend that Dorinda had made since Matt broke off their fledgling romance, and she had pried Dorinda away from her desk and out of her cocoon, into the mainstream again. After Matthew Cooper walked out of her life, Dorinda had unconsciously become stuck in a very lonely place, and Daria had sensed it. She said it was because she'd been in that same place when her younger brother died. She'd recognized something in Dorinda, and reached out to her, and their friendship was created out of that kinship. But as much as it had been a comfort, it had never been a sad thing. It reaffirmed Dorinda's faith in sisterhood. She didn't know if that extended to Matt—her first best friend.

"Ronnie seemed like a nice guy." This was her chance to explain about Ronald Clarke. But Dorinda couldn't bring herself to admit he hadn't been her date.

"He is," she said, then cast about for a different topic of conversation. "Are you still teaching at New York Tech?"

Matt followed her lead. "Yes, what about you?"

"Do you want the long version or the short?" she asked. It felt so familiar and yet so foreign sitting with him like this. Dorinda was not surprised to hear he didn't know where she worked. Her information on him came from her parents, through his parents, and vice versa. Her parents probably never mentioned her work to the Coopers. They didn't understand what she did and so just told people she was a computer genius. But his family was different. His mother was a school teacher, his father the principal of the high school they'd attended. It was one of the many things that had first drawn them together. He loved her family's nonconformist behavior. She envied his mother's involvement in his life, his father's authoritarian clothes and manner. It had created a kind of empathy between them, since each would have cheerfully switched parents with the other. She marshalled her thoughts, trying to decide if she should tell him her entire work history, since college, so he'd truly understand the dilemma she currently faced.

"After college I started work in the computer division at Con Ed, but I couldn't handle it. I couldn't stand going into the office every morning, the bureaucracy, the idiocy. So I quit. And while I was thinking about what else to do, Con Ed offered to pay me to do a few training sessions. Some friends started calling me about their computers, and then the programs and networks at their companies. In the end, I had a little freelance business going, until Bob Anderson called me and said he was going to put together a bunch of hackers and freelancers like myself and handle the business end for us. So we could do what we wanted, and not deal with the bull. So I agreed. Now Bob wants to give the company what he calls a face lift. I feel like it's more like major surgery. He wants to change our image completely. He put out an interoffice memo which involves some pretty far reaching alternatives to the way my colleagues and I currently work. We'll be less autonomous, and he wants us to look more mainstream, too." She grimaced.

At work, Bob Anderson was refusing to respond to any of the e-mails he'd received in response to his memo. That got all of the programmers into an uproar. They seemed to expect Dorinda to lead the rebellion, which she might have been happy to do, except she had other problems that were occupying her attention—first Ronnie, then Matt.

"I went to work for him in the first place because I didn't want to wear a suit or deal with office politics and that is, of course, exactly what's happening."

"Are you thinking of leaving?" Matt asked.

"Yes. It sounds sort of odd but I guess I feel like my autonomy may be worth it. I wanted to work for him because I didn't have to worry about things like my image and running an office, and if I leave, of course, I'll have to do just that. But at least I can do it my way."

"But he hasn't really done anything yet, has he? Maybe

you should just wait it out, talk to him. You could end up getting exactly what you want."

"I could, but I don't have a good feeling about this. I think the change is inevitable."

"Take a stand. You're a very persuasive person, and you've got a lot of people behind you. Try reasoning with him."

"I don't know. I'll certainly think about it. But I know something is going to have to give. I can't handle all of this right now."

"Oh? What's making you so tense?" Matt asked.

He was the answer to his own question. Seeing him again had thrown her off balance. The wedding, and her family and friends who seemed to have stepped up their campaign to convince her to date again ever since Gwendolyn announced her plans to marry. She couldn't say any of this to Matt, of course, who couldn't know about her determination not to date. The comparisons with her twin were inevitable, but they made Dorinda feel as if she was lacking. Or perhaps, she suddenly realized, the pressure she felt was building from within. Maybe everyone was just saying the same things they'd been saying all along. It certainly sounded all too familiar. It could be that she herself was hearing their advice and feeling their concern more because she was comparing her vow of abstinence with her sister's recent marriage vows. The realization struck her so suddenly that she couldn't deal with it right away. She tucked it away and turned her attention back to Matt.

"I'm always like this," she said. "Don't you remember?"

"Oh yeah," he said, smiling.

"That's why they call me The Worrywart," she reminded him.

"I forgot about that."

"I met a girl in college whose father called her Yenta for the same reason," Dorinda said.

"Two of you—now, that's a scary thought," he teased. "Did you become good friends?"

"Actually we were never very friendly. My best friends are mostly from the old neighborhood. Do you remember Tamika and Claire? They lived on our block."

"Sure," he said.

"And my friend Daria, she's a trip. You don't know her." Dorinda wondered if they'd ever have the chance to meet. What would they think of each other?

"You remember Gerome?" Matt asked.

"Sure." How could she forget him. He'd been her rival for Matt's attention for years. He was Matt's other best friend, a kid with a single working mother who was never home and never had any food or anything else in the house. He'd been tough, rough, and often just plain mean. But he'd been smart. He'd been in all the advanced classes with Matt and herself, and they'd had a bit of a competition between the three of them over scores and grades.

"Are you still in touch with him?" she asked.

"Yes. I spend a lot of time with him."

"How's he doing?" Dorinda asked when he didn't continue.

"Not very well. He enlisted remember, in order to get the money for college, and he was sent to the Gulf."

"Oh," Dorinda said, feeling sympathetic in spite of herself.

"He's got Gulf War Syndrome. It ruined him. He can't work. He can't stay with a woman. He had a kid, and he hardly sees her."

Dorinda didn't know what to say. She'd never met anyone with the disease but she'd read about how debilitating it could be. "I'm sorry," she offered. Matt's clouded expression changed a little.

"I'm going over there after lunch. He's never going to believe we had lunch. You could come with me, if you want."

Seeing Gerome again was an interesting proposition, but not today. "No, thanks. I have class. Karate," she explained when he looked at her inquiringly.

"Are you still into that? I thought your parents said you quit."

"No, I just stopped competing. It's a lot more popular now. I'm not the only woman in my class anymore."

"You must be a blackbelt by now, huh?"

"Yeah," Dorinda said modestly.

"Mom told me you got your arm broken once."

"It figures my folks would mention that," she said wryly. Her parents were even more disdainful of her karate than her career, so Dorinda imagined they'd lost no time telling people when she'd stopped competing—though she didn't think they'd ever mentioned it when she was involved in the tournaments. They were pacifists and didn't approve of her avocation. Gwen had gotten into it for the exercise more than anything else. They both liked the fact that it combined the physical and the mental. They learned how to defend themselves, as well as some Eastern philosophy. It had been one of the few times she and her twin had presented a united front to her parents. They left her alone after that.

"How can you still be so intolerant of your parents?" Matt shook his head. "They're so great."

"I love them. We just don't understand each other," Dorinda explained. "I guess we never will."

Marry, and with luck
It may go well. But when a marriage fails
Then those who marry live at home in hell.
                                            Euripides

8.

The next day, her mother called, frantic because Gwennie had returned from her honeymoon—a week early and
without Herbie. Dorinda couldn't imagine what could have
possessed Gwen to return home, rather than going to her
own place, unless her husband was there, but Janine
assured her that that was not the case. A friend's house
would have been preferable to their parents' house. Especially since Gwen wouldn't tell anyone what had happened,
not her parents or her brothers.

Dorinda's presence was not requested by her twin. It
was Aunt Willie who suggested to Earl and Janine that they
call Drin. It had happened plenty of times before. Eveyone
in the family called one twin when they didn't understand
the other.

Her parents, completely at a loss, had been persuaded
that Dorinda's presence couldn't hurt. She herself was not
so sure. The house was strangely quiet when she arrived.
Given that her parents could make a meeting with their
accountant into a full Irish wake with drinking, food and
all the neighbors invited to share in the family personal

business, she'd expected to find at least the family members present, arguing and shouting and wringing their hands. But only Willie was home.

"I sent them out," her aunt told her. "They weren't doing any good here, and I thought maybe you two could use some peace and quiet. To talk."

"Thanks," Dorinda said with heartfelt sincerity.

She knocked softly at the door of her and her twin's childhood bedroom, which had been the guest room for ten years now. It still had twin beds with matching spreads but otherwise, all trace of their residency there had been erased.

"Gwen, it's Drin," she said softly. She almost wished her sister would turn her away as she had the rest of the family.

But she called, "Come in."

Gwendolyn was sitting on the edge of one of the twin beds, a tray on her knees with a manicure kit spread across it. Dorinda entered slowly. The walls were a clean white, decorated with soft watercolors. The wallpaper had a black and gold floral print. When the twins had shared the room, it had often been painted two different colors, once half deep purple, the other lilac. Drin had given a blow-up of a popular Einstein photo a prominent place on her side of the room, and Gwen had hung a Twyla Tharp poster above her bed. Earl had kept some of his children's favorite toys and games—in storage for his grandchildren, he said—and their mother had small jars with their baby teeth in them and a portfolio of their childish artwork, but most of their possessions from the years when they lived in this room had been discarded long ago. Gwen still had her dolls, and Drin's fairytale collection had a place of pride on her bookshelf at home.

"Hi," Dorinda said tentatively.

"I don't know why they called you. I told them it was over."

"That's why they called me," Dorinda said, smiling— sympathetically, she hoped.

Gwendolyn's attention was centered on her fingernails. They looked perfect to Dorinda, but seemed to present quite a dilemma to her twin, who was immaculate, as usual. Her hair was styled in a french braid that curled over the nape of her neck. Her clothes, in stark contrast to Dorinda's wrinkled blouse and ragged jeans, were an elegant ensemble. Her ivory linen skirt was topped off by a matching linen jacket over an amethyst silk blouse. Her hose probably cost a hundred dollars. Gwendolyn didn't wear No Nonsense pantyhose. She'd gone on a shopping spree before the wedding and bought beautiful silk and satin underthings and if Dorinda knew her sister, that same dainty lingerie lay against her sister's chocolatey skin at this very moment.

Dorinda took in the perfect picture her twin presented while she waited for an answer to her little joke, and when none was forthcoming she went and sat across from Gwen on the other bed.

"May I ask *why* it's over?"

"We weren't compatible," Gwen said, apparently unconcerned.

"In what way?" Dorinda probed her twin.

"In every way."

Dorinda sat silently, watching her work on her cuticles, and waited. Finally, Gwen continued. "I don't know why I didn't see it before. You did, didn't you?"

"See what?" she asked, but Gwendolyn didn't even look up at her.

"He didn't change or anything. He was exactly the same man I fell in love with, and married a week ago. But *everything* he did got on my nerves. The way he talks. The things he talks about. He's so self-absorbed. Even when he asks how I am, it's all in relation to him. Wasn't Hawaii just as he described it? Didn't I love it as much as he did? Wasn't I so happy we'd gotten married? And those stupid jokes of his. He has such a strange sense of humor. It got on my nerves." It was difficult for Dorinda to refrain from nodding her understanding. After all, she completely agreed with her sister. But, as Gwendolyn had said, she'd fallen in love with this man when he'd acted the same way. "He chews with his mouth open and when I asked him to stop he said he couldn't. He wouldn't even try. He makes strange noises in his sleep. And to top it all off, he was exactly the same way in bed!"

"That could not have been a surprise."

"No, but he was so self-serving. He actually asked if it was good for me. I told him if he didn't know, he'd better start paying more attention."

"But it was, right?" Dorinda asked delicately.

"Huh?"

"You were satisfied with his performance."

"Yes, except for that smirk on his face."

"Did you two argue?"

"No."

"Something must have happened."

"We didn't fight exactly. I tried to talk to him about how I felt and he became furious."

"So you left?"

"Not right away. I was so angry with him after that that I could barely stand to look at him, let alone talk to him, and he acted like he wasn't upset at all. He ignored it. Just went on as if nothing had happened."

"Did you try to talk to him after he calmed down?"

"No. I knew I'd made a huge mistake and I just wanted to put it all behind me."

"So you left?" Dorinda felt sympathy for her twin, but she was also frustrated with her. "Did you tell him it was over?"

"I may have mentioned it."

"Well, did you or didn't you? It's a simple question. Did you sneak out in the middle of the night without a word, or did you pack your stuff in front of his face and flounce out of there?"

"I don't flounce," Gwen declared, insulted. "And I

didn't sneak around. He was out. He went to some plantation on the other side of the island."

"So you didn't tell him," Dorinda said with a sigh.

"Well he's back at the hotel by now. He'll know when he doesn't find me there waiting for him." She looked inordinately pleased as she thought about that and Dorinda gave up on the pointless line of questioning.

"So what's next?" she asked her sister.

"I haven't figured that out yet. A divorce seems like the first logical step."

"You're certainly calm about it," Dorinda commented.

"I feel like I've been on a rollercoaster for weeks. Up, down, happy, sad, ecstatic, miserable. It feels good just to feel . . . nothing."

That gave Dorinda pause. She'd seen no sign of tearstains on her face, or redness in her eyes, just this maniacal obsession with her nails, but for the first time, she realized Gwen was really hurting. She wanted to give her a hug, but everything about her body language told Drin that consolation would not be welcome.

"Um hum," she cleared her throat. "Maybe when your . . . when Herbie gets back, you'll feel differently. When you see him again . . ."

Gwendolyn still didn't look directly at her, but Dorinda couldn't go on with the thought. As cool and collected as she looked, Dorinda suspected she felt like one raw, exposed nerve. Now was not the time to apply common sense.

"Do you want me to tell Janine and Earl?" Gwen looked at her quizzically. "Mom and Dad?" she tried again. "Our parents."

"I know who they are. But why in the world would I tell them? They'll just tell me marriage is not to be taken, or left, lightly. Willie will say try and try again and the boys . . . they'll be the worst. I'm sort of surprised that you haven't said it."

"Said what?"

"I told you so."

"I don't even really understand what's going on here. Why would I say that?" Dorinda felt slightly offended.

"Come on, admit it. You love being the smart one. The humble one. The one who never makes mistakes."

"Are you serious, Gwen? You think I like being called The Worrywart."

"Don't you?"

"No." Dorinda was starting to get irritated. She had spent the last half hour coaxing her twin sister to unburden herself and had been careful to be non-judgmental. Now she was being accused of she didn't know what by the ungrateful brat.

"I'd rather be the Princess," she muttered under her breath. To Gwen she just said, "So I shouldn't tell anybody anything."

"That's right," Gwen said.

Her life seemed to be on an inexorable downhill slide. She was on tenterhooks at work, waiting to see what her boss would do next. And her mother and father called each day to report on Gwen, and to ask her for her interpretation of her sister's slightest comment. She tried to explain, nicely, that she wasn't the best translator of her twin's cryptic statements, which consisted primarily of plans to remodel her apartment and expand her very successful salon, but they weren't interested in excuses, they wanted answers.

Dorinda had already visited her sister's place of business twice that week. On Monday she'd gotten her hair cut. Gwendolyn was, understandably, suspicious when she first appeared at the salon. Dorinda's last visit to a beauty parlor had to have been made seven or eight years before. She hated fussing with her hair, nails or anything else. She kept her hair one length, cut straight across her shoulders, and almost always pulled back, out of her way. The red tints in her hair were completely natural, she didn't even use henna to bring them out.

Gwendolyn had given up on trying to beautify her sister years before, although Dorinda did usually go to Gwen when she needed a mature, elegant look for a job interview or other important event. In the past few years, even the most formal events had all been work related.

"I'm seriously thinking of changing jobs," Dorinda said when her sister greeted her, a look of surprised inquiry on her face. It was the only semi-believable excuse she could think of to cover her real motive in coming which was, of course, a spying mission for her parents.

Gwendolyn nodded, but she didn't look convinced. "I'll have Jamilla do you. She's very gentle, and she won't go overboard. I know how you hate that." Dorinda had been traumatized at the age of thirteen by a terrible haircut inflicted on her while she begged the hairdresser, weeping, to stop. "I only wanted a trim, I didn't want *bangs,*" she had sobbingly repeated over and over all the way home. Only Gwennie had understood. Her parents said it would grow back and her brothers just teased her, but Gwennie had consoled her, surprising her with a gift of a Yankees baseball cap. Dorinda wore it religiously for half a year as she waited for her hair to grow back. Her twin's empathetic response hadn't been nearly as much of a shock to Drin as the fact that she'd spent some of her carefully hoarded bicycle money on the unexpected gift. She had never before or since felt closer to Gwen than she had at that moment.

Certainly, right now, Gwen wasn't feeling very charitable toward her sister. With a rueful smile at Gwendolyn's retreating back, Dorinda followed Jamilla to the changing room. Gwen's salon was as elegant as her sister could make it, which meant that it was probably the classiest joint this side of Manhattan. The decor was modern yet there were no hard edges; black and white photographs of models and beautiful children hung on pastel walls. The sinks were pink and spotless, the chairs white and plush. Customers were greeted at the door and offered beverages, then ushered into a lush changing room and given soft cotton robes to wear so their blouses or dresses wouldn't be dampened or wrinkled. The carefully selected music was soothing without being banal.

When she emerged from the changing room, Gwen was at the front of the store, behind the counter on which sat the phone and appointment book. Dorinda sat down in the chair Jamilla led her to and leaned back, taking a deep breath and enjoying the luxurious aroma Gwen called her secret weapon against stress. The delicate fragrance was certainly soothing, a hint of incense mixed with lavender potpourri and the faint tropical fruit smell of shampoo. Dorinda, unexpectedly, relaxed.

Maybe Gwen had something here. She insisted that a day of caring for oneself should not be torturous or in any way associated with a visit to, say, the dentist, but should be, instead a feast for all the senses. She had always dreamed of becoming the next Elizabeth Arden with a magnificent spa-like beauty parlor in which women could enjoy a day of pampering themselves and go home feeling they'd been renewed and revitalized. As teenagers, Dorinda hadn't thought much of Gwendolyn's schemes, but as an adult, she appreciated the sense of purpose and complete determination with which her twin pursued her goals.

Dorinda had been to The Beauty Spot before, for the grand opening and to set up the computer and teach Gwen how to use it, and had gradually come to admire the unique atmosphere Gwen had created in her beauty parlor. It was a pleasant place. The employees chattered good-naturedly with each other and the customers and Dorinda lay back as Jamilla washed her hair. She was very tenderheaded so to divert herself away from Jamilla's pulling and prodding, she eavesdropped on the conversations going on around her.

Old Mrs. Chase was having her hair dyed. "My Larry was a pill on our wedding night, but I must say that that's one area of our marriage that *improved* when the honeymoon ended. It took time, but we've got it right, now, and in 21 years, I've never been unsatisfied." Apparently she'd heard Gwen cut her honeymoon short.

"My first husband was not bad between the sheets but my second husband . . . Faugh," said her companion.

"Is that why you got rid of him so quickly, Mildred?"

"That was part of it. Also he was an idiot." The two elderly women cackled in glee. Dorinda marvelled at these women's apparent unconcern with what was happening above and behind them. They acted as if the women putting curlers in their hair were completely deaf. But the stylists responded to their conversation with smiles and nods and even the occasional comment of their own.

"Gwendolyn, dear, I thought you were so mature for your age. Opening this place and running it single–handed." Mrs. Chase said, her tone clearly implying that Gwen's recent actions did not reinforce that impression. Gwen nodded and continued the work she was doing at the high counter by the front door.

Dorinda's heart went out to her.

The woman she'd called Mildred, whom Dorinda knew she'd seen at church, but didn't think she'd ever spoken to said, "Young people these days don't realize patience is a virtue. Marriage isn't something that works out overnight."

If Drin had been her sister she'd have asked Mildred why she'd been married three times if she was such an expert on the subject, but her training didn't permit her to disrespect her elders, so she held her peace.

Mrs. Chase nodded her agreement. "You can't blame Gwen completely. Things have changed. If they had had these no-fault divorces back when Larry and I were first wed, we wouldn't have lasted one year, let alone twenty–one."

"There's another country heard from," Dorinda muttered under her breath.

Jamilla heard her. "They don't mean anything by it," the hairdresser said softly.

"What business is it of theirs," Dorinda said, offended on her sister's behalf.

Jamilla shrugged, "They're in here every week and I'm sure they think of Gwen as family," she said patiently. "Besides, Gwen won't listen to any of us. Mrs. Chase may be a nosey old hen, but she does care and maybe Gwen will listen to *her*." She certainly wasn't listening to her family.

Dorinda found the thought that Gwendolyn could have formed such close relationships with her clients somewhat disconcerting.

"Has she said much to you?" Dorinda asked.

"Not really. Just that Herbie had better not come looking for her when he comes back. As far as she's concerned, he's history."

"That's more than she told me," Drin admitted. "She just said it because I said he'd be back and she couldn't avoid him forever." Jamilla just nodded. "Well what do you think happened?" Drin felt guilty talking about family business to a virtual stranger, but Jamilla was her sister's friend as well as her employee.

"She thought he was sprung on her, that he'd dote on her forever, but Gwen hasn't been involved in this kind of relationship before." Jamilla, Drin knew, was divorced with two children around six and four years old.

"Men change when they get that ring on your finger. No matter how devoted they are—and I think Herbie is—they don't have to try so hard to show you you're the center of their universe once they get that ring on your finger."

"He's got her now," Dorinda said.

"And he figures he can relax a little bit. He's proven he's committed, he loves her."

As if an echo of their conversation, Mrs. Chase said, "Gwennie honey, you've got to give the man time to adjust to being married. He's never done that before."

"Neither has she," Dorinda said aloud, before she could stop herself.

"Women handle these things better than men." Mildred discounted that argument.

"Women handle nearly everything better than men." Dorinda recognized Ronnie's voice. She turned around to look at him and found him standing by the counter where Gwen was working. He must have just arrived.

Ronnie was working with Gwendolyn to create and market her line of beauty supplies for black woman. A marketing expert, he'd seen the potential and the need for such products just as the major players like Revlon and Max Factor had.

It was odd seeing him here. At Monday night's session at The No Name, her friends had put the pressure on. They wanted her to date Ronnie, whom they had named The Best Man, and with whom they were convinced she could finally break her streak of bad luck. Nothing Dorinda said could convince them that she agreed with their assessment of his sterling character and his obvious sincerity and that it wasn't him, personally, she was rejecting. It wasn't even her track record with men that held her back. It was her recent experiences at the wedding and since then, with Matt, that made her doubtful of the advisability of choosing this moment in time to start dating again.

She didn't have anything to prove. To anyone.

She nodded her hello, feeling like a drowned rat. Water dripped down from her hair on to her terrycloth bathrobe. Jamilla, standing above and behind her, worked quickly but carefully, separating the mass of curls her wet hair had become into manageable sections with the aid of silver hairclips which Dorinda could feel dragging at her scalp. Then she clipped the ends of thin swatches of hair and let them fall onto Dorinda's towel-wrapped neck. Ronald Clarke didn't stay. He went into the back of the salon, with Gwendolyn beside him.

The minutes ticked by while Jamilla blew her hair dry, but Gwen did not reappear. The older women were finished and gone before Jamilla had gotten halfway through with Dorinda's hair. Two other women came in for their appointments, but they read magazines rather than talked. Dorinda would have been bored, if she hadn't been so busy trying to figure out how to get Gwen out in the front room again without Ronnie. Her twin might be willing to talk about her marital problems in front of Jamilla, but she didn't think Gwen would appreciate being questioned in front of her business partner.

Gwendolyn never came out. Dorinda suspected she was hiding. As if on cue, Gwen and Ronnie emerged from the back just as Dorinda was paying her bill.

"Do you have time for a cup of coffee?" he asked. Dorinda gave him points for being smart enough to wait until her hair was blown dry before he approached her and she didn't feel so much like a show poodle now that she was out of the stylist's chair. Still, inwardly she groaned.

"Umm, well, I . . ." she stuttered, seeing the faces of her friends in her mind's eye. Daria, Tamika and Claire would never forgive her for turning down this chance to innocently explore the possibility of dating The Best Man. "Okay," she finally agreed.

"Are you sure?" he asked, smiling at her hesitation.

"Sure," she said with a self-deprecatory smile of her own. "Why not?" All she could think as she walked beside him down the street to the Ivory Coast Cafe was that she had better get some serious brownie points for this.

"Is this all right?" he asked, as he gestured toward a

table by the plate glass windows that made up the front wall of the store.

"Sure." There couldn't be any harm in having a cup of coffee with the man. This way, she couldn't be accused of being *afraid* to get to know him.

They made small talk as they waited for their coffees and Dorinda forced herself to relax. It was not much different from her luncheon Saturday with Matt, except, of course, she barely knew this man. But then, she didn't exactly know Matthew Cooper inside and out anymore.

"I haven't seen you at the salon before," he said.

"Usually I have Gwennie do my hair at home," Dorinda explained. "But at the moment, my parents can't, uh, seem to stop, umm, questioning her."

"She's having a hard time of it, I think," he said. "She hasn't told me what happened, but I wonder if she's thought this all through."

"Hmmm," Dorinda muttered. Gwendolyn usually didn't worry about thinking things through. She reacted instinctively. And it had always worked for her before.

"How are *you* doing?" he asked.

"Fine. Thanks." They'd already done the round of how-are-you-I'm-fine so she wasn't sure what he expected her to say. She certainly didn't know him well enough to go beyond the standard answers.

"No, really. This must be hard on the whole family," Ronnie said.

"It's a little strange," Dorinda conceded. "But for the most part we're just worried about Gwen."

"That's understandable. Something like this happens to other people, not family. In fact, I keep thinking of all the television shows where one of the characters had one of these week–long marriages. You don't think it can really happen in everyday life." It was the perfect opportunity to tell him about her own sad history with relationships, and the reasons behind her no-dating policy, but just as Dorinda was about to speak, he added, "But you can't give up, you know. My girlfriend and I split up after six years together, but I still want to meet a girl, get married, have kids, the whole thing."

If he hadn't been so sincere, it would have been hokey. Dorinda couldn't think of a comeback for that one. Finally, she said, "You're an optimist, I see."

"You're not?" he asked.

"No," she said firmly.

On her second visit to The Beauty Spot she had her hair box—braided. It was a complicated and time—consuming process. She had extensions added to bring her shoulder—length hair halfway down her back. There was something decadent about having someone else "do" her hair. The washing, the brushing, even the cutting, which she certainly couldn't do herself, seemed like something Dorinda should have been able to handle on her own. It made her feel intensely feminine and yet uncertain of her femininity. Getting her hair cut made her feel especially insecure. At one and the same time, she felt decadent and vain, while she put herself and her appearance at someone else's mercy. Her hair was perhaps not her most valuable asset, but was certainly a vital one to how she felt about her appearance. A woman's hair, someone once said and Willie had repeated, is her crowning glory. Glorious or not, Dorinda felt more confident when she wore her hair in the style to which she was accustomed to seeing in her mirror. It was not, she strongly felt, a safe area for experimentation.

But she had to speak with her sister, and this was the only way she could think of to do that. They were stuck together for the next four hours or so, while Jamilla poked and pulled at her head.

"Gwen, come on over here for a minute?" Dorinda asked after about an hour. She knew her twin must have seen through her excuse for this visit easily, since she was famous for wearing her hair in one neat, easy French braid, a style she'd sported since high school. Dorinda didn't care. The first time she came to The Beauty Spot she had felt not only out of place as a spy, but also quite ineffective, as Gwen wasn't talking. Not to her. This time, she was going to get some answers.

"If everybody minded their own business," the Duchess said in a hoarse growl, "the world would go around a deal faster than it does."

Lewis Carroll

9.

"Nice 'do,'" Tamika commented as soon as Dorinda came into the No Name. Dorinda was getting used to her new hairstyle and actually found it was even easier to care for than her old hairstyle. All she did was wash it and go—no brushing, no untangling the knots that formed so quickly in her thick hair, no pinning it back. Although her mission had led to this one unexpected bonus, she hadn't achieved her objective. "I spent six hours at The Beauty Spot and got nothing but these braids. Gwen's not talking."

"I figured it out!" Tamika yelled. "I forgot to tell you."

"What?" Dorinda asked, regarding her skeptically.

"What happened to Gwen. I figured it out."

"So tell us," Daria commanded.

"Remember when you guys were saying that the thing that freaked you out about marriage was the idea of waking up to the same face for forty years?"

"That's the kind of thing single women say—not engaged or married women. There's a thin line between wanting to commit and not wanting to. Once across that line you don't worry about stuff like that," Claire said calmly.

"Why not?" Daria asked.

"You must have felt that way at least once," Dorinda said. "Certain relationships are like that. If you're in lust, or infatuated, or whatever, then it's no problem to think of cutting yourself off from all other men. You've found one that *seems* completely satisfying."

"Uh–uh." Daria shook her head.

"I have," Dorinda said.

"Like who?" Claire asked.

"Jeff Hubble," Drin said promptly.

Daria groaned. "That trifling fool?"

"I know it was silly, but when he kept talking marriage all the time I started thinking about it—and the fidelity issue just wasn't a big deal. I didn't want anyone else. I was concentrating on how we could make a go of it."

"Did you forget those dents he left in your butt when he dropped you?" Daria asked.

"I didn't know that." Dorinda glared at her. "Not then," she ground out between gritted teeth.

"I wouldn't mind," Claire suddenly said. "I'm not talking about marrying Fred or anything, but if I were, the idea of never sleeping with someone else does not freak me out."

"Gwen must have felt the same way." Claire said. "Otherwise she wouldn't have married Herbie . . . I mean if she was going to freak wouldn't she do it when she was standing up there in front of God and everybody."

"But I read somewhere that some women suffer the jitters after the wedding. They're too busy planning before or something."

"Where did you read that, Tamika?" Daria asked dubiously.

"I don't know," Tamika said, disgusted. "But I did!"

"She doesn't need some vague, unsubstantiated rumor,"

Daria declared. "Drin's looking for an explanation. What she needs is real data—facts, hard evidence."

"Daria's right, girl," Claire said. "This made–up stuff won't help her."

"I didn't make it up. Anyway, I don't see you guys coming up with any better ideas," Tamika said grumpily.

"Hey, I haven't got a clue," Daria admitted. "It's a complete mystery to me."

"Me, too. But it's one I've got to solve," Dorinda said, frustrated. "My parents are working my nerves."

"Tell them to talk to her."

"They've tried. She won't say anything except that she and Herbie aren't compatible."

"She thought they were a week ago."

"Apparently she changed her mind."

"No kidding, Claire. But why?"

"Maybe he talks in his sleep and she found out something about him that she didn't like."

"He didn't need to talk in his sleep. Gwen has a whole list of things she can't stand. The way he eats, the jokes he tells, the way he laughs, et cetera," she informed them.

"Talk about the honeymoon being over," Daria said.

"So where is he?" Claire asked.

They all looked at her.

"I don't know," Dorinda said slowly. "He should have gotten back by now."

"Even if he stayed the second week without her, weren't they due back yesterday?" Daria asked.

"Yeah." Dorinda's mind was working furiously. Maybe talking to Herbie would help. She had to find him.

By Tuesday she'd done it. It was not difficult to find Herbie Wright. He'd returned to the apartment he was going to share with Gwen and he was a mess.

"How long have you been back?" Dorinda asked him.

"A couple of days." If the shape of the apartment was any indication, he'd been wallowing in self-pity ever since he arrived. Empty pizza boxes littered the table, half–

empty cartons of Chinese food sat on the coffee table, clothes had been dropped and left where they fell. A pair of boxer shorts hung on Gwennie's favorite statue.

Gwen had fixed her new home up before the wedding and Dorinda had helped her move some of her things in. Gwen had the walls painted white, and bought comfortable, elegant furniture including the leather couch, on which, apparently, Herbie had been sleeping.

"Have a seat," he offered. Dorinda shoved the newspaper off the armchair and sat. "After Gwen left me, I waited at the hotel thinking she'd be back. Then when I realized she wasn't coming, I decided to keep right on having my vacation. When will I ever get to Hawaii again, I figured. So I tried." His eyes filled with tears. Dorinda had to look away. "I couldn't do it though. After one day of pretending I was okay by myself I cashed in my ticket and came home. I couldn't take it."

"Have you tried to call Gwen?"

"I—I tried. She wouldn't take my calls." He was trying not to cry, but he was failing. A sobbing, distraught husband was more than Dorinda felt capable of handling and she stood up to leave.

"Look, here's my home number. I've got to get back to work, but we should talk some more."

"Will you help me?" he pleaded.

"Oh sure," Dorinda said without enthusiasm.

"Thank you. Thank you," he repeated as he walked her to the door. "I can't live without her. Tell her for me, will you?"

"Right," Dorinda said, escaping gratefully into the summer sunshine outside the apartment.

She didn't know what to do. She hadn't had any particular plan in mind when she went to see Herbie; she'd just thought he could help somehow, perhaps just by shedding some light on the situation. But it might even have been a mistake to go. It appeared he was looking for help from *her*. When she thought of those eyes filling with tears and that jaw working to hold them back—the only evidence she'd seen of his desire to keep some semblance of dignity—she felt overwhelmed with guilt. She'd *never* wanted their marriage to work. She had to admit, there'd been a tiny part of her that had been pleased that the honeymoon hadn't gone as well as the couple had hoped. They'd been so sure of themselves, so sure of each other that she'd envied them, and wished them just a little bit of bad luck. Not that she would have wanted the complete dissolution of their marriage. She still didn't. They had made vows to each other, not long ago, and Dorinda didn't think Gwen should turn her back on those lightly.

Her mind worked furiously as she tried to decide how to pass the information she'd just gotten on to her sister. Should she just tell Gwen straight out? Should she accuse her of selfishly destroying the man she had so recently claimed to love? Or should she arrange a meeting between the two of them? Perhaps a phone call?

Dorinda could imagine the disaster that could occur if she chose the wrong course. Maybe if Gwen knew how Herbie was suffering, she'd give him another chance. However, if she forced Gwen into a meeting it could turn ugly. He could cry all over her and she could respond to his distress by walking away. He might even lose it and try to kill himself, and her. As unlikely as these possibilities seemed, if someone had told Dorinda two weeks ago that her sister's marriage wouldn't last a week, she would not have believed it any more possible.

What could she do? Daria was sympathetic when Drin told her about Herbie's pitiful state, but she had no suggestions to offer. Dorinda even called Rachel, but her sister's closest friend was as stumped as she was. Gwennie hadn't opened up to her either, despite Rachel's attempts to pry. The bottom line was she had no idea how Gwen would react to the news. After that, Dorinda figured it would be useless to call any of the other bridesmaids and finally decided to call Aunt Willie for her advice.

First she swore her to secrecy. "Whatever happens, Willie, I'll tell her what she needs to know," she insisted.

"Fine, fine," her aunt promised. "What is it?"

"I went to see Herbie," she announced.

"I'm impressed. How did he look?"

"He's completely fallen apart. He cried, Aunt Willie, and begged me to help him get her back."

"Sorrows make us all children again. Emerson," Willie said.

"He's living like a pig in their apartment. I'm telling you, if Gwen sees what he's doing to the place, the marriage will *definitely* be over."

"Don't say that. Hope springs eternal in the human breast. Man never is but always *to be* blessed."

"I don't want to give up, but I can't figure out what to *do*. If I tell her she might not appreciate it and if I just show up with him, she might hate me."

"She wouldn't hate you, but I agree she could certainly get angry. Once I said something uncomplimentary about Stan, and Josephine didn't speak to me for two years."

"That's *exactly* what I'm afraid of," Drin said.

"Life seems to be a choice between two wrong answers. Sharon McCrumb," Aunt Willie said. "If you don't try to help, you'll never forgive yourself, and if you do, Gwen may never forgive you. She's barely talking to you as it is."

"Barely, but still talking," Dorinda said. "I just can't decide if she'll be happier to put this behind her or if this is her way of taking time to figure things out. I don't want to foist Herbie on her."

"The strongest principle of growth is human choice. George Eliot. You'll have to give her the choice," Willie said.

Dorinda couldn't handle another trip to the salon, and she really didn't want to talk to Gwen again in their old childhood bedroom where she felt as though she'd be sucked into that vortex of childhood memories and teenage insecurities again, so she called her the next morning before work.

"Hello?" her sister said when she answered the phone.

Dorinda launched right in. "Gwen, it's Dorinda. I talked to Herbie."

"I don't want to hear about it," her twin said.

"Oh. Maybe later?"

"Mmm," Gwen responded noncommittally. "Was there anything else?"

"Well, oh, how are you doing?"

"Fine." Gwen was silent for so long, Dorinda thought she might have hung up the phone. But then she said, "Did you have a nice time with Ronnie?"

"Oh, ah, yes," Dorinda replied, caught off guard. "He's a nice guy."

"Yeah, he is, but I thought you swore off men."

"It wasn't a date, it was just coffee. I was going to tell him I don't date anymore but he launched into this whole schpiel about still believing in love and marriage and everything and I just didn't have the heart."

"I'm staying out of this," Gwendolyn declared. "He's my partner, you're my sister; I don't want to be involved. But I hope you know what you're doing, Drin," she warned.

"I'm not doing anything," Dorinda protested.

"He likes you. He told me. He said you were adorable, and I'm quoting."

"I did tell him I wasn't interested in a relationship the minute he asked me out."

"Was that before or after you went out for coffee with him?" Gwen asked sarcastically.

"Before, but we weren't out. Not the way you mean. It was just 'I've got a few minutes free, let's have coffee together.' Nothing more. What do I have to say to make you believe me?"

"It's not a question of *me* believing you. It takes more than a simple statement to persuade a man you're not interested. If he likes you and you're friendly, he'll take that as a yes, no matter what you say. You know that."

"I can't be nasty to him. Ronnie's too sweet. But I'll just keep saying no. He'll have to get the picture eventually," Dorinda said, to reassure herself as much as her twin.

"If you really believe that, those braids are tighter than I thought," Gwen said dryly. "Never underestimate the size of a man's ego."

"I'll remember that," Drin promised, then paused before adding tentatively, "Is that what you did?"

After a moment's hesitation, Gwen answered, "Probably."

"How did—?" Drin started to ask.

Gwendolyn cut her off. "I've got to go to work."

That evening, and for the next two nights, Dorinda went to the gym to release her pent–up aggression by working out like a demon. If her life continued in its current course, she was going to be so fit, *SHAPE* magazine would want to interview her.

Every day brought another small crisis.

On Wednesday, Ronnie called and left a message with Donna suggesting they get together again. The cat was out of the bag. Donna told Daria, of course, and Daria couldn't keep it to herself.

She pounced. "You sly dog! You went out with him."

"Just for a quick cup of coffee after I got my hair done. He was at the salon, working, when I went in," Dorinda tried to excuse herself. "It wasn't a date."

But her protestations fell on deaf ears. Instead of taking the pressure off, her safe little session with Ronnie had the girls convinced that she couldn't resist him, despite herself.

On Thursday, Matt left a similar message. After Daria gave her an earful about that one, Dorinda called Donna into her office and forbade her to pass her messages along to her best friend. Donna was annoyed at being treated like a secretary and retreated into stormy silence for the rest of the week.

That wasn't the only source of aggravation at work. Tension was building between the programmers, too, and on Friday, two of the more testosterone–driven males actually ended up in a fist fight. Dorinda immobilized them by using the skills she'd perfected during the past few weeks' intensive training.

If only she could have used her karate to keep her parents in line, she might not have finally blown up at them later that day. Just as she was going home, they called her and asked if she'd spoken to her sister that day.

"Mom, Dad, give it a rest, okay? Gwendolyn is a grown woman and she has to handle her marriage herself. I don't know what's going on in her head any more than you do."

"Do you think Herbie could have . . . done something to her?" Earl asked delicately.

"No," Dorinda said definitely. "He's completely broken up about this, I told you that."

"But some men are full of remorse after they, say, hit their wives."

"I've spoken to him, Mom." She could have added, *"Every day, unfortunately,"* but she kept that to herself. "He was blindsided. If he had any idea what he could have done, he'd have figured it out by now."

"It's just not like Gwen to behave so impulsively."

That did it. Drin's temper flared. "Are you kidding?" she asked. That described Gwen *exactly*. "She always acts on impulse, and reacts on impulse. This is how she's handled every mess she ever made in her life. The *only* reason I'm trying to help is because, for once, she isn't trying to justify herself to you people."

"Don't speak to your mother that way," Earl commanded.

"Yes, sir," Dorinda snapped at him.

"Dorinda!" Janine exclaimed. "Earl doesn't deserve that."

Dorinda could have screamed in frustration. "Look," she said as calmly as she could. "Just leave me alone. I'm not going to forget about this situation. You do not need to call me twice a day. It doesn't help anything to speculate about what could have happened. Gwen said that nothing happened. Maybe nothing is all we're gonna get. There's a good chance, in my opinion, that the marriage is actually over, and we're not going to bring it back to life. Gwen and Herbie will work things out or they won't."

"We hate this," Janine said.

"We want to help her, but she won't let us," Earl added.

"We've made ourselves available to talk, if she wants to open up to us. You guys are giving her room and board. There's nothing more you can do for the moment. I'm doing my best but I'm not sure what, if *anything*, I'm going to do next. If I come up with some brilliant idea, I'll tell you. So just let me go to karate class and work out, okay?"

"You should go home and take a long soak in the tub with the eucalyptus oil I gave you, Drin," Janine said.

"I will," Dorinda promised. "After."

"Are you going to come to watch the game this weekend?" It was the finals, and the first game could end up setting the tone for the rest of the championships.

"I don't know yet, Daddy," Drin answered. "Maybe."

When she got home from karate class, there was another message from Ronnie on her machine. He had gotten two free tickets to *The Lion King on Broadway* and asked if she'd like to go see it with him. It was a play she really wanted to see but not pay for, because she didn't approve of the Disney company's policies or politics. If she hadn't had that little chat with Gwendolyn, she'd probably have accepted in a heartbeat. He'd called twice already, each time casually asking her if she'd enjoy going with him to an interesting event—first an art festival, then a lecture at the library. She refused politely each time, hoping he would get the message, but this was a tempting offer.

She wouldn't deal with it tonight, Dorinda decided. She'd call him after she got a good night's sleep.

Saturday morning dawned bright and clear and Daria called to ask to treat her to brunch—a peace offering Dorinda was eager to accept.

Daria was waiting for her when she arrived at the restaurant Drin had chosen. It was her favorite cafe, and had a pretty little garden in the back.

"Isn't this nicer than the No Name? Why do we always hang out there, anyway?" Daria asked.

"Because I can't take you anywhere," Drin said. Her friend looked down at herself—she wore a simple dress, in a style made classic during the forties, with huge shoulder pads that made her look very Joan Crawford.

"Me?" she asked.

"You. And you know it has nothing to do with the clothes you wear. You dress a lot better than I do. I was referring to your behavior, and you know it."

"Truce?" Daria asked.

"All this is for me?" Drin asked in return.

"Just for you," Daria said.

"Truce," Dorinda agreed and sat down opposite her friend.

"Can we talk about it?"

Dorinda had never seen Daria act diffident before. It made her feel magnanimous. "Okay. But no nagging."

"Nag? Me?" Daria proclaimed in mock indignation. "Never! No, I just wanted to explain."

"Okay, but after we order," Dorinda suggested, picking up the menu.

"I got you a mimosa. It should be here any second."

"Thanks." Within moments the mimosas had been served and their meals were ordered.

"So," Daria began, Dorinda nodded her approval. "I'm sorry that I invaded your privacy and talked about you with Donna. Does that cover it?" She sounded contrite.

"You've forgotten one small detail."

"What's that?"

"I was annoyed that you and Donna gossiped about me—"

"I don't gossip," Daria interrupted.

"Your real crime wasn't talking to Donna, or Tamika and Claire. It was deciding you knew what was best for me. I don't need you guys to tell me who to go out with, or torment me about whether I go out at all. You jumped to the conclusion that I was dating again when all I did was have a conversation with a friend of my sister's."

"And coffee, and lunch with Matthew Cooper," Daria pointed out. "You must admit it looks like you're changing your game plan."

"As Aunt Willie would say, appearances are deceptive. I was just being friendly. You have male friends."

"Yes . . ." Daria agreed, but Dorinda knew she wasn't persuaded.

"Admit it. If Tamika, or Claire, or Donna, or anyone else, had coffee with a family friend, you wouldn't make it into a budding romance. You just do that with me because you think I'm wrong about not wanting to date."

"Okay," Daria breathed a sigh of relief. "I admit I was doing some hopeful thinking, but it's only because I love you." She blew a kiss at her and Dorinda couldn't help but laugh.

"I love you, too. But I don't tell you how to live your life."

"All right, all right. I give up. You're determined to die old and alone. Who am I to stand in the way?"

"I don't plan to die alone," Dorinda said, as the waitress arrived with their meals. "I plan on taking you with me."

"That's beautiful," Daria said, wiping an imaginary tear from the corner of her eye.

"So you can stop worrying about me finding a man."

"Apparently you have no problem finding them; you just can't seem to enjoy them."

"Show me one guy who you think could be as good a

friend to me as you are, and I'll consider breaking my own rule."

"There are a couple of guys I could name who would like to be friends with you, or more," Daria said, supportive as ever.

"Why are you so evil?"

"Me? I'm just telling you what I think."

"I have nothing against the male sex in general, but unlike you, I just don't have any luck with them. And I really can do without the hassle. I can't do like you do. If I'm going to invest my time and energy in a relationship, it has to be for more than dinner and a movie."

"Hey, babe, I'm just test–driving mine. It doesn't mean I won't eventually settle down."

"Your way is fine, for you. It's just not for me. With my luck, if I took someone out for a test drive, I'd crash."

"We all do, sometimes, but it doesn't mean we can't enjoy the ride," Daria retorted. "Damon was a jerk. Jeff Hubble was a jerk. But not all men are like them." Dorinda understood what her friend was trying to say. Her experiences with Damon hadn't turned her off men completely. It just left her wide open to the skin–deep facades of the Jeff Hubbles of the world. "The Best Man, for example, sounds like a man who could keep his head in an emergency."

"Ronnie's fine," Drin started.

"So fine," Daria agreed.

"I mean, he's just fine. He's okay. Matt wasn't a jerk, either, but he was still . . . a disappointment."

"Anyone can disappoint you. Even me. And I'm the perfect date."

"Oops, that's right." Dorinda snapped her fingers. "We're married, aren't we?"

"Marriage is pretty serious. I don't think I'm ready for that kind of commitment," Daria claimed. "I've got places to go and men to do. We're both young, hot, happening babes. You should be playing the field, too."

"What kind of husband are you, anyway?" Dorinda complained. "You sound more like a pimp."

"I'm not the husband," Daria protested. "You are."

"I am not."

"You're butch. You chew people up and spit them out. Like our boss. You even beat guys up. I'm definitely more of a wife than you are."

"We could both be the wife," Drin suggested.

They looked at each other. "Nah," they said at once.

Dorinda was on her way to karate class on Sunday morning when she stopped to answer the phone. "Hi, I'm on my way out the door," she said, thinking it was her parents.

"I can call back later," Matt said. "When will you be home?"

"I should be around this evening," she said reluctantly. "After six."

"Fine, I'll talk to you then." He hung up before she could respond. Dorinda carefully put the portable telephone back on its stand. Then she deliberately took it off the recharger and turned it on. She had been meaning to discharge the battery, and recharge it fully, Dorinda rationalized. It seemed like a good weekend to be unreachable by phone.

If she'd realized that he would stop by when he couldn't reach her, she might have taken a different plan of action, but she didn't know until it was too late.

I hate and love. You ask, perhaps, how can that be I know not, but I feel the agony.

Catillis

10.

Matt was standing in her doorway when Dorinda answered the ringing of the doorbell. "Hi," he said.

She was even more astonished to see him than she had been that morning when he called. "Hello," she managed to say. "What are you doing here?"

"I couldn't reach you. Your answering machine seems to be broken. You said you'd be here tonight, so I thought I'd take a chance and drop by."

Drin was dressed for her workout in sweats and a T-shirt which she would exchange for her gi when she arrived at the gym. Of course, he looked great in his jeans, but she didn't think she could carry off the casual look the way Matt could. She just looked like a slob.

"Come on in," she asked, when she couldn't think of anything else to say. "I forgot you were going to call and I'm recharging the phone's battery," she lied.

"I thought you might have gone out and left the phone off the hook, but . . ." Matt let his voice trail off.

As they walked through her apartment, she tried to see it as it might look through a stranger's eyes, although it was strange to think of Matthew Cooper as a stranger. At least it was clean. The large living room had a bit of a lived—in look. Since she hadn't expected any guests, there were newspapers and books everywhere, and even some clothes that she'd been planning to donate to charity on a chair in the corner. The computer table, as usual, was in chaos. However, it wasn't too bad.

It wasn't one of those frilly apartments with a lot of keepsakes and clutter everywhere. She shared her mother's appreciation of wooden African sculptures, and had picked up a piece or two over the years, which sat on shelves on the far wall, above the couch. Tall bookshelves of dark wood stood on either side of the cream sofa, which was covered with a simple blue afghan that Josephine had crocheted for her. The coffee table was glass, with a pedestal of the same dark wood, and facing it was a rocking chair and a cream—colored armchair which she'd worn to the exact shape of her fanny over the last few years. The door to the bedroom stood open beyond it, and through it one could see the television stand, and the large windows that looked out into the boughs of a huge oak tree, which she loved for the shadows it cast on her walls.

The kitchen was also visible from the living room. Luckily, she'd just cleaned it the night before, so the gray tiled floor and the white Formica counters were as clean as the shining white refrigerator and stove top. There wasn't even a dirty coffee mug in the sink. Though she might have lost a point or two on her personal appearance, her apartment didn't look too bad.

"Would you like a drink, or some coffee?" she asked.

"Coffee would be nice," he said. He followed her into the kitchen. "You don't have to make it just for me."

"No problem."

He watched her spoon the coffee into the filter and put water in the pot without saying a word. Finally, when she had the coffeemaker going, she asked, "So what's up, Matt?"

"I had a really good time the other day."

She felt flattered, but that wasn't enough. They could have old home week another time, and she might have enjoyed it, but at the moment, she wasn't feeling very charitable toward him, or anyone else. The situation with her sister, her parents, Herbie, and everything else made her feel helpless, which annoyed her to no end. Everything in her life had spun out of control, and she didn't need another blow to her ego—which was exactly what she would get if she spent any time with Matt, Drin was sure.

"I enjoyed seeing you, too," she said. She was determined to be offhand; polite and nothing more.

"I was hoping we could try to . . . I don't know, re– establish some part of what we had."

"I thought we did that," she said. Dorinda poured his coffee, and added milk and two sugars, then cursed herself for remembering how he took it.

"I didn't want to wait another ten years to see you again. I want to try to be friends again."

Maybe it was all the stress she was under with Gwen's situation, and at work, but the conversation was beginning to make her angry. "Is that all you're here to say? Let's be friends? We tried that before, remember?" Her tone was sharper than she intended, but she was irritated by his lack of feeling. Couldn't he see that he wasn't welcome? Didn't he realize that she had a life, problems to deal with, and his presence wasn't helping? Once, a long time ago, he would have sensed it. When they were kids, it seemed he could read her mind. Now he couldn't even pick up on the most obvious signals.

"Things are different now," Matt said simply, and that was it.

The tenuous control she'd had over her temper was gone. "*That* was the reason you came here?" Dorinda asked. "*That* was so urgent you couldn't wait to reach me on the phone?" She felt deflated. She'd expected some great revelation and this fell far short of the mark. "I think you'd better go," Dorinda said.

"You're angry. Why?" he asked. "What did I say?"

"Angry? Not yet. Irked, annoyed, irritated, yes." She managed to keep her voice even, this time.

"Did I miss something?" he asked.

Drin stared at him in disbelief. "Oh no," she said, sarcasm dripping from her lips. "I just don't feel like reminiscing anymore," she answered.

"Reminiscing?" he echoed. "Is that what we were doing? I thought we were talking about the future." His earnest expression defeated her. She felt suddenly drained, deflated.

"I don't feel like having this conversation right now," she said flatly. After all she'd been through this week, her feelings were too close to the surface. Her nerve endings felt exposed, and every word he said grated on them further. She didn't want to argue. She didn't want to explain. She just wanted him to leave.

"What conversation? Hi? Nice to see you after all these years." He made no move to get off her couch.

Dorinda stood. "Look, I can't believe you came here to give me the let's-be-friends speech, but okay, it just proves your people skills haven't improved. Ten years later you're still the same immature, obtuse boy that dumped me for the prom queen." Clearly, he hadn't gotten any more sensitive to her feelings.

"I don't know what I said but I'm sorry." The apology came too late.

"I'm trying to be polite, but you are not getting the point so maybe I should be more direct. We have nothing to discuss."

Finally, he rose from his seat. He was going.

"Can I call you later?" Matt asked.

"What for?" Dorinda replied, uneasily.

"I feel like . . . I took a wrong turn somewhere. But I'm

not ready to give up on us. Not now that I've seen you again."

"I'm sorry. You chose a bad time for this," Dorinda said without emotion.

She wasn't going to get what she wanted from Matt. That much was clear. Seeing him again hadn't helped her at all. In fact, she was probably going to need a massage to loosen the muscles in her neck and back. She didn't need any extra tension in her life right now. She led him to the door. He didn't respond to her statement until he stood just outside her doorway.

"You're wrong," Matt said. She started to swing the door closed. He stopped it with his hand. "I've changed. I'll prove it to you. I am a much better friend these days."

"Good for you," Dorinda said, and gave the door a push. He let go and it closed in his face.

As soon as the phone's battery had recharged, Dorinda called Daria to tell her about Matt's extraordinary visit. "You wouldn't believe who came by here tonight!" she began.

"I'm not in the mood for twenty questions, girlfriend. You got something to tell me, just spill it," Daria said impatiently.

"If you're not interested . . ." Drin knew her friend wouldn't be able to resist the challenge in her voice.

"Come on, who was it?" Daria asked.

"Matthew Cooper, believe it or not." Dorinda still couldn't get over the fact that he'd shown up at her door.

"What? Why?" Daria sounded as astonished as Dorinda felt.

"To say he missed me all these years and he wanted to start over, as friends."

"What the—" Daria sounded properly stunned.

"I still can't believe it." Daria could picture her friend shaking her head.

"What did you say?"

"I said no thanks—what do you think I said?"

"Of all the exes, you always talk about him like he was some kind of god and computer whiz all in one."

"So you thought I might want him?"

"I wasn't sure. I'm sorry. I'm glad you didn't, though."

"No chance. I thought he was all that and a bag of chips once, but I'm not sixteen anymore. I know what he is."

"There it is, girlfriend," Daria congratulated her. "I'm proud of you."

"Why would you think I'd even consider . . . No, forget that. I don't think I want to know."

"I never saw you two together, but Claire and Tamika told me how close you were. I just thought he might be the reason you don't date anymore."

"He's as much of the reason as the rest of the duds I've dated, but I don't want anything from him. Except maybe some closure. I'd love to have him on his knees, grovelling for my forgiveness."

"I like the attitude. You'll be back out there, ready to give those men as good as they get in no time," Daria said.

"Will you forget about my dating habits for a minute? What did we just say, at brunch yesterday? I wouldn't have even called you if I thought you were going to get back on that."

"I'm sorry, all right. Old habits are hard to break."

Dorinda let it go. "I still haven't gotten over him showing up on my doorstep."

"How big a jerk is this guy, anyway?" Daria asked.

"About as big as they come," Dorinda responded. "I just can't figure out what he thought I'd say. 'Oh yeah, I've missed you, too. And by the way, want to spend the night? Pick up where we left off?' "

"Sounds to me like his elevator does not go all the way to the top floor," Daria said colorfully.

"I guess that's as good an explanation as any," Dorinda replied. "Well, hopefully that's all cleared up."

"Hopefully?"

"He *said* he's going to prove to me he can be a better friend than he was last time."

"That wouldn't be hard to do," Daria said sarcastically.

"He's got an advantage over the other contenders vying for the position. He's been there before. Not that there are any contenders," she added hastily. But it was too late. She'd given Daria the opening her friend needed to mention, for the thousandth time, that there were men who were eager for a chance to change her opinion of the opposite sex.

"Let us not forget Ronald," Daria said.

"Don't start that again," she begged.

"Okay, okay." Daria soothed. "I just don't want this little visit from Matt to sink you any deeper into your cloister. I know you don't want his nasty butt up in there, but that doesn't mean you have to be alone."

"I'm enjoying celibacy. It's got some real advantages," Dorinda said feelingly.

"I knew you were going to say that. Understand that I'm not giving up on you, girl. We're going to get you hooked up, yet."

"Dream on." Dorinda laughed. "And speaking of dreams, I know you like to turn in early on Sunday. I'll talk to you at work tomorrow."

After she hung up the phone, she felt restless and edgy. She had picked up the book *Inc. Yourself* during the week and this seemed the perfect time to finally take a look at it. Her mind was working a mile a minute and she figured she might as well make good use of the seething energy left by her near argument with Matthew. She could turn her residual anger into something productive.

She hadn't gotten through the first chapter before she started skimming through the sections on paperwork and monies available to minority–owned business. Then she found the instructions for creating a business plan. Her usual methodical approach would have been to read the entire book, and then turn back to this section, but she didn't feel quite herself at the moment. She started jotting down notes on a business plan of her own. It was tough, but absorbing, and an hour after she sat down, when the doorbell rang, Drin didn't think to ask who it was.

For the second time that evening, Matt Cooper stood outside her door. "I definitely screwed up," he said.

"Uh huh," she agreed, not sure what specifically he was referring to, but sure that the confession was warranted.

"May I please come in?" he asked.

"I guess so," Dorinda said ungraciously. She stepped out of his way, but didn't move away from the door. He closed it behind him, then faced her. She stood, arms folded across her chest, and waited for his explanation.

"I really am sorry for the way things just went. Almost as sorry as I am for letting you walk out of my life ten years ago."

"Oh." She felt her anger and tension start to slip away with the sincere apology. "When I said I missed you, I really meant it. It wasn't just casual conversation. We grew up together. We were part of each other. I thought it would always be that way. I didn't know what I was giving up. I didn't know how to say good-bye at all. And I didn't have the faintest idea how much I was going to miss you."

This was what she'd been waiting for. Hoping for. "I did," Dorinda said softly.

"What?" Matt looked shocked.

"I knew. But there wasn't a damn thing I could do about it." She looked into his eyes. They grew dark as comprehension dawned. "I knew how much I was going to miss you."

"You did?" Dorinda couldn't look away. She nodded wordlessly. "Oh, God," he groaned.

She didn't know who moved first, but an instant later his arms were around her, and hers were wrapped around his waist. Her last thought before his lips descended on hers, was that this was the way it was always meant to be. Then she didn't think anything at all. She was pure sensation. She remembered every time they'd touched like this. The feel of his mouth over hers was so familiar, it was as if no time had passed since the last time. They were a part of each other. They belonged together.

The feel of his hands against the flesh at the small of her back woke her up a little. "What about your girlfriend?" she murmured against his lips.

"We're not exclusive," he said.

The simple statement sent a draught of cold water through her veins. "That's it?" she asked. He didn't seem to have noticed that anything was amiss. One of his hands slid up her back and under her braids to grasp her nape, but she pulled her head back, out of reach of his mouth. "You're kissing me like my lips are the last you'll ever see, touch or taste, and tomorrow you're just going to call her like nothing ever happened?" she asked, incredulous.

"Not tomorrow." He still hadn't opened his eyes, but his lips curved in a wry grin. Dorinda was not amused. She waited for him to realize that she was no longer kissing him. His eyes opened when it finally occurred to him. "I was kidding, Drin," he said immediately.

"Not funny," she said. She was upset. He was only proving that he wasn't the man that she once thought him. He was a typical, unfeeling, oversexed moron.

"What?" he finally asked. "You're worried about Francie?"

"No, I'm worried about me. I can't believe I could even consider making love to you."

"Francie knows that I see other women. She sees other men. That's how she wants it."

"She seemed pretty possessive when I met her," Dorinda said.

"You must have misunderstood," Matt said. "She couldn't be jealous of me. We've only been going out for a couple of months. It's not that serious."

"But it could be. I mean, she could think that it will be."

"No," he stated.

"No?" Dorinda echoed.

"No way. She knows I don't feel that way about her. As you said, we don't have that much in common."

Dorinda didn't know what to think. She wanted to believe him. "So why are you together?"

"We have a good time. She's fun. She thinks I'm fun."

"And that's all? You're sure?"

"Sure, I'm sure. Even if I hadn't met you again, I knew the relationship wasn't going to last much longer."

Amazingly, Dorinda was convinced. "Are you saying you were planning to break up with her?"

"She was getting to that stage. When I saw you again, I knew it was just a matter of time."

"Me?" For some insane reason, she was incredibly touched by the revelation.

"You," he said sincerely. "Of course, you."

This time, she was conscious of moving toward him, of Matt opening his arms and pulling her closer. He kissed her cheek, the tip of her nose, her eyes.

He growled, "I want you." He was still kissing her when he asked, "What about your boyfriend?"

"Who?" Dorinda said, completely engrossed in relearning the line of his jaw.

"The guy you were with at the wedding. I forget his name."

"I wasn't with anyone," she said, dreamily, rubbing her cheek against his.

"You weren't?" He traced her cheekbone with one tentative fingertip, sending a shiver through her. "I thought you were there with the best man."

"No, I barely knew him. I just let you assume he was my date because I didn't want you to know I didn't have one when you had Francie with you."

"I thought you were together," Matt breathed into her ear.

"I know, but I wasn't. He's my sister's business partner."

"That's good," Matt said, kissing the corners of her mouth.

"I've never gone out with him, except for a cup of coffee."

"Coffee?"

"Forget it, it's a long, unimportant story," Dorinda said, and she caught his lower lip between hers and sucked on it provocatively.

"Tell me later," Matt said, and kissed her neck.

His lips were hard, but soft, like his skin, which she remembered all too well. Drin eagerly unbuttoned his shirt and slipped it off his shoulders. He let it fall, busy with her T-shirt, which he lifted over her head in one swift, smooth motion. Then his arms wrapped urgently around her.

It had been so long. She moaned as their naked flesh met, and he gasped and kissed her even more hungrily, devouring her. When they'd kissed for an eternity, they finally took stock of where they were, and she led him into her bedroom. She needed him now. Nothing could have stopped her from making love to this man tonight.

But she hadn't forgotten the past. Even when all other thoughts flew from her mind and she was pulsing with need for him, her heartbeat pounded out two words over and over again. "He left. He left." She let go of his hand and turned to face him, searching his face. Her fears couldn't compete with his eyes, and his mouth. They burned her skin wherever they touched.

She was conscious of every movement he made, aware of him on a level that was deeper than his skin. She saw his broad brown chest expand with each breath, his eyes flicker from her eyes to her lips to her neck, the muscles in his arms flow one into the other as he lifted his hand to her shoulder, and flow back again as he stroked her arm lightly, until his hand rested behind her elbow. He pulled her gently into his body again, and lowered his head to kiss the hollow between her neck and her shoulder.

She nuzzled his jaw, and her hands came up to splay across his chest. Her palms drew out the heat in him, her fingertips grazing the dark hair that shadowed his pectoral muscles. He smelled of shaving cream and toothpaste, and she smiled and said, "You cleaned up for me." It was an old joke, from their first date, when she'd insisted that after school, and before their first romantic dinner, he had to go home, change his clothes, and shower, or it wouldn't be a 'real' date.

"You'd do it for any other girl," she had said then.

He'd argued. "But we're going to a basketball game at school. All we'll be able to smell are old gym socks anyway."

"Not when you pick me up," she'd insisted.

So he'd done it, and shown up with his hair still glistening from the shower, and a dab of shaving cream in one of his ears, grumbling, "What's the point of going out with my best friend if she's going to turn into a regular girl. You never cared what I smelled like before."

"I never got this close before," Drin had said, and stepped up to him and kissed him—knowing her two brothers were probably peeking around the livingroom wall and snickering, and her parents were going to hear about this later.

But the past receded as she catalogued the differences in his body now against her memory of him. His jaw, even after a shave, was darker. The stubble on his chin was visible, this close up, and she could feel it a little. At sixteen, his skin had felt as smooth as her own. She couldn't feel his bones beneath his flesh anymore, either. His arms were much thicker, his shoulders deeper, his abdomen a wall of muscle.

The biggest change was in his eyes. They were deeper and so much more knowing. When he looked at her body, when his fingertips found her breasts, it was with an assurance, a conceit, he hadn't had then. The wonder of the experience they'd shared—exactly forty–seven times . . .

she'd been sixteen; she'd counted—had been replaced with a different kind of awe.

This was Matt, loving her again; his hands touching her in places that hadn't felt a man's touch in so long. Her knees went weak, and he held her up, and nearly carried her to the bed. He sat her down and knelt before her, to remove her sneakers and socks, and then skim her sweatpants down her legs. She hoped he wasn't comparing her body to the one he'd made love to at sixteen. She was fleshier, certainly rounder everywhere, though karate kept her in pretty good shape. Her legs weren't sticks anymore, but padded at the thighs and hips. As she neared thirty, her abdomen had resisted all her efforts to retain her youthful concavity and had swelled, as nature intended.

Without surgery, she would never again look like the fourteen–year–olds in the underwear ads. She was proud of her body, but nervous under his questing eyes that he'd find it lacking in comparison to his memories of her. He stroked her thighs, kneading them gently, then leaned forward and kissed her kneecap where, she suddenly noticed, a purplish bruise had formed—probably the result of yesterday's kickboxing workout.

He stood and unzipped his jeans, then stooped to remove them. She scooted back in the bed, making room for him to join her without once taking her eyes off his magnificent body. As he straightened up again, she admired his long, strong legs which had also filled out nicely, and followed them up and up, and sighed in satisfaction, and reached for him as he joined her in the bed and pulled her close to him.

She could feel every inch of him against her as they met and melded together, still a perfect fit, if even more forbidden to each other now than they had been in high–school. Her arms and legs twined around him and he slid against the core of her body, sending a tremor through her. She wanted him inside of her, now, but he just continued kissing and stroking and teasing her with his tongue and teeth and hands until Drin bit his shoulder in desperation.

"Ow!" he said, sounding shocked. "What was that for?"

She realized they hadn't spoken in a long, long time and she laughed because the first words she wanted to say were "Hurry up!"

"What's so funny?" he asked, still rubbing the spot she'd bitten. She told him. He, obligingly, fulfilled her request.

When she awakened the next morning and remembered how she'd acted, Dorinda was mortified. If she had to do something so stupid, why couldn't it have been with anyone but Matt Cooper? She would have sworn that nothing on earth could make her behave so brainlessly. Despite her friends' constant reminders that she was young, healthy, with all the usual urges, she hadn't felt out of control. At least not until the previous night. She hadn't even really missed sex all that much since she'd sworn off men almost two years before. Why did this have to be the way she proved everyone else right, and herself wrong?

He stirred beside her, and she jumped out of bed and ran for the bathroom. Once inside, she locked the door and turned the shower on and climbed in. She washed automatically, desperately trying to think of a way out of this. It had been a mistake. If she was going to get involved with someone at this point in her life, it would by no means be this man. He had already demolished her world once. He might not have meant to do so, but he had hurt her so badly that she couldn't imagine letting anyone else ever get that close again. Not even Matt himself.

As soon as she turned the shower off, she heard him call, "Good morning."

"Oh no, oh no, oh no," she chanted softly, wishing herself out of the bathroom and out of this apartment. It didn't work. "Uh ... morning," she called out, leaning back against the door, thinking maybe she could just hide in there until he left.

"Are you coming out of there anytime soon?" she heard him ask.

"In a minute," she trilled. She had to get to work, but she hated going back into that bedroom wearing nothing beneath her robe. Although she was covered in thick terry cloth to her knees, she felt vulnerable, exposed. But she had to face the day ahead and she was as ready as she was going to get.

He was awake and sitting up in the bed, covered from the waist down by her white sheet. Now that her mind was back in control of her body, she was surprised that she still felt a frisson of awareness of the long, nude body beneath those sheets. She forced it out of her consciousness, and looked away. Facing him was the hardest thing she'd ever done, and her eyes searched the room, the floor, the window, anything but him.

"How are you?" he asked tentatively.

"Fine. Just fine," she answered. Then thought to make her way to the closet. Trying to keep as much of herself as possible behind the open closet door, she slipped her underwear on under her robe, then her jeans. She grabbed her top. "I've got to get to work." Drin let the robe drop to the floor and quickly slipped her camisole and blouse on over her head.

"Like that, is it?" he asked. "You're just going to run away?"

"What do you want me to do?" He couldn't be any more pleased about what had happened between them than she was. Up until last week, she'd have bet he hardly remembered her. And even last night, his aim in coming to her home hadn't seemed to be seduction. He had said he wanted them to be friends again, and she still believed he had meant it.

"Nothing." He held up his hands in a gesture of surrender.

"What did you think? We'd wake up this morning and act as if nothing had happened?"

"I didn't think that far ahead. In fact," he rubbed his eyes with the palms of his hands. "I wasn't thinking. Period."

Dorinda had to admit, she didn't exactly have a plan either. She just wanted to get out of here, out of this. "I guess we're both guilty of that. Not thinking, I mean. Our . . . hormones just took over. My only excuse is that it's been a long time, and I was feeling a little . . . tense. I'm sorry."

"No need to apologize. Really. I was there, and you—" he looked around at the floor, and she instinctively reached over and picked up his pants and threw them to him. He turned his back to her, and pulled them on as he stood. "I'm the one who is sorry. I, we, shouldn't have . . ." He shook his head, looking down at his feet. Then he started around the bed.

Dorinda froze, until he leaned over and picked up his shoes, then sat on the bed to put them on. She finished dressing.

"Well, I guess we needed closure," she said, with a lame attempt at a laugh.

"Yeah, sure," he said, but he didn't sound convinced.

After the intimacy they had shared the night before, it was sad that all she wanted to do was to cover up, and to get away from those deep brown eyes. But, sad or not, she had to get rid of him. She needed to figure out what had happened here, and what she was going to do next.

"I've really got to go," she said. She turned to leave.

"Drin?" he called.

"Yes?" She stopped in the doorway, but she didn't turn back.

"I really am sorry. I didn't mean for this to happen."

"I know."

All the way to work on the subway, she replayed the evening over in her mind. She'd been angry, upset with everyone and everything, and with herself. She'd grown angrier when she'd seen him. But his second visit, his admission that he was still attracted to her, had made her anger dissipate. It was all she'd wanted to hear him say for years. She'd pictured it. If she'd known he was going to be at Gwen's wedding two weeks ago, she probably would have imagined the whole scene—without the fake date, the awkward ride home, the argument, or any of the unpleasant elements of their reunion. Just him, saying as he had the night before that she was the one he should have chosen all those years ago, that she felt right in his arms in a way no other woman ever had.

That old fantasy had seduced her, not Matt Cooper. She had only herself to blame.

> Where so many hours have been spent in convincing myself that I am right, is there not some reason to fear I may be wrong.
>
> Jane Austen.

11.

When Dorinda arrived at work, she jumped into a client's emergency head first, desperate for a distraction from her thoughts. She didn't emerge again until nearly quitting time, when Daria stuck her head in the office to ask if she was ready to go to the No Name.

"I'm not sure I'm going to make it tonight. I've been dealing with the bank people all day, and I haven't even had a chance to check my e-mail."

"Do it tomorrow," Daria said. "Come on, it's Monday night. You should unwind."

"I'll be along in a little while," Dorinda reluctantly agreed. "Save me a place."

She delayed for a while, but she was going to have to face her friends eventually, so she finally closed up her desk and headed for the bar. It was only after she got there that she decided she was not going to tell them about Matt. A twinge of guilt assailed her, but she rationalized the decision by reminding herself that her sex life was none of their business. They were grown women, well past the age where locker room talk was justified. If she told them about Matt and herself, they'd just crow over her fall from grace, and she didn't need to hear the collective I-told-you-so.

She felt badly enough already. She didn't want to think they might have been right all along. This had just been an aberration, a once in a lifetime thing that no one could have anticipated. Dorinda still didn't feel like she'd been wrong about dating. After all, it hadn't been a date. Exactly.

When she met the girls at the No Name, they ended up having the usual conversation; highlights of the week's events, friendly banter about their questions and quandaries, and yet another reiteration of their conviction that Drin should consider dating the men who had been asking her lately. For some reason, as she walked home, a question Daria had asked, stayed with her. "I think I understand this no-dating rule, in the abstract, but men are coming out of the woodwork, and you still say you're not interested for all the same old reasons. Aren't you tempted to see what the sport is like these days?" her friend had queried.

"No," Drin had answered. "Nothing's changed as far as I can see." She felt like she'd been lying, though. There might have been no change in the dating 'scene', but there had been a change in her. She wondered if her friends had sensed it, and that was why so much of their conversation had centered around the question of her dating lately. They had always driven her nuts with their conviction that they were right and she was wrong, but it seemed to Dorinda that this harping on the subject everytime she spoke with them was something new. And the pressure to succumb to the pressure was growing . . . inside her.

Perhaps it was the girls' latest debate, or maybe it was her lapse with Matt, but when Ronnie called her again about the *Lion King* tickets, Dorinda decided to break her own rules and go out with him. It had been so long since she'd been on an actual date that she felt about sixteen years old again as she prepared for the evening out. Her reflection in the mirror was somewhat reassuring. She chose to wear a tailored black suit that looked chic and elegant, and gave her a veneer of sophistication.

She hadn't spoken to Matt since Monday morning. He'd called once, and left the simple message, "Let's talk." Dorinda hadn't gotten up the courage to call him back yet. Tonight's date would be a preparation of sorts for the conversation she knew she couldn't put off forever. If she could get through this date, she figured, she'd be able to get through anything.

She met Ronnie for dinner before the musical at a French restaurant in the theatre district. Her first glimpse of him both reassured her and threw her even further off balance. He looked good. Sexy. Confident. Male. Intellectually, she knew that spending the evening with Ronnie couldn't be all that difficult. He was a nice, interesting man who was about as unthreatening as a person could be. Emotionally, she was a wreck.

"Hi," he said, taking her jacket. He was sensitive, sweet, and quite charming, and she was confident he'd do his best to put her at ease. She told herself she had to stop worrying and loosen up. Recent events hadn't exactly filled her with self-confidence. She'd embarrassed herself at her sister's wedding, in front of the four men who had had a profound influence on her. Two weeks later, she'd somehow ended up in bed with a man who had once broken her heart. *Relax!* she commanded herself.

"Nice place," she said to Ronnie, struggling to put all thoughts of Matt out of her head. She glanced around at the elegant restaurant, which consisted of a huge art deco room filled with large round tables. Each table was covered with a pristine white tablecloth and glistening silver, and a crystal bud vase with one red rose rising over the beautiful place settings.

"The food is wonderful. They also know that most of their patrons are going to catch a Broadway show, and they're quick. And it's only a five–minute walk to the theatre from here."

"You've thought of everything, then," she said, teasingly.

"I try," he said, in the same tone.

She smiled, and Dorinda could almost see him exhale—in the Terry McMillan sense. She sat back in her chair.

"You look lovely," he said. She was wearing a black linen pants suit and had already shrugged out of the jacket, revealing her blue satin camisole-type blouse. It was a comfortable outfit that looked classy, and had gotten her sister's seal of approval the first time she'd worn it. She wanted to compare well to Gwen tonight since Ronnie had a lot of contact with her twin through their work together. Dorinda had been compared to Gwendolyn by men all her life. She might not know how she was going to get through the evening, and she wasn't sure how she felt about Ronald Clarke, but Drin was vain enough not to want to suffer in comparison to his business partner.

"Thank you," she said. "You look nice, too."

"Thank *you*," he acknowledged her compliment with a nod.

He cleared his throat. "So," he said, and she braced herself, but he only joked, "I think this is going pretty well so far, don't you?"

"So far, so good," she agreed, relieved. If he kept it light, she could handle this.

"I was a little nervous," he admitted sheepishly. "Since you told me you don't really date."

"You can't be nervous. I feel like I've forgotten how to do this," Dorinda quipped. "It's been so long since I was out with a strange man I was afraid I would forget how my fork worked."

"I'm not really that strange," he said conspiratorially.

"No, of course not," she chuckled.

"You're doing fine, by the way."

"Just keep telling me that," Dorinda said.

He laughed, but then there was an awkward pause between them. At least, it felt awkward to her. "Remind me, what comes next?" she asked.

"I haven't been out on a first date myself in six years," Ronnie said. "We'll have to figure it out together."

She'd forgotten about his recently ended relationship with his long–term girlfriend. The reminder made her want to put him at ease, as he was doing for her. "So, how's business?" she asked, since that was usually a safe question. He spent the next half hour giving her a quick summary of the history of the cosmetics industry. She was surprised by how interesting it was. In her mind it was tied up with models, and beauty queens, and advertising, and she hadn't given much thought to the science or the politics of the business.

It was always fascinating to learn about something from someone who was truly excited by their subject, and Ronnie was as passionate about his venture with Gwendolyn as her sister had ever been, although he didn't share her particular interest in women feeling better about themselves and their appearance. "I think women look lovely without all that gook on their faces," he said. "But if they're going to buy it, and use it, I'd like to offer really wonderful choices for women of color. I believe we can produce more variety, all safe, hypoallergenic, and without using any animal testing," he enthused as they finished the meal.

"That sounds great," Dorinda said sincerely.

"I hope I haven't bored you," he queried.

"Not at all. It's been an education. Just one question. What's your position on lipstick?" she asked.

"What?"

Just one question.

She held up her lipstick. "Do you mind?"

"How could I?" he chuckled. "You're my target market."

They had a little time before they had to leave for the theatre, so they talked about other plays and musicals they'd seen while they sipped the restaurant's creamy cappucino, and then they strolled toward the theatre.

"I love this," Dorinda said, as they came to the corner of 46th Street and Broadway in the heart of Times Square. The sky was just beginning to darken above the colorful neon signs and huge billboards that shone down on them.

"So do I," Ronnie agreed. "I often think of moving into the city, but I love Brooklyn, too." Ronnie had moved to New York from Ohio, after business school. She knew he'd been invited to join one of the prestigious executive training programs, but after his year with Chase Manhattan, he'd decided he preferred working for himself to toeing the line at a large corporation. It was another thing they had in common. Dorinda had been recruited by some major corporations for her computer skills, and Ronnie had been a prime specimen for one of the token spots for African Americans in the banking business.

"I love my neighborhood. It's more like a small town than a part of the most populated city in the country. And Manhattan is only a subway ride away. I don't have to live in this dirty, crime-infested city, but I can enjoy it. I think we get the best of both worlds, don't you?"

"Yes," he said. They walked down a couple of blocks to the theatre, through the heart of New York City. The lights of The Great White Way seemed to grow brighter every moment, as the sky kept growing darker. Drin felt a part of the excitement, like the many tourists who stood about gawking, and the actresses and playwrights who struggled to work here, and everyone else who worshiped this mecca of the theatre world.

They had house seats, the perfect seats to enjoy a Broadway show in one of its bigger theatres. They were not right on top of the stage, but about ten rows back and in the center of the orchestra. Dorinda loved these theatres, the plush seats, towering ceilings, and, of course, the huge stage, hidden behind forty-foot red velvet curtains, which slowly parted as the house lights dimmed. Ronnie took her hand for a moment and gave it a squeeze, and she turned her head to look at him. He was looking up at the panorama unfolding onstage. He looked like a young boy, taking in the lively music and colorful costumes of the characters on the stage, his eyes wide.

Dorinda felt oddly protective of this sweet, sensitive man. Then her attention turned to the spectacle unfolding in front of her, and she forgot about Ronnie, work, Gwen, her parents, and even Matt as she became completely engrossed in the music and dancing onstage.

"I was a little worried that I wouldn't like it," she told Ronnie as they emerged from the theatre onto Broadway. "I hated the movie."

"I have two nieces back home who love the show," he said. "I know a lot of it by heart, and I've always loved the song "The Lion Sleeps Tonight." But I wasn't expecting it to be as good as it was. The costumes, the acting and dancing, were so original. Kids may enjoy this show, but it's definitely something you appreciate more as an adult."

"It was one of the most innovative productions I've ever seen," Dorinda agreed. "The movie was so racist, but I thought the musical was just gorgeous. I have nothing against Whoopie Goldberg or Sinbad, but I hated that the bad guys were all played by minorities, with very recognizable accents. The dialogue even included popular slang phrases that were meant, I think, to identify the hyenas as black and hispanic."

"I don't know if it was done on purpose," Ronnie said. "They got the best talent available for the parts, I'm sure. And a Brit played the worst character," he added.

"Jeremy Irons did play Scar, but he was also a lead, with some of the best lines in the movie. He was much more sympathetic than the hyenas whom he controlled, by the way."

"Okay, okay," Ronnie held up his hands in surrender. "I give in. It was a racist film. But the play was nothing like that."

"No, it wasn't. Those actors and dancers were incredible.

And those costumes were like nothing I've ever seen. How did they make those people look like giraffes?"

"Stilts, I think," Ronnie said. "I'll call my nieces, they'll know. They're the ones who told me I had to see this show."

"I never see anything by Disney anymore, since the media exposed their treatment of their workers in Haiti. But I am glad I got to see this. Does that make me a hypocrite?"

"Do you support the spending of government dollars to develop the arts?" he asked.

"Yes, as a matter of fact, I do," Dorinda said. "Why?"

"Then you're supporting one cause, even if you're a little unsupportive of the other. Every stage production you attend, every art show, all of it is supported by the NEA in one way or another, and our support is necessary to keep our elected officials from deciding to cut those funds any further than they already have."

"That's true," Dorinda mused. "I hadn't thought of it that way. I think you've found the perfect rationalization for me. I should support companies like Disney to some extent, since they are producing art." Ronnie nodded, very well-satisfied with himself. "Actually, that brings up an interesting point," Dorinda continued. "Since I don't believe in censorship, but I do believe in supporting the arts, then how can I express my dissatisfaction with a company like Disney, without crossing the boundary into the area of censorship?"

"I guess you've only got your vote. Everyone has the choice of not paying for art that they don't approve of, but they don't have the right to stop someone else from creating or selling their art. I guess our representatives are left with the burden of drawing the line."

"Oh God, that's a frightening thought," Dorinda said. They had been walking for some time, talking, and she realized they had just passed the second of two subway stations at which they could have caught their train home. "Where are we going?" she asked.

"I thought we'd walk down to the village and have dessert on Thompson Street," Ronnie said.

Drin nodded and they fell into step together as if it were the most natural thing in the world to do.

"So, are you interested in politics?" she asked.

"Why do you ask? Is this a test?" he responded.

"No, no." Drin laughed. "You mentioned supporting the arts with our tax dollars, and I wondered if you were active in politics."

"I'm embarassed to say, I'm not. I believe in thinking globally and acting locally, but I never have the—"

"Time," they said together. "Me, too," Drin admitted ruefully.

"My father always said; never talk politics, religion, or sports with a woman. It's bound to get you into trouble."

"My Aunt Willie gave me similar advice, years ago." Dorinda felt at ease with this man, despite all her earlier misgivings.

"Looks like we've got even more in common than I thought," Ronnie commented.

They continued talking straight through the walk to the cafe, and shared a dessert of Italian pastry and the taxi ride home, without ever having an awkward moment of silence. Then, as he walked her to her door, Drin ran out of things to say. She didn't want to ask him up to her apartment. They hadn't set foot inside her building yet, and she already felt ill at ease—and it wasn't the sweaty-palmed-hoping-for-a-good-night-kiss kind of tension that filled her.

Apparently he felt exactly the opposite. "Since you danced with me at Gwen's wedding, I wanted you to touch me again."

"I have a confession to make," Dorinda said.

"To me?" he asked, raising his eyebrows in surprise.

"I wasn't exactly trying to get your attention at the wedding, but I did need your arm." He looked completely baffled. "I was pretending you were my date, for the benefit of my college boyfriend. He was there with his wife," she added, hoping he would understand.

His smile just widened. "I'm glad I was useful," he said.

"You're not annoyed?" she asked, surprised.

"I think it was adorable," he responded. "You're adorable."

"I've been called plenty of things," Dorinda said, smiling nervously, "But I've never been called that before."

"You're kidding," he said, genuinely astounded. "But you're so tiny, and funny, and smart, and . . . I don't know, it's one of the first words that springs to my mind when I think of you."

"You don't know me very well," Dorinda admonished gently.

"I'd certainly like to remedy that," Ronnie said, in his gentlemanly way. She couldn't help but smile. "Are you laughing at me?" he asked with a mock threatening growl.

"Not at all. You are just such an odd mixture. One minute you're so smooth, and sophisticated, and the next you say things like that."

"Like what?"

" 'I'd certainly like to remedy that.' " she said in her deepest voice.

"What's wrong with that?" he asked.

"Nothing. Nothing at all. It's just . . . you sound like some guy from an old forties movie."

He grinned. "Hey, those guys were the coolest."

"Sure they were," she said sarcastically.

Dorinda was grinning back at him when he leaned over and kissed her, gently. He pulled away immediately, to look down into her eyes. Whatever it was he saw there, he took as an invitation, because he kissed her again. He held the kiss longer this time. Dorinda relaxed against him, and casually kissed him back, waiting for the heat, and desire, to consume her as it had when Matt kissed her. It didn't come. She felt comfortable, even content, in Ronnie's arms, but there was none of the need she'd felt when Matt and she had explored each other's lips.

Ronnie slowly pulled away. "Mmm," he murmured. He hadn't felt anything lacking in the kiss apparently. When he spoke his voice was a soft growl. "That was nice."

"It was a nice . . . surprise," she said gently. She looked up at him, and watched his eyes slowly lighten. When he focussed on her again, she could see his disappointment as he realized she hadn't been as moved by their embrace as he had. She also sensed his acceptance.

"Was it?" he asked. He didn't comment on her qualification of his statement, but instead made a joke of it. "I always like to give my dates a surprise gift when we get home. That way, even if they didn't have a great time, they'll probably agree to go out with me again, just to see what I'm gonna do next."

"I thought you hadn't been on a date in six years," Drin tossed back in the same light tone.

"I didn't say this method worked," was his quick retort.

"So how often have you felt the need to give your dates a consolation prize?" she asked, coyly.

"Well, I'd feel bad if they had to walk away empty-handed."

"And do they all get the same thing?"

"Kisses? Oh, no." He shook his head. "Sometimes it's whatever I happen to have in my pocket. A handkerchief, or a candy bar, or something."

"Nice guy," Dorinda commented.

"I try," he said modestly.

"Well, I had a lovely time. Door prize and all," she said as she put her hand on the door handle.

"Me, too. I'll call you," he said, accepting his dismissal gracefully.

"Good night," Dorinda said, pushing the door open.

"Good night," he turned to walk away. "Dorinda?" She

turned back to find him watching her. "I hope we can do this again."

She nodded, then escaped by slipping inside. She didn't want to do it again. But she didn't have a single good reason why not.

> Women never have a half hour in all their lives
> . . . that they can call their own without the fear
> of offending or of hurting someone.
>
> Florence Nightingale

12.

The past had come back to haunt her with a vengeance. Dorinda received a wedding invitation from another ex-boyfriend whom she'd seen at Gwen's wedding, Thomas Grayson. Her relationship with Tom had not been like the others. It had been harmonious, he'd been supportive, and they'd been completely honest with each other. Unfortunately, the fairy tale hadn't lasted, though. They weren't in love, and eventually he ended it. He wasn't happy where they were, he said, and no matter how hard she tried, Dorinda wouldn't be happy if they moved on to the next step. And she had tried. They had both done their best to grow together, stay together. They'd followed all of the advice in the popular books. It hadn't worked.

In fact, Tom was the reason that she'd decided to stop dating altogether. Her heart wasn't broken when he let her go. It was almost a relief. And she realized she'd been with him for the wrong reasons. She had loved him, and she believed he had loved her. They had been there for each other, but they had not been in love. She didn't want, ever, to make that mistake again.

It seemed that love, for her, was one mistake after another. She didn't want to deceive herself again, nor did she want to hurt anyone else. While she hadn't been dating, she'd been safe. Now, she'd given Matthew Cooper the power to hurt her again. And Ronnie was vulnerable to her. It wasn't an acceptable situation.

Then Matt tracked her down, at work. She didn't even let him into her office. When Donna told her that he was waiting for her at the reception desk, she went out to meet him.

"Hi," Dorinda greeted him, with a smile, and with her hand stretched out for his handshake. She wasn't fooling anyone with this act and she knew it, but she felt more comfortable treating him like a client who had dropped in unexpectedly. She gestured toward two large blue foam chairs that faced each other across a modern glass table top, which formed the waiting area. The conference room was too lonely. Dorinda preferred to remain in plain view of the receptionist, and anyone who came into the office. They slowly sat across from each other.

"Dorinda, I think we should get together and talk," he said, as soon as they were seated.

"Of course." She kept her phony business-y smile plastered on her face, and nodded.

"You choose the time. I'll be there."

"The No Name Bar, on Willoughby. Tomorrow night." She kept her gaze level and inquiring. He nodded. "Fine, I'll see you there," she confirmed.

"What time?" he asked, as they both stood.

"Eight o'clock?"

He was gone as quickly as he had come, and she went back to her office without speaking to Donna. Amazingly, she did not hear from Daria until lunchtime, and even then she was just offered an invitation to lunch. Apparently, Donna had obeyed her edict, and hadn't told her friend about her unexpected visitor.

She fobbed Daria off. "I'm going to eat at my desk."

Drin often had her meals in her office, and Daria didn't question it, so she was left alone with her thoughts through the noon hour. She was completely preoccupied with thoughts of the date she'd made with Matt. She had no idea what she was going to say to him.

She was on the verge of panicking as the hour drew near the next night, when he called and cancelled their appointment.

"I've got to go see Gerome," he said, in explanation.

"Fine." This was one meeting that Dorinda was thrilled to avoid. He was the one who had insisted they talk. It hadn't been her idea.

"I'll call to reschedule."

"Fine," she said, and gently hung up the phone. His cancellation only confirmed his disinterest. If he'd had any intention of trying to continue their relationship, or work through their differences, he would not have decided to see Gerome rather than meet her as arranged, she reasoned. He saw his old friend all of the time, while theirs was a unique situation. She knew now all his urgency had just been for show. Perhaps he'd just wanted the one thing they never seemed to get—closure. Dorinda refused to stew over the incident. It was history. She had too much to think about, and to do, to waste any more time on Matt Cooper.

She had awaited eagerly any further word from Bob Anderson on the changes he'd proposed in the office. Feeling as though she were the eye in the center of the maelstrom, she'd fielded all the inquiries and complaints of the other programmers and employees, but she had no firm answers. Bob could only say 'Let's wait and see,' and Dorinda didn't think she could comply with that request. If her boss couldn't come up with answers, she'd have to devise some of her own. It seemed her best bet was to start making plans to leave the company and start up her own. She had done her research. All that remained was to do it.

Before she got the opportunity to tender her resignation, the situation at home took her life over again. Her mother called. "Gwendolyn is looking for an apartment, Drin, but she still won't talk about the status of the marriage. We don't want her to go apartment shopping, put down a couple of months' security, move in, and then discover she's made a mistake. We're going to do an intervention." Her mother and father believed in interventions, and they took credit for saving the lives, marriages, and children of many of their friends because of their proactive behavior. Proactive was, in fact, their latest catchword.

"Jeez, Mom, she's not an alcoholic or a junkie. She's not under the influence of any cult, or even any of those paperback psychology books you and Dad love to foist on us. She's just doing what seems right to her. Can't you just leave her alone?"

"No. We've got her under our roof, and we're not going to waste this opportunity. Will you come?"

"If I say no, will you call it off?" Dorinda asked desperately.

"No way. She's our daughter. We've got to get her to open up and talk about this. Self-awareness is the first thing to go in a crisis, and it's the most important tool in making decisions. We're going to try to get through to her, whether you help us or not."

Dorinda had to go. Little as she had in common with her twin, she knew Gwen would hate having this kind of confrontation with their parents about as much as she'd like to use sulfur-based chemicals to straighten hair. After going to the gym to work out her pent–up frustration, she went to dinner on Friday night, as prepared as possible for any weird New Age rituals her parents might have come up with.

After dinner, it began. "Gwen, we have all decided that we need to speak with you, seriously. Whether you will talk to us or not, you're going to have to listen." Her mother's wide brown eyes were intent on Gwendolyn's face. Her lithe body leaned into her daughter, as if she could coax confidences out of her by sheer force of will.

"Oh my God, don't tell me—" she said wearily.

"It's an intervention," Drin confirmed.

"Now are you going to listen to us and try to *hear* what we have to say?" Janine asked.

"Just get it over with," Gwen said, resigned.

"Earl, you start," Janine commanded.

In his most soothing basso tones, their father began. "Sweetheart, it kills me to see you like this." He sat next to Gwendolyn on the couch and took her hand in his. She didn't resist, just sat looking at him blankly. "I am not sitting in judgement on you or your actions. I love you, unconditionally. Anything you decide to do, we'll support. But we need to know where you're coming from. What happened with Herb? Are you planning on getting a divorce, or is this just a trial separation?"

Janine interrupted. "If she wants to answer our questions, she will. This is not an interrogation, honey. Tell her how her actions are affecting *you.*"

Earl nodded. "You're right, of course," he said to Janine. Then he turned to Gwen again. "I feel so helpless, so powerless. It's a father's job to protect his children, but I see you hurting and don't know how to protect you, my strong, beautiful daughter. It makes me feel terrible. My heart is breaking for you. Less than a month ago, we walked you down the aisle and gave you away, and now for some mysterious reason, you've decided to take it back. I invited the Wrights into this family, and you've made that a lie, too. I feel shaky. I've never been on shakier ground. How can you do this to me?" As heartfelt as his plea was, Dorinda could barely keep herself from haranguing him and her mother for attacking Gwen when they should be supporting her. But she held her peace. The rest of the family all wanted to proceed in this way. She couldn't overrule them. She could only try to exert some damage control.

Gwendolyn didn't respond to her father, and he stood,

and gave his seat to Janine, who started in, "Gwennie, we don't want you to feel we're attacking you." Dorinda couldn't help making a sound under her breath. Her mother turned accusing eyes on her, and she pretended to cough. "We're on your side. We feel terrible about this, but you're our daughter, and we love you so much. We don't want to lose you, and I feel as though you're slipping away, more and more each day. We're hurt by it. Your whole family is suffering. And we thought you should hear how your actions are affecting us. I don't want to accuse you of being thoughtless, because I know how easy it is to get caught up in one's own problems and forget that the people who love you are waiting to help."

"Janine, I don't need your help," Gwendolyn said firmly.

"This mumbo jumbo isn't going to help her," Dorinda said.

"Drin, let your parents finish. Honor your mother and father. Wiser heads will prevail . . . " Willie advised, shaking her graying head.

"You're just making it worse. You say you don't want to attack her, but you should hear yourselves talking about how she's hurting you."

"That's how an intervention is done," Janine explained painstakingly.

"I'm well aware of that. I grew up in this house, remember. I'm just saying this isn't necessary. Gwen will figure out what she wants to do on her own. She's made it perfectly clear that she doesn't want us to interfere. I think we should respect her wishes."

"You don't have to act like you know so much better than anyone else," Gwen said. Dorinda felt like she'd been slapped. She was trying to help her sister, and instead she had made herself into a target.

"I don't do it on purpose," she said, looking to her parents for help.

Janine shook her head. "She's always been that way. She was like this when she was just a little girl. Remember at parties, Earl, how she used to carry around the ashtray and make everyone knock their ashes in it . . . when she wasn't lecturing us on the dangers of smoking."

"Oh yeah," Earl laughed. "You were so cute," he said to Dorinda. "You were afraid the house was going to catch on fire."

"This isn't supposed to be about me, this is about you guys," Dorinda exclaimed.

"Why do you always have to control everyone and everything? Why don't you try using a little of that iron control on yourself? You don't always have to tell everyone how to do everything the right way. Your way," Gwen responded.

"I'm just trying to help," Drin said, feeling betrayed. "Sometimes I'd love to have someone to tell me what I should do."

"Like you'd listen," scoffed Gwen.

"It's true, honey," her mother agreed. "We stopped trying to give you advice a long, long time ago. You were always so independent, even as a baby."

"As a baby?" Dorinda was losing it. "As a baby, you say I was independent. *I was a baby*. Why would you let me do that? You were the parents. And all I can remember is how much I *wanted* your advice."

"You didn't seem to," her mother replied.

All those years, she'd hated being the grownup, the adult. It had been devastating when her parents didn't seem to have the same interest in her life, or her decisions, that they did in Gwen's and her brothers. She couldn't believe that all this time, they thought that was how she wanted it. "But . . . but," she spluttered.

"We've gotten off the track here, somewhere," Janine said. "We're talking about you, tonight, Gwennie."

"I *heard* you, Mother, Father," Gwen said disgustedly. "And I'm sorry that I've hurt you. I didn't mean to, but . . . I don't see how I could have done anything but what I did. I can't explain about Herbie. You wouldn't understand if I tried. So can't I just say I'm sorry and leave it at that?"

"Gwen," her father started to say.

She cut him off. "I *am* sorry." She looked around the room, at her mother, her father, Aunt Willie, and at Dorinda, but Drin just looked away. "I've got to go." She left, and no one moved until they heard the door shut behind her.

Then Willie said, "I didn't get to say anything."

"You could have jumped in there and helped me out," Dorinda muttered under her breath.

"Self pity in its early stages is as snug as a feather mattress. Maya Angelou." Aunt Willie said. "That's all I wanted to say."

"Well, what was *that?*" Dorinda asked. "I wasn't the one who was supposed to be under attack, Gwen was."

"No one was under attack." Her mother tried to soothe her.

"So what *was* that?" Janine and Earl only looked at her helplessly. "Gwendolyn managed to get out of it again. She used me as a diversion."

"Maybe she tried to divert our attention from her to you in a cry for help. You can't blame her for that, Drin."

"You bet your ass I can." Dorinda could understand her sister's motivation, and she might have been able to forgive her methods, but she was not going to forget, or forgive, her criticism.

All the way home, Dorinda was occupied with a plan for a little intervention of her own. If she was going to be accused of being a controlling bitch, she might as well deserve it. That night, while working out, she nearly injured her sparring partner, and still she seethed. It wasn't revenge. Well, not strictly revenge. This evening's session had convinced her to go ahead and get Herbie together with his reluctant bride, without her knowledge if necessary.

She enlisted Ronnie in the scheme. It went off as

smoothly as if she'd been planning it for months, rather than hours. First, she told him she had a surprise for Gwen, and he arranged for her twin to work a little late at The Beauty Spot. When he called and gave her the all-clear, Dorinda brought Herbert Wright to his new wife's office. Then she went into the main room, where Ronnie was waiting.

"Thanks, Mr. Clarke," Drin said. "I was worried you wouldn't approve."

"It's Bond, James Bond," he said playfully.

"You're laughing now, but if Gwendolyn finds out you were involved in this, you may be sorry."

"Nah," he dismissed her warning. "She knows you and I only have her best interests at heart."

"You're really a sweetheart, you know that," Dorinda said, settling into one of the raised stylist chairs. She was feeling pretty good. There hadn't been any loud noises, shouting, or sounds of breaking crockery from the office yet, and they'd been in there almost five minutes. Maybe this was going to work out. "Are you always this optimistic?"

"Almost always," he said. He stepped towards her. She hadn't realized how close he was. In only one or two steps he was beside her, then he was bending over the chair, and her, and planting a big, soft, wet kiss on her smiling mouth. Dorinda reached up and put her hands on his shoulder, closed her eyes, and let him taste her. Her lips parted. He tasted good, like coffee with cream and sugar. Like the color of his skin. It was late in the day, and his chin wasn't as smooth as it had been the night they'd gone out. Razor stubble rubbed against her cheek, but the friction was not unpleasant. She let her mind drift, and just felt him, his hands running up and down her arms, his teeth, and lips and tongue, tasting and tugging at her mouth. It was very pleasant, very comfortable. Still, there was no hint of the intense heat that had been generated when she'd kissed Matthew Cooper.

There had never again been anyone like her first love

for her. Physically, she'd found him so compatible, she couldn't help comparing all men, even ten years later, to him. Now, only a few days after their sexual reunion, Dorinda could catalogue the differences. Matt's lips were firmer, more demanding, his mouth hotter. He, too, had explored her mouth with his tongue, but more deeply, more completely.

Ronnie pulled her up out of the chair, into his body, and she found his shoulders weren't as wide as Matt's, the muscles in his arms were more wiry, less dense. He didn't feel as substantial as Matt, as solid. They were both tall men, but his proportions were different. Matt had been long–waisted, as she was, putting their hips at nearly the same height. Ronnie's legs were long, and his waist was much higher than hers, and it felt odd to her. She was a short woman, and she'd been with plenty of men who dwarfed her, but today the difference between their heights made her feel less womanly and more childlike.

She wanted to feel ultrafeminine, as she had with Matt, but she didn't. She felt like she had with the first boy she'd ever kissed, before Matthew even, an experiment in the eighth grade. Now, as then, she was waiting for that moment when she forgot who and where she was and was swept away by sensuality and desire. It didn't come. There was no spark between them.

At least not for her. Ronnie was so engrossed in what he was doing, he didn't hear the office door open. Dorinda had to push him away, hard. Herbie followed Gwen out into the room.

"We're going out," Gwen said, without emotion.

"To talk," Herbie added. He didn't look too happy.

"That's . . . good," Dorinda offered hopefully.

"I'll lock up here," Ronnie said.

The other couple left, and Ronnie smiled ruefully at her. She turned her back on him and walked away. Dorinda felt more comfortable when she'd made a little distance between them. Ronnie's smile had already begun to fade.

"I'm sorry." She turned and tried to think of the right words for this unfamiliar situation.

"For what?" He watched her consideringly.

"I don't guess you've noticed, but . . . I don't feel, I mean, I'm not very attracted to you."

"Not very? Does that mean you feel some attraction?" When she hesitated, he probed further. "You did seem to feel something. I did notice your tongue was in my mouth."

"I wanted to. I want to," Dorinda tried to explain. "I think you're a great guy. You have everything a woman could want in a brother. You're beautiful, and you have a good heart, and you're ambitious like me . . ."

"You like me," he said, grimly.

"I do. And I wish I liked you more, because you are probably the nicest man I ever met."

"That's the kiss of death," he said, apparently recovering his sense of humor. "I can tell you for a fact, nice guys do finish last," he said. He was smiling, but a trace of his earlier grimness showed through.

"I don't know what to say," Dorinda said apologetically. "I can't believe this happened. I always thought if I started dating again, I'd be the one getting the let's-be-friends speech."

"Hey, it works both ways," he said lightly.

Dorinda was so grateful that he was taking this well that she wanted to say more than just a simple "thank you," but everything else sounded lame—or patronizing.

"I'll lock up," Ronnie said. "You go on. I'll see you later."

"Good-bye," Dorinda said and walked slowly out of the shop.

This was the second time she had walked away from a perfectly nice guy because her foolish heart wouldn't cooperate with her sensible mind. Tom Grayson had been so sweet that it had pained her to let him go. They met at a party six months after she broke up with Jeff Hubble, and he asked for her number that night. He'd been polite, and attentive, and she'd agreed despite having reservations, because she'd been single for about six months. But she hated dating. When their second and third dates were as fun and friendly as the first, they'd started seeing each other exclusively.

They were both twenty–six years old, and both at exactly the same place in their lives. They had decided on their careers, and were happy with them. He was stable, responsible, and loving. He was not an Adonis, like Ronnie, but he was cute in a cuddly teddy bear way, and he was honest and straightforward. They wanted the same things: to fall in love, settle down, and think about starting a family. He wanted two children, she wanted four, and they agreed that three was a perfectly reasonable compromise.

They'd been together six months when they decided to move in together. It had been a practical, rather than a romantic decision. They spent all their time at her place anyway, and he was tired of toting his clothes around in his knapsack. There hadn't been any fanfare. He moved his favorite armchair into her livingroom, next to her couch. They bought a new entertainment center from Ikea and built it together, then moved her small television set into the bedroom, and his larger one onto the newly constructed unit.

Not too long after that, they started talking about marriage. It had been summertime, she remembered, about two years ago now, and they'd both been invited to friends' weddings all through the spring, summer and fall. It seemed like the right time. They were good together. They wanted the same things. It was the next logical step in their relationship.

It took an amazingly long time to agree on a date, and to start telling their friends. They decided on a long engagement so that planning the wedding would be made easier. Then they relaxed; their futures settled. It was Christmas time, and the next spate of weddings was scheduled for June. They were going to wed the following February, on Valentine's Day. That way, they'd never forget their anniversary. It had been Tom who had started to question their plans. He kept trying to bring up the subject, but it made Dorinda nervous. That was when he knew that he wasn't the only one with some serious doubts.

It was over before the fall. There was no big argument, no endless debate, just careful consideration of the subject, and for each other. They loved each other. But they hadn't been in love. Dorinda suggested staying together, but calling off the wedding. Thomas didn't want that. Moving his furniture into her place had been a symbolic gesture to him. It was a prelude to the forward movement of their relationship and if they weren't going to move forward, he had no desire to stay where he was, literally or figuratively. He had to move on, and begin the rest of his life.

He had been correct. They had not had a future together. But she wished so much that they had. Just as she wished now that she felt more than friendship toward Ronnie.

Dorinda said a silent prayer. She didn't know if it was the kind of prayer the gods listened to. It was all mixed up in her head. There was the verse about not wanting to fall in love with any more scumbags, and a chapter about not wanting to sleep alone for the rest of her life. There was also a barely discernible wish, which she finally recognized as the equivalent universal human plea, "Don't let me die old and alone."

She felt ill. What was the matter with her? She took in the beautiful spring day as she walked home. The streets were lined with gingko trees in all their Eastern perfection. Other hardy city plants grew out of the cracks in the sidewalk, and any other dirt they could find not completely covered over with cement. But the comforting surroundings didn't soothe her inner turmoil. She had always blamed Matt for the fiasco with Tom, because she had always blamed Matthew Cooper for everything that went wrong in her love life, but now that she'd seen him again, she realized that he could not wield the enormous power over her that she'd always given his memory. She had to acknowledge her own part in this pattern she seemed destined to relive. Matt was just a man.

She might have chosen Damon in reaction to Matt, and Jeff in reaction to Damon, but Thomas was not at all like them, nor was Ronnie. It was she who had thoughtfully considered the advantages and disadvantages of getting involved with them, then chosen to go out with them. She had evaluated them and herself, including the fact that she enjoyed their personalities, and admired their gentle sweetness, and felt comfortable with them. She had begun relationships with them, then weighed them up and then let them go. But perhaps she was the one who lacked some vital element to her character. Dorinda had accused Damon and Jeff of being afraid of commitment, but she had to admit she did seem to chase away the men who weren't afraid of it, and pursue men who were.

By the time she got home, Dorinda had a pounding headache. And there were messages on her answering machine from all the people who hated her. Aunt Willie suggested she remember the respect due her elders, honor her mother and father, and take seriously her responsibilities as her sister's keeper. When Willie started quoting from the Bible, Drin knew she was in serious trouble. Meanwhile, Gwen had also called to say, sarcastically, that she really appreciated Dorinda playing God with her life. Matt had called to reschedule their meeting. He asked her to meet him tomorrow night at The No Name again. And, finally, Herbie called, sounding miserable.

She listened to his message. "Thanks for trying to help, Drin, but I don't think it's going to work. Gwendolyn and I just go around in circles. I asked what I did and she says it's not about me. I asked what's her problem and she says *I* am."

She took an aspirin, got herself a cup of tea, and called her brother-in-law. "Herbie, tell me what she said."

"I did most of the talking. I apologized for being an insensitive, selfish idiot, like you suggested. She didn't seem angry. I thought she was listening. But then when I asked her to come back to me she said, 'I don't think it will work for us.' "

"No explanation?"

"Well, I sort of asked the same thing, and she said it was because I was a selfish, insensitive idiot. I mean, she said I already knew the reason and I asked if it was because I was selfish and insensitive."

"Did you mention that she hadn't been exactly a paragon of those virtues herself?" Dorinda asked.

"What do you mean?"

"Well it was not exactly unselfish, or very sensitive of her to leave you in Hawaii without a word."

"But you said not to," he wailed. "I distinctly remember you saying that I had to take all the blame and not attack her because that was what everyone else was doing. So I told her it was all my fault, but I would change."

Dorinda shook her head. He was hopeless. "You didn't *say* that."

"Of course I did. What's wrong with that?" the poor man asked.

"Men always say that!" The words came out more forcefully than she intended. Dorinda took a deep breath and said more calmly, "How can you say you're going to change when you just said you didn't know what you did wrong?"

"Hmmm, well," he mumbled.

"No wonder you ended up going around in circles; what kind of logic is that?"

"I wasn't being logical, I was trying to get my wife back. I grovelled, just like you said."

"You were supposed to just keep saying how sorry you were. *That's* what I suggested. Not make some stupid promise you had no intention of keeping."

"But I did!" he objected. Drin sighed, exasperated. Why was she doing this? She didn't even like the man.

"Forget it, Herbie. I don't want to argue with you."

"I didn't call to argue with you. I just wanted to thank you."

"She didn't mention divorce, did she?" Dorinda asked, grasping for straws.

"No . . ." Herbie said slowly.

"Then we won't give up yet. You sit tight and think about every single thing you said and did the day before she left you, no matter how small. It probably wasn't any one thing that made her so upset, but if you can remember exactly how the argument started, I might be able to figure out just what straw finally broke this camel's back."

"Okay."

"And Herbie."

"Yes, Drin?"

"Write it all down. Everything you can remember," she ordered. It would be easier to sort out this mess if she didn't have to spend too much time talking to Herbie.

"Okay," he said obediently.

"Bye," she said.

"Good-bye," he said. "Sis." Dorinda sighed. He was so pathetic. But he was the one Gwen had chosen, and she didn't think her sister had fallen out of love with him. At least, not yet. She'd seen them together when they came out of Gwen's office earlier, and there'd been hope in both pairs of brown eyes.

The real art of conversation is not only to say the right thing at the right place but to leave unsaid the wrong thing at the tempting moment.

Dorothy Neville

13.

Sunday morning, Dorinda turned off the alarm clock and slept in. She had thought about going to church this week, but she found she still couldn't handle the thought of going back there—to the scene of the crime, as it were— and facing the whole neighborhood. These people had known her and her family since she was born, and were bound to want to ask her how Gwen and Herbie were doing, and if she had a date yet. She couldn't face the curious gazes of all those little old ladies, like Mrs. Grace, who had treated her since she was a small girl as if she were one of their grandchildren.

She didn't call Gwen or Matt back. Gwendolyn's untouchable princess act was grating on her nerves. As for Mr. Cooper, she hadn't decided whether to keep their appointment this evening or not. She definitely didn't want to speak with him, but she didn't want him showing up on her doorstep again. In the end, he called her.

"Hello?" Dorinda answered the phone, unsuspecting.

"Drin?"

She'd have known that voice anywhere. "Hi, Matt."

"I, ummm, I'm calling to say I'm sorry, but I can't make it tonight."

She should have been angry, but she only felt deflated, almost as though she'd been looking forward to seeing him again, like she was being denied an anticipated treat. And that was about as far from the truth as she could imagine. These little encounters with Matthew Cooper were no treat.

"Uh huh," she said.

"I really do want to talk, um, about what's happening between us."

"There's nothing happening."

"Well something happened. But I've got to . . . I have to pick Gerome up. He's been crashing since the other night. You know?"

"Sure," Dorinda said shortly.

"He drinks. It's really bad for him, unhealthy, and he was on a binge and I tried to stop him. When I saw him, I thought he was just going to sleep it off. But he must have taken a train down to D.C. He goes down there sometimes, to protest, and . . . ummm . . . other things. When he's been drinking, he sometimes goes a little nuts."

"A lot of guys do." She tried to sound harder than she felt. Despite herself, Dorinda was starting to feel sorry for both of them: Gerome, for being sick, and Matt, for trying to take care of him.

"I'm not trying to make excuses. I'm just trying to explain. I really did want to talk this thing out with you, but I can't tonight. I've got to get Gerome at Penn Station, and bring him home. Make sure he's all right. He didn't say much on the phone, just that he was coming back on the six–thirty train."

"I understand. We'll get together another time."

"Unless, maybe, we could leave it open. I can come by after. If he's okay. He might be fine again. I just couldn't tell because he got off the phone so quickly."

There was no way she was 'leaving it open' for him to

drop by and throw anymore curve balls at her. "I don't think that's a good idea." She thought for a minute. She did want to get this over with, and who knew when Gerome would recover. "I could come with you," she heard herself say and groaned inwardly at her stupidity.

"Where? To Penn Station? I don't think that's such a great idea," Matt protested. She should have just agreed, but instead of being relieved at having him turn down her impulsive, idiotic offer, she found herself saying, "I can help you with Gerome, if you need me to. If he's okay, we can talk after we drop him off at home."

"When he's on one of his benders, it can be pretty bad," he warned.

"Gerome and I have known each other since we were five years old. He didn't need to drink to get pretty disgusting."

"This is different," Matt said feebly.

"Pick me up on the way," Dorinda commanded. "I'll be here waiting."

"Fine, then," he said reluctantly. "I'll see you at five–thirty."

"See you later, Matt," she said, not quite sure what she was letting herself in for.

"Bye," he said abruptly and hung up.

Dorinda wasn't sure how smart she had been, pushing her way into this situation, but she knew Matt wouldn't let her alone until they talked. This way, at least, she had some control over the situation. She could see him with Gerome and decide for herself if his concern for his friend was completely real, or was just an excuse to delay the conversation he said he was so eager to have.

When he pulled up in front of her building, she was waiting outside. "Hi," she said brightly, hopping into the front seat. It was a rare luxury to ride in a car. She didn't need one to get around Brooklyn. New York's public transportation system was one of the best in the country. It ran all over the city and the boroughs, and it ran twenty–four hours a day. In an emergency, she could flag down a taxi at any corner. Dorinda had lived here all her life, and never owned a car. "Nice day for a drive. The bridge or the tunnel?"

"The bridge, I think. I can't handle the tunnel during rush hour. Drin, are you sure about this?"

"Don't worry about it. I'm a big girl now."

"I know." He gave her one last considering look, then turned face front and started to drive. "I don't know how to prepare you for this. Gerome is never very good company, even when he's clean."

"I'm prepared for the worst."

They drove on in silence for a while, until Matt finally said, "Why did you want to do this? I had the feeling you would just as soon never see me again." When she looked at him inquiringly, he added, "The last time I saw you, you were nearly falling over your feet you were in such a hurry to get out of there."

"In a way, you're right. I probably wouldn't have called you. But I figured when you showed up at my office, I'd better plan on seeing you soon, on more neutral turf. I didn't want you surprising me again." He raised his eyebrow. "First you showed up at my place, then at work. I didn't know where you'd pop up next."

"Oh," he seemed satisfied with her explanation, and Dorinda left it at that.

They had come through downtown Brooklyn with the rush hour traffic and reached the bridge to Manhattan. The Brooklyn Bridge was a one of a kind architectural triumph, built under the auspices of three different engineers, each of whom took over when their predecessor could no longer fight the elements that resisted the efforts of man to triumph over nature. Its very existence was miraculous, and in the mighty pylons below them were plaques dedicated to the men who'd died raising this arch of steel and cement out of the soft silt of the Hudson River.

They drove off the bridge and into the steady flow of cars, taxis and buses that always filled the streets of the city, but Matt wasn't concentrating on the traffic. He wasn't finished. "So you never wanted to see me again after we ... uh ..."

"Well, not right after, but when I woke up the next morning, that was my basic instinct," she said bluntly.

"Why?"

"Why?" How could he ask her that?

"You heard what I said. Why? It's a simple question."

"Why wasn't I happy to sleep with you? Because we are not together. We haven't been together in a very long time. We have not seen each other in years, and the last time we did see each other it was not a particularly pleasant experience for me, since you were dancing with another girl while I stood there, watching."

"But you said you understood."

"I understood there was nothing I could do about it, because there was nothing you could do about it. You fell in love with that ... with Joan. I got it. You were very clear. I didn't think I'd ever be whole again. Now I am. And I'm not going to give that up. It took a long time for me to get here, and I'm not going backwards. Not again. Going to bed with you was definitely a step in the wrong direction."

"I don't want us to go back. We were immature kids then. We didn't have a clue about relationships. We're adults now."

"I still don't have a clue. Maybe I'm retarded. I don't get the relationship thing in general, and I cannot imagine trying to have any kind of relationship with you."

"I thought we were still friends, at least."

"We are acquaintances. Our parents are good friends. That means we're not going to ever get rid of each other completely. Believe me, I tried. But even if we have to see each other, at family occasions or on the holidays, we don't have to be anything more to each other than what we are right this moment, which is nothing special."

"You are special to me," he said.

"Give me a break," Dorinda replied, incredulously.

"I told you. That night. I meant what I said."

"What, that you wanted me the minute you saw me again? So what? We had some unfinished business between us. Maybe you wanted to try and regain something that was lost. Dead," she said stoically.

"It didn't feel dead. It still doesn't. How can you pretend you weren't affected by it?"

"I'm not. I admit it. I wanted you, too. I wanted that one last moment, that last good memory. Maybe I hoped it would erase all the bad memories. I didn't want your last memory of me to be of some crying, desperate kid. I'd rather have you think of me as a fantastic lover. The one who got away." They had reached their destination, and he slowed.

Dorinda spotted a place to park. "There." She pointed.

"Is that how you think of me?" he asked blandly.

"No, that's how you said you thought of me. And I liked that. I was flattered. After being dumped by my best friend, I didn't think too much of myself. It took a long time for me to feel like I was worth anything. It did my ego good to hear you say that." He finished parking the car and turned to look at her.

"So it was an ego boost?" It was his turn to sound incredulous.

"Not just that." She relented. "I wasn't thinking that clearly. It wasn't some twisted revenge, and it wasn't just the past. It was feeling good again. Feeling like a part of something again." He got out of the car, and she opened her own door up and got out.

He came around the car. "If I make you feel like that—?"

She cut him off. "Let's not talk about this anymore, now. We're here to get Gerome, and I don't want him hearing any part of this."

"Fine, Drin," he said, agreeably enough. "Later." Dorinda didn't think he meant the word to sound like a threat, so she tried to shake off the sudden chill it evoked in her. But when she shot a sidelong glance up at his face as they entered the bowels of the train station, his chiseled jaw was tight.

When the six–thirty from Washington, D.C. pulled into the station, they were waiting on platform fourteen. The station was busy, people bustling around them, noise bouncing off the tall ceiling and marble floors. The renovation of the old building had taken years, but it left Penn looking new, modern and clean, something that would have been hard to imagine a few years ago, when the bums and panhandlers had dominated the cavernous station.

The dull silver commuter train pulled in slowly, and immediately the passengers poured out. It didn't take Matt long to spot Gerome, who had some difficulty getting down the tall train steps with his crutches. As he went to help his friend, she followed more slowly. She was shocked by Gerome's appearance. He'd never been a big guy, but he was skin and bones now. His long brown dreds swung halfway down his back, but his complexion was so grey he'd never be mistaken for a brother from the islands.

"Okay, Ger?" Matt was saying as she joined them. Matt had righted him, and he'd gotten his crutches firmly under his arms again.

"Hello, Gerome," Dorinda greeted him as Matt stepped aside.

"Holy shi—" he started to curse, but that threw him off balance again, and only Matt's supporting arm kept him from falling over. "Drinda, darlin', is that really you?" he said in amazement.

"In the flesh. It's been a long time." She couldn't tell if his unsteadiness was caused by drink, or if he was always this weak.

"So you came to babysit, too?" he asked.

"Let's get you home," Matt said. "The escalator's out of order again, so we'll have to get you up the stairs."

"You're not carrying me, man. I'm sick of that shit. If these assholes don't want to put in elevators, the porters should carry me up those damn things!" Gerome raged.

"You can get up by yourself. I'll help you," Matt said patiently, ignoring his friend's outburst. When Gerome looked like he might continue his diatribe, Matt gave him a quelling glance.

Gerome visibly sagged. "Okay," he said, more calmly. The torturous process of getting up three flights of stairs took a lot out of both men. Both were sweating when they reached the street, and all three of them stopped by tacit consent and took a rest.

"It's good to see me again, huh, Drinda?" Gerome asked.

She had already decided he wasn't drunk, though he might have a bit of a hangover from his binge. His pronunciation was clear, even if all she'd heard so far were obscenities. "I always wondered how you turned out," she said.

"Now you know," he responded. "You were right about me all along. I was a screw–up, and I still am. If it weren't for your hero here, I'd probably be lying in a gutter somewhere, or maybe I'd be another John Doe in the morgue by now. You were right about the army, too."

"It's time we got going," Matt said, without emotion.

Dorinda wasn't about to let it go. She spoke as they walked down the street to the car. "You know more about the military than I do. You were there. But I'm sorry this happened to you. I don't want any soldiers to get hurt, just like I don't want to see civilians get hurt. That's part of why I'm a pacifist."

"I don't need your pity," he said resentfully.

"I can see that," she said, giving up.

"Knock it off," Matt said.

But he wouldn't let it go. "Ms. Drinda got *her* college degree, I bet. You didn't let those scholarships go to waste, did you?"

"Not at all."

"She's thinking of starting her own business," Matt informed him.

"Good for her," Gerome said nastily.

"I'm not ashamed of it," Dorinda told him. "I worked hard to win those scholarships, and I worked hard in school. You could have done the same thing, but you chose not to."

"I know I screwed myself over," he said. "I don't need you telling me."

"Just thought I'd remind you that I had nothing to do with this, since you seem determined to take it out on me," Dorinda said.

"Time for you two to call it a truce. I'm not listening to this all the way back to Brooklyn," Matt warned.

They settled into the car in silence. Dorinda was embarrassed at having been needled so easily into the verbal sparring with her old nemesis. The ride home was quiet, giving her plenty of time to think about her conversations with both men. She made a mental resolution to behave in a more adult manner, no matter what they said to her. As before, she couldn't help admiring the view as they drove back over the bridge. Without the city lights behind it, she noticed the bridge's construction more. The heavy wire struts were laced with red and white lights, which sparkled like hot stars against the night sky. Her eyes automatically followed them up to the top of the arc that towered over the marble arches which stood like sentinels, each guarding one end of the structure.

Matt drove them along a circuitous route to Gerome's apartment building in a low rent district not too far from her own apartment. Downtown Brooklyn did not have the residential look of Dorinda's neighborhood. Although the newly revitalized Metrotech complex, containing the high-rise where she worked, was not far away, its glory did not seem to have spread to this seedy nearby street. They passed mainly five-story buildings housing a mix of discount stores that sold odd assortments of common goods: clothes, cleaning supplies, hardware, cosmetics, office supplies, toys, et cetera. Poor quality goods at rock bottom prices. Above the stores, in the near-tenement apartments, were families barely eking out a living. Gerome lived in a three-story building above a thrift shop which was closed. When he'd struggled out of the car, Gerome immediately went on the offensive. "No need to come up, Princess. I know how you like to have Matt all to yourself."

"We're both coming up," Matt said. Dorinda didn't say anything at all. She was trying to be understanding, reminding herself of the pain that Gerome must be in to need to lash out constantly in this way.

The studio apartment was quite sparse. A nondescript couch, a bed, a small card table with four chairs around it, and a television on top of a small bookshelf comprised the furnishings. Gerome made himself comfortable, while Matt checked the refrigerator.

"Would anyone like a soda?" he asked.

"Sure," Dorinda and Gerome said at the same time.

Matt smiled as he gave them each their drinks. "You two should talk to each other. You're not as different as you think. You share the same views on the military, if for different reasons. And you're both determined to control your own lives."

"She was always a control freak," Gerome accused. "I'm just trying not to let them take away what little dignity I have left."

"We're a little old for name calling, don't you think?" Dorinda asked.

"Did you protest Desert Storm?" he asked.

"Yes," Dorinda answered. "Why?"

"I just thought you might have." Gerome seemed less aggressive now that he was home, and Dorinda tried to relax as well.

"So what were you doing down in D.C.?"

"A little protest of my own," he said. "I was stupid enough to enlist because I wanted to go to school on the GI bill, but sometimes I go down to the recruiting office and show other young black brothers that it's a mistake. Better to pay for college *any* other way."

"Do they listen to you?" she asked.

"Generally, no. But I am living proof of what can happen to them, and even if they go into the army, they might be more careful and less trusting than I was."

"I think that's great," Dorinda said. "You're turning what happened to you into something good. That's impressive, Ger."

"Thanks," he said, but he didn't sound particularly grateful. He sounded like he didn't want her there.

"I guess I'd better be going," Dorinda said. "Mission accomplished." Gerome waved at her, unconcerned.

Matt looked from her to Gerome and back, clearly torn between staying with his friend and leaving with her. "Ger, I'm going to give Dorinda a ride home. Okay?"

"It's only a few blocks," Dorinda demurred. "I'll jump in a taxi."

"I don't need a babysitter," Gerome said to his friend, without rancor. "Go ahead."

"Okay. I'll call you tomorrow." Matt went to the door and opened it for her.

Dorinda hesitated in the doorway. She turned back to her reluctant host, wishing that things had gone more smoothly between them. "It was nice to see you again," she offered.

He ignored her. "Matt, thanks for picking me up."

"No problem. Talk to you soon," Matt said. "Bye."

The sky had turned that cobalt shade that presaged the coming of total blackness. The stars were faint beyond the streetlights. They walked to the car in silence.

Dorinda's emotions were confused. Her pity for Gerome was tinged with resentment, which spilled over onto her companion. She got into the car, and Matt started to drive while she turned over the evening's events in her mind. She had discovered the truth. Matt had not casually cancelled their 'date.' He felt responsible for Gerome. It was written all over him. She thought back to what he'd said in the car on the way to Pennsylvania Station about them still being friends. If his relationship with Gerome was any indication—friendship to him was a very committed relationship. Dorinda didn't think she was too good at those.

"Matt, about what we were saying earlier, I want to explain."

"Yes?" he asked, intent, apparently, on the road before them.

"Before. When we were together. I felt like you belonged to me. I have never been as sure of my emotions as I was at that time. But I finally realized that when I left, the way I left, I not only lost a lover, but I lost a best friend. It was such a shock when I found out I was wrong that I've never completely trusted my own judgement since."

He didn't look at her. "You weren't wrong. I felt the same way. That is how we were supposed to feel."

"No. I don't think so. When I was little, and I didn't fit in with my crazy family, I knew there was something wrong with me. And you were the only person I understood. You loved me, and I loved you for it. And when I grew a little older, and I realized that everyone was always going to like Gwendolyn more, maybe love her more, you were the only thing I had that she couldn't even touch. And when I grew old enough to understand that my parents were different, and it wasn't just me who didn't seem to fit in their world, I fit with you. You belonged to me and I belonged to you."

He pulled the car over, but he didn't interrupt. The words spilled out of her, unstoppable. "And when I was sixteen, and you told me you loved me, I felt like I had finally come home. I was a part of you, the way you were a part of me—the most important part. And then you fell in love with someone else. I thought I was going to break into a million pieces. I didn't think I would survive it."

"Will you come in?" he asked. She looked out the window and realized he must have driven her to his house.

"Haven't you heard a word I said? I'm trying to be nice about this, but you're making it extremely difficult." She made no move to open the door. If she had to, she would walk home, but she hoped that wouldn't be necessary. She just had to get the one fact through his thick head. She wasn't interested.

He didn't get it. "I'm just trying to get back with you. I shouldn't have let us drift apart; I just didn't know what else to do. We were only seventeen when you left for college."

"I understand," Drin said patiently. "You have good intentions here. Listen to me. I'm not blaming you for the past anymore. Okay? You're forgiven. Beyond that, I'm not willing to go. I don't see why I have to keep saying this."

"Because I won't accept it. I'm sorry for the other night. Not that we made love, but that we did it instead of talking. But it's done, past, we can't change it. I'm not going to let that one mistake get in my way."

"We're not kids anymore. You said it yourself, we're adults now. You know how the world works. You don't get very many second chances. We blew ours," she said somberly.

"We didn't blow it. We . . . I don't know . . . suffered a minor setback. It was actually very—"

Dorinda jumped in. "Don't say it." If he said the sex was great, she was going to have to hit him.

"What? I was just going to say it was illuminating. I didn't think I had that kind of recklessness left in me. I haven't been that out of control since . . . I don't know when. Have you?"

"I don't know you well enough to discuss this with you," Dorinda said repressively.

"You knew me well enough to do it, but not well enough to discuss it with me?" he asked.

"*It.* Have you regressed completely? It? It's called sex. And it's a normal, human need. That's all."

"So why can't we discuss it?" he asked in a calm, reasonable tone.

"What do you call this?" Dorinda asked.

"Avoidance?"

She had had enough. "I've tried." She opened her car door, and stepped out. He flew out of his door and around the car and met her on the sidewalk. "I'm going home."

"Get back in the car. I'll drive you," he said.

"It's only a few blocks, and I could use the fresh air," Dorinda said keeping her tone calm and even.

"When I take a girl out, I see to it that she gets home safely. It's my training." When Dorinda didn't respond, he pressed a button on his keys and the car beeped at them. She heard the locks click. "I'll walk you."

"Fine." She was tired of this seemingly endless debate. He was a good man, and she had truly appreciated the glimpse of him she'd gotten tonight. It was a credit to her judgement that he was still the honest, sensitive boy she'd known. And she was completely convinced of his sincerity in wanting to reestablish their friendship. She even thought she understood how he could have made love to her a few nights ago, just as she had made love to him, because of their past. It had been an enlightening evening, but Dorinda just wanted to go home and empty her mind. She didn't want to think about Matt, or Ronnie, or Herbie, or Gwendolyn, or work, or dating or not dating. She didn't want to think. Period.

He walked her home, and stopped outside the door to her building, but Dorinda didn't wait for the conversation to begin again. She nearly ran inside.

> You don't learn to hold your own in the world by standing on guard but by attacking, and getting well hammered yourself.
>
> George Bernard Shaw

14.

The next day, Dorinda quit her job. It was a typical midsummer Monday morning. She woke to bright sunlight streaming through her bedroom window, and for a moment, she lay there, savoring the promise of a fresh new day. She watched white clouds blow across the blue sky. Then the events of last night, then the last few days, then the last week, slowly overcame her lazy contentment. The decision to quit came over her even more slowly. It was born as she showered and dressed for work and grew as she sat eating her breakfast cereal. She contemplated the possibility as she sat on the subway on her way to work. And it blossomed as she walked into her office.

She went right to her desk and wrote out her letter of resignation as if she were on automatic pilot. Even as she handed the envelope to Bob, Dorinda felt as though she were not really there. But it felt right. She couldn't hold off on making the decision any longer: whether she should stick with safety and security, or whether to leave that behind and hope to strike it rich. It was strange how the situation at work mirrored her situation with Matthew.

Dorinda was tired of walking this tightrope. She could take the safest course, and deprive herself of the chance to enjoy all the profit from her endeavors, or she could take a chance and hope the gamble paid off in ways she couldn't begin to imagine.

That night at their regular Monday night drinks date at the No Name, Dorinda dropped her bomb. "I quit."

She sat back and enjoyed Tamika and Claire's shocked expressions. Daria had been there, but Dorinda didn't know what she really thought. She had intended to warn her friend before actually going through with her resignation, since Drin had been the one to recommend and then hire Daria to work as Anderson's bookkeeper, but her best friend had not been around. Drin hadn't been able to wait. They had had no chance to talk privately since but Daria didn't seem upset. She looked amused.

"You go, girl," Tamika said.

Claire didn't say anything. She was processing the information.

"I already put out some feelers, and generally I think my accounts will go with me. They know that I'm the one who does the work for them—Bob never tried to take the credit for that," Dorinda rushed on.

"Until now," Daria said dryly. She'd been dragged into the spreading paranoia at the office against her will, and she had said she was tempted to leave the company herself the previous week.

Dorinda waited anxiously for a sign of approval from Claire. "I have a good idea of what my billing will be, and the overhead shouldn't be too high in the beginning. I'll be working out of my home. Bob owns the computer at work, but all my files are on the one at home since I do a lot of work from there. And I know my little Dell can handle the load, for now."

"It sounds like you thought it out thoroughly," Claire said finally with a nod of approval. It was one of the highest compliments Claire ever paid anyone. "How did your boss take it?" she asked, smiling.

"Bob was shocked. He must have seen it coming, but he wasn't at all prepared. I wasn't feeling all that ready either."

"Don't believe her. She was a rock," Daria said. "I saw them talking later. Everyone saw them. He pounced on her whenever she came out of her office."

"Not at first. I couldn't believe I was doing it—I never quit a job before. But then he had the nerve to ask me if I had thought about this."

"I was not sure of myself up until that moment, but when he started talking to me like he was my father or something, I knew I was out of there."

"You should have seen her," Daria said. "She was icy cool. He was pitiful," Daria said happily. "He could barely speak."

"But when he finally realized that I was totally serious and this wasn't some impulsive, spur of the moment emotional outburst he got serious, too. He offered me a raise."

"That must have felt good," Claire said.

"I enjoyed it," Dorinda said modestly.

"She had this strong black woman thang going on," Daria said in her best street accent.

"He even promised to let me handle my accounts without interference."

"Were you tempted?" Tamika asked.

"Not really. I felt guilty when I turned him down, but by then I was floating somewhere above the whole scene. I left my body and admired myself in action, I swear. And the guilt couldn't compete with the high."

"Adrenaline rush," Claire pronounced. "I thought your pupils looked a little large."

Tamika leaned in closer. "Wow, look at that," she said, staring into Dorinda's eyes. "They're little black basketballs!"

"It was fun. I have to admit it," Dorinda said.

"It was fun to watch," Daria added.

"I wish I'd been there," Tamika said.

"It won't last," Claire declared cynically. "You are going to wake up tomorrow with a slightly different take on the situation."

"Let her enjoy it for now," Tamika scolded her.

Dorinda shrugged. "If I crash, I crash. Meanwhile, I did it! I'll be nervous about it later, I'm sure, but for now I just want to enjoy it. I felt so ... aggressive, so butch. I always thought of myself as non-confrontational, but it was a trip!"

"You're starting to scare me, Drin," Claire gave an exaggerated shudder.

"I love it," Tamika exclaimed. "I want to try it."

"You love your job," the practical Claire reminded her. "Besides, I don't think this is a permanent condition."

"We heard you the first time, Claire," Daria said. "Stop being such a party pooper."

"Okay, okay." Claire conceded defeat, smiling tolerantly.

"I feel like I've got back control of my life," Dorinda sighed satisfied. "I never would have dreamed it could go so well."

"I'm happy for you," Tamika said.

"Me, too," Claire chimed in.

"You're a true woman," Daria declared. "A toast," she announced. "To success."

"To success," they all intoned as they raised their glasses.

Dorinda, still caught up in the excitement that had gripped her, tapped her glass loudly against the other three. "For all of us."

Tamika said, "From your lips to God's ears."

"To that strong black woman thang," Claire added.

The next morning, as Claire had predicted, Dorinda's euphoria had faded, and anxiety took its place. She hadn't had too much to drink the night before but she could feel a humdinger of a headache coming on. However, there was no way she was going to call in sick. She couldn't bear to be seen as weak after the previous day's show of strength. She put on a pair of dark glasses and reported in for the first day of her last two weeks at the office building she'd called a second home for the past six years.

Dorinda found herself looking at everything differently. Every stick of furniture, each employee's demeanor, even the model of the phone was compared to a model in her mind in the office she planned to soon open.

"I feel half gone already," she told Daria at lunch in a nearby diner, over her cup of tea and English muffin.

"Was Claire right? You look hung-over," Claire pursed her lips and shook her head as she examined Dorinda more closely. "Or is this an anxiety attack?"

"Not yet, Daria," Dorinda tried to explain. "It doesn't seem real to me yet. Maybe when I walk out of that place for the last time it will sink in completely."

Within a couple of days she sent letters to her clients, informing them of the split between herself and Bob Anderson. She only said that she was excited about a new venture she was starting, and she'd contact them with a prospectus at a later date. She didn't mention any reason for leaving, but rather concentrated on the positive aspects of her past association with the firm and her expectations for the future success of both her employer and herself.

She spent half an hour at the county clerk's office and officially became DF Computer Services Company. At home she ordered a new phone line to be installed for her new business and designed stationery to be printed at her local copy shop. It seemed absurdly simple to begin her own business.

Dorinda was just starting to become accustomed to her entrepreneurial role when she was contacted by her liaison at Chase Manhattan, her biggest client. Randy Lawson was usually a very easygoing man, but he was clearly nervous as he questioned her about her availability to the bank after she completed her final two weeks at Bob Anderson's firm.

"Don't worry," she reassured him. "I'm not deserting any of my accounts. I'll still be at your disposal. The transition shouldn't even affect you guys."

"Transition to what?" he asked.

"It's a bit premature to discuss this now, on Bob's time and on his phone. My last day here is next Friday. How about if we set up a meeting for the following Monday morning? Then I'll make my pitch."

"You're not going to get married or anything, are you?" he blurted out.

"No," Dorinda said, keeping her voice even with an effort. They wouldn't have asked a man that question. But because she was female, they felt no compunction about invading her privacy—sticking their corporate noses in her personal business. She would have told Lawson what she thought of his chauvinist bull, but this was the wrong time to antagonize her liaison to her biggest account. Besides, he'd probably just take it as proof that he was dealing with an emotional, overwrought woman, so she just said reassuringly that he, and Chase, had nothing to worry about.

"Idiots," she spat, when she told Aunt Willie about the conversation.

"Never underestimate the bigotry of Corporate America," Willie advised.

"Who wrote that?" Dorinda asked.

"No one. I just said it," Willie answered. "I stole the form though."

Dorinda recognized it from a popular idiom about the general intelligence of the American people. "Oh," was all she said.

"Do you think they'll continue to use you?" her aunt asked.

"Sure. I'm not getting married or anything," Dorinda said sarcastically. "Damn them."

"The crocodile doesn't harm the bird that cleans its teeth. Linda Hogan."

"Hey, their money's green. Take it and run. Maybe they'll actually learn something through this process— namely that even women of marriageable age can do the job."

"I want to go out and get married, just to spite those narrow-minded, prejudiced old farts. They can't be allowed to discriminate against women because they want a family."

"Unfortunately they can, they always have and there's a good chance they always will."

"That sucks."

"May I quote you?" Willie said facetiously.

"Of course. I have others like them, too. Work sucks; Men suck, arugula sucks," Dorinda offered.

"Arugula?"

"All those vegetables I never heard of before 1985 irk me."

"I know," Willie nodded sagely. "It's the little annoyances in life that eat away at the sparkling inner light we're all born with. People think it's traumatic childhood experiences, and big events like disappointment in love or death, but it's the slow erosion of bile eating away at the soul that does it." That, Drin recognized as an original Willie statement. She couldn't figure out why her aunt spoke in axioms when she had such an original point of view and a refreshing way of expressing herself. "Speaking of that inner spark, it sounds like quitting was an invigorating experience. Don't forget that feeling." Willlie advised.

"After today's little communique from my biggest client, I have the feeling it's going to be difficult to keep my enthusiasm level up."

"Don't forget I'm here for you. If you ever need a shoulder to cry on, or a little ego boost."

"Thanks, I will," Dorinda said gratefully. Even though

Willie had slipped back into maxim-speak, the emotion behind the axioms was sincere. Even if her aunt's quotations drove her crazy sometimes, she could always count on her aunt to say the right thing.

"Have you heard from your sister lately?" Willie asked.

"No. I've got to call her," Dorinda replied. "She's pretty ticked off at me for that stunt I pulled, setting her up with Herbie."

"Hey, you were just trying to help them work out their differences. The marriage may only be a month old, but it's still a marriage, and anyone who cares about Gwen has to try to save it."

"Maybe," Drin said doubtfully.

"You did the best you could," Willie consoled her.

"Yeah." She might not have the same loyalty to the institution of marriage that her elderly aunt had, but when two people stood up in front of the entire congregation of their church and all their friends and relatives, and pledged their love, Dorinda figured they shouldn't break up because of one stupid fight. She sighed. "I'll call her."

"Good," Willie said, satisfied.

They said their good-byes and Dorinda hung up the phone, then she stared at it for a long moment before deciding she'd had enough strife for one day. She'd call her twin sister tomorrow.

But the next day she woke up late and had to rush to work, and was immediately involved in a crisis at, of all places, Chase Manhattan Bank. That night she left the office satisfied that her most profitable client had been dazzled by her expertise and reminded that she was, indeed, indispensable.

She took a long hot bath when she got home, and then brought the phone into the bedroom to call Gwen. She got comfortable on the bed, looked at the glass of red wine on the bedside table and consciously resisted the urge to down it before she made her phone call. She hadn't spoken to her twin since she'd received Gwen's angry message after she'd blindsided her with Herbie at the salon. Every time she thought about calling, she remembered that Herbert still hadn't given her the summary she'd asked him for—of everything he'd done and said to Gwen before she left Hawaii so abruptly. She was hoping that once she got that, it would inspire a plan, give her a direction for her next move. Until then, she didn't know what to say or do.

Herbie hadn't called either, much to her surprise. It had been over a week since she'd asked him for his written recollection, and his urgency had been unmistakeable. She didn't know what was going on with either of them. Dorinda sighed and punched her sister's number into the portable telephone.

Gwen answered it on the first ring. "Hello?"

"I thought I would get Mom or Dad," Dorinda said stupidly.

"They're not here right now. Do you want me to tell them you called?" she said stiffly.

"No, no. I called to speak to you."

Gwendolyn didn't try to disguise her impatience. "So?" she asked.

"I owe you an apology."

"Okay," Gwen said without hesitation.

"I'm sorry that I interfered, between you and your husband. I just thought it might be good if you two talked."

"You might have asked me," Gwen said, but her voice sounded a little softer, Dorinda thought.

"I was afraid you'd say no."

"I probably would have," her sister responded.

"Mom and Dad were bugging me. You were moping around, not talking, so they couldn't bother you, and of course, that meant they called me all day every day."

"Don't try to blame this on our parents. Herbie told me it was your idea."

Great. I told him not to blame her, so he blames me instead, Dorinda thought. She picked up the glass of wine and took a big swallow. "Gwen, I just thought that you couldn't have fallen out of love that quickly. It was a week! You had to have some feeling left for the guy."

"I did. And I do. We're trying to work it out," Gwen told her.

"You are?" Dorinda said, jumping out of bed and nearly spilling the wine in her excitement.

"Yes," Gwen said. She couldn't be sure from the sound of her voice, but Drin thought she might even be smiling. "Herbie caught me at home the next night, and we talked about the honeymoon. We were both expecting too much, I think. I know I was."

"Gwennie, I'm so happy for you."

"Nothing is settled yet," her sister admonished. "But I think we may be able to try again. It's funny. Here I thought that I was the one who couldn't handle the changes in Herbie, and it turns out that he felt exactly the same way."

"What changes?" Dorinda settled gingerly back on the bed, and took another sip from her glass.

"He was just more . . . himself. So was I, though. We both thought we knew all there was to know about each other when we took that walk down the aisle, but we were still holding back from each other. We got married pretty quickly, you know. We were still in the first throes of passion."

"I noticed." Dorinda let out a little laugh. She could picture Gwen's outraged expression and quickly added, "But I'm not the type to say I told you so."

"Sure you are. But in this case, I'll forgive you. Maybe we should have waited. But we didn't because we each thought the other was perfect—just what we wanted. Nobody's perfect, Drin. Nobody. We were just play–acting, then playing house. It may be silly to you, because you never pretend with men; you just are who you are, but I'm used to acting a certain way with guys. Especially guys I'm really interested in. It's just like with Mom and Dad. I always try to act exactly like I think other people want me to. You just say what you think, and do what you want. I'm the good girl.''

"So neither of us is perfect. You make me sound like some soap opera character pretending I'm good when I'm not. I admit I'm far from perfect. But face it, I'm not the evil twin either.''

"Get over yourself. We're talking about me, now. When I left on my honeymoon, I felt like a different person. For the first time in my life, I didn't worry about what someone else wanted. But I may have taken it a bit too far.''

"That's what high expectations can do to a girl,'' Drin joked.

"Just you wait 'til it's your turn,'' Gwen warned. "You'll be worse than me.''

"I'm sure I will,'' Drin said. "If, or when, I get married, I *am* marrying the perfect man, and on *my* honeymoon, I'm going to have exactly what I want, when I want it, the way I want it.'' She was only half joking.

"Mmm hmmm,'' Gwen murmured. "That's what I thought,'' her sister said dryly.

It is one of the blessings of old friends that you
can afford to be stupid with them.

Emerson

15.

Dorinda didn't think about Matt much that weekend.
Except when she couldn't help it. Thoughts of the man
did intrude at the oddest times. The sight of a man on
crutches made her think of Gerome, and Matt's loving
care for his friend. She rented a romantic comedy on video
called *Love Jones,* and even though the characters' lifestyles
were about as dissimilar as they could get from her own
and her friends' she couldn't help picturing Matt's strong
face when the jealous, insensitive commitment-phobic boyfriend begged his love to take him back. It was his face
she saw on her sparring partner at the gym, whom she
actually knocked out this time.

She dreamed of him, too. Sexy dreams that didn't immediately fade when she awakened in the morning. Dorinda
figured that since he'd stimulated her sexual self after it
had been dormant so long, it was normal that her subcon-
scious should put his face on her dream lover's body.

Unfortunately, thoughts of him abounded at her Monday night meeting with the girls the following night. Now
that the general excitement about her career change had

died down—at least, for them—the subject of dating inevitably reared its ugly head once again. They'd already heard Claire's weekly review of Fred's endearing idiosyncrasies and his general perfection.

"What happened with Matt?" Daria asked.

"Nothing? Why?" Dorinda asked guiltily.

"I heard from someone in the office that he'd been by. It wasn't Donna, so don't get your panties in a twist," she rushed to add, when Dorinda sucked in her cheeks. Daria and Tamika had already reported that they had nothing new or different to report on the sex and romance front. Of course, that was considered normal and absolutely okay, whereas Dorinda was going to be raked over the coals if she told them about Matt.

She took a deep breath. "He came by because he wanted to give me the 'let's be friends' speech."

"I thought he already did that," Daria said. "What's he really after?"

"Absolution?" Dorinda said, shrugging.

"I thought you guys parted amicably," Claire said.

"First he drove you home from the wedding, then he showed up at your house, and now, the office. I think he might be interested in more than friendship," Daria mused.

"Whoa, back up. When did he show up at her house?" Tamika asked.

"Oh yeah, I guess I forgot to tell you about that," Dorinda muttered.

"He went by there, uninvited, a couple of weeks ago, I guess." Daria looked at Dorinda for confirmation.

"Three, I think. It was right before Gwen cut her honeymoon short, and that sort of knocked the incident out of my mind." Nothing could have been further from the truth. She'd consciously decided not to tell the crew because after she'd called Daria to tell her about it, Matt had come back, and they had done the wild thing all night. There was no way she could have forgotten that visit, or the follow–up. She would never tell her girls about that lapse.

"Anyway, he came by the office, unannounced, to give me the 'lets be friends' speech. And that's all there is to it," she lied.

"Persistent little toad, isn't he? If he were interested in more, would you consider it?" Daria asked.

"Not a chance," Drin said vehemently.

"Why not? You said you still liked him," Claire said. "After the wedding."

"Except for his taste in girlfriends," Tamika remembered.

"I might have been willing to let bygones be bygones, if he were different, but when he dropped by my house, it proved he was still an insensitive moron."

"Some women might find all this attention flattering," Tamika pointed out.

"How would you like it if one of your exes, say Charlie, dropped in on you all of a sudden," Drin countered.

"After we made peace? I guess I wouldn't mind." She was sincere.

"Even if it was to give you the same old speech?" Drin pressed.

"I could handle that," Tamika said, nodding.

"I think the guy's an idiot," Daria said loyally. Of course, she didn't know that Drin had slept with him—making his irrational behavior somewhat more understandable. But whether she'd sent out mixed messages or not, it was still his bad behavior that was annoying her. "Then he said he would prove that he had learned to be a better friend."

"It sounds like Matt really wants to get back in your good graces," Claire remarked.

"He says he missed me," Drin told them.

"And what did you say?"

"I told him I missed him, too." Finally, a completely true and unvarnished statement. Her relief was short–lived.

"But you told him you were over him, right?" Tamika asked.

"I am soooo over him." Dorinda felt a small pang of guilt. Was she lying to herself now, too, as well as everybody else?

"And you told him so, in so many words," Daria pressed.

"Not in so many words, but he got the picture." Of that, she was sure. She hadn't heard from him since he left her at her doorway, Sunday night. Of course, it had only been one day. Still, she'd made herself very clear, and he had left her without a word.

"So now that that's settled, maybe Ronnie would be a good practice date," Tamika suggested.

Dorinda couldn't keep any more from her friends. "I went out with Ronald Clarke a couple of weeks ago." She explained about how he'd helped her to trick her sister into seeing her husband. "And it worked. She's working things out with Herbie," she announced triumphantly.

Her friends were not diverted so easily. They all spoke at once. "You went out with the Best Man? When? Where did you go? How was it?"

"He had free tickets to *Lion King,* so we went to see it, in Manhattan. But when he kissed me goodnight, there was no chemistry between us."

"After all this time, your chemistry is probably all clogged up," Daria said. "You could give it one more shot. Like jumpstarting a dead battery. It would be worth it, I promise you."

"You cannot possibly promise something like that. And anyway, I already told him how I felt about dating, in general, and him, in particular. He was cool. I think he may be the one man in the world without an oversized ego."

"You found the one?" Tamika joked. "Come on, girl. You can't just let him get away."

"He won't ask me out again," Dorinda said with certainty.

"If he did, would you go?" Claire asked.

"He sounds too good to be true," Daria said dubiously.

"There," Dorinda jumped on that as an excuse. "He's probably got so many problems, he's learned to disguise them really well. The minute we started going out, I'd find out he kept his mother on ice in the closet or something equally twisted."

Even Claire thought she'd taken it one step too far. "He's known your sister for years, and he was with a woman forever—right in her face. She'd know if there was anything seriously wrong with him."

"Face it. You're a chicken-hearted lily-livered crybaby, who wouldn't know a good thing if it jumped up and bit her on the ass." Daria shook her head in helpless frustration.

"There's a good reason for my . . . cautious behavior. It's called history. I've got the teethmarks on my tush to prove it."

"You think you're so logical and reasonable," Tamika said. "But Daria's right, you're just scared."

"Fear serves a purpose, it protects you from danger," Dorinda countered smugly.

"Well . . ." Claire said, then hesitated. With an apologetic glance at her old friend, she continued. "Rational fears serve a purpose. Irrational fears can hurt us."

"Who gets to decide which is which?" Drin asked. "Me? Or you guys?"

"We do," Daria and Tamika said simultaneously. Claire laughed, and Dorinda found herself joining in.

But she was shaking her head when the laughter died down. If they were going to try to persuade her she should date again, they'd fail. She'd tried it. It didn't work for her. "I still think I've made the only sensible decision under the circumstances. I'm not interested in Ronnie, or Matt. I tried it," she added as Daria started to interrupt. "And anyway, I'm too busy with other things, like putting my sister's marriage back together and opening my own business, to even contemplate the horrors of dating."

"That's your problem, right there," Tamika said.

"Which one?" Dorinda asked facetiously.

"You've got the wrong attitude."

"I'm just trying to keep the mood light," Drin said.

"About dating, you fool," Tamika corrected her. Drin rolled her eyes at her friend's implication that she could possibly have misunderstood which topic was under discussion.

"It's always about dating. I swear if I said I was going to start dating again, you wouldn't have anything left to talk about."

"We only get on your case because you're so bad at it. But we could help you. We're all single women, with different tastes in men, and you're not covering your share of the market."

"Good, maybe their value will go down, and I can pick one up cheap, later."

"I give up," Tamika said.

"Good. Anyone else?" Dorinda challenged.

Claire bowed out of the fight. "Hey, it's your life."

"Even if it is all work and no play," Daria said.

"Are you trying to imply something here? I'm not dull. I'm a scintillating conversationalist with a great sense of humor. Try to find a man with both of those qualities."

Daria, as usual, had to have the last word. "You already did. The question is: what could convince you to go out with him again?" Daria probed.

"Matthew Cooper? Nothing. Why would I put myself through that?"

"If things didn't work out, you'd get to dump him this time," Tamika said coyly.

"That is ridiculous," Drin said.

"I think she may have something there," Claire said. "You won't be able to forget him and move on until you've resolved this once and for all."

"It's resolved. I have no interest in dating him or anyone else."

"What about Ronnie?"

"That was a mistake. And it was all your fault. I should never have broken the golden rule. I'm not looking for a man."

"Honey, he's a straight, handsome, black man with a good job and a great personality. He likes you. You may not have been looking, but you *found,*" Daria suggested.

"I think what the girl is trying to say is—"

"I know what she's trying to say." Drin cut her off. "It's the same thing she always says. And you, and you." She looked pointedly at each of them. "How many times do I have to tell you all you're wrong?"

Claire looked at her speculatively. "*Has* Matt mentioned anything about getting together?"

She hesitated slightly, which gave her away. She saw the dawning comprehension in three sets of brown eyes. "Yeah," she admitted. "But we just went to pick up a friend from high–school at the train station."

"Is this part of the proving he's a better friend routine?" Daria asked.

Dorinda knew that this was the moment to confess. If she just told them that he'd asked her out to talk, but then he'd tried to cancel because of Gerome and she'd been the one to suggest they meet up anyway, her other prevarications might go unnoticed. Instead she lied. Again. "Maybe," she said slowly, drawing the word out, as though turning the idea over in her mind.

"So you went out with him, and Ronnie . . . I think it's safe to say we're getting to you," Claire concluded.

"Getting *on* me, you mean. You are working my nerves, and you know I don't need that."

"You just don't want to admit you were wrong," Daria said.

"Because I wasn't," Drin insisted. "I'm not. And these two 'dates' if you want to call them that, they prove my point, not yours. For one thing, they reminded me why I didn't want to do this in the first place, and for another, they were further examples of what's wrong with me. I didn't even want The Best Man. And Matt . . . well that's a can of worms I don't want to open."

"Why not?"

"Seeing him, just seeing him, it hurts. I am better alone."

"You are alone, alone," Daria said.

"I'm not alone. I've got you guys."

"For now," Claire said.

"This is just temporary," Tamika added. "I'm only hangin' with you all 'til I find myself a man." She looked challengingly at all of them. Everyone laughed.

Better by far you should forget and smile
than that you should remember and be sad.

Rossetti

16.

It was Dorinda's week for getting flowers. Her office mates bought her a beautiful bouquet. Then she received a dozen pink roses and a cheerful card from Herbie. She didn't have any surface space left in her small office when the window box filled with impatiens arrived with an apologetic note from Matt.

"I shouldn't have tried to rush things," he wrote. "Get it?"

She couldn't miss the not-very-hidden message contained in the offering. As far as Dorinda was concerned, they'd rushed into bed, but more time wouldn't have made any difference. If he'd spent weeks, or months, trying to reestablish their friendship before they slept together, she'd still feel the same way she did now. It had been a mistake.

Bob Anderson came puffing into her office soon after Matt's flowers arrived. "The university," he whispered urgently. "They're thinking of redoing the computer lab."

"Great," she said, as enthusiastically as possible, under the circumstances.

"They specifically asked for you." That sounded more like a Matt Cooper apology. She remembered all the times he told her that buying flowers was no way to tell a woman what was in your heart. They signified, he believed, growth and beauty, not remorse. She had thought daisies were a lovely gift then, and she'd have preferred the flowers now. They were simple and sweet. The offer of the job was just going to be one big headache.

When Matt called later, presumably for her expression of gratitude, she only told him, "If you wanted to give me a job, why couldn't you wait a week. Or at least ask me first. I told you I was thinking of leaving the company."

"I know. I just thought this would give you more power in the negotiations."

"I gave Bob two weeks' notice. Friday is my last day," she explained.

"I made it clear that we only wanted to deal directly with you," Matt said. "We can still give the deal to your new company."

"I can't do that," Drin said. "I was working for Bob when the offer came in. It's his. It wouldn't be ethical to try to bypass him just because I'm leaving."

"He's going to lose business when you go. There's nothing you can do about that," Matt argued reasonably enough.

"That's old business; this is new. I wouldn't feel right about it. He could even sue me. Don't try to help me, okay, Matt? I can take care of my career myself."

"Let me sit down with you and Anderson. I'm sure we can work something out."

"I don't think that's such a great idea," Dorinda demurred. She had images of the two men talking about her, and around her, and for her.

"I was trying to do something nice. Give me a chance to make this up to you, Drin?" Matt said. "We're the client. It wouldn't be that strange for us to request a meeting, would it?"

"Nooo," Dorinda said hesitantly.

"I'll call Anderson and set it up."

That was how Dorinda found herself sitting at a table Friday afternoon with the two men in her life who were doing their best to drive her insane. Bob looked self-satisfied, if a little bit nervous. He lived for business and liked nothing better than the edge-of-his-seat tension of making a deal. This particular negotiation had an added bonus, in that he hoped it would change Dorinda's mind about leaving. He knew that she and Matt knew each other, but he didn't know they'd dated. Dorinda didn't feel it was any of his business, and since it didn't really change the situation, she just hadn't brought it up.

Matt had his own agenda. There was a promise in his deep–set brown eyes when they met hers. Like Bob, he was looking forward to this, for reasons of his own. This was his chance to prove to her that they truly could be friends again. She didn't believe it. She could not look at his square jaw, his broad shoulders without remembering how they felt, and she couldn't be friends with a man who made her feel this way. Just sitting in this room with him, looking the way he did, was torture.

Matt seemed to have more than sex on his mind. He wanted to be best friends again. It might have been nice to be so coveted, except that Dorinda was feeling completely claustrophobic. She took some deep breaths while the men exchanged pleasantries. This was important to her future. She had more to gain, or lose, from this than either of them.

"Bob," Matt began. "I understand Dorinda is leaving to start her own consultation firm."

"We've been discussing that," Bob acceded.

"We want her working with us on this. We'd go directly to Dorinda after she opens her new office, but none of us wants to create an atmosphere of distrust here." Dorinda waited, with bated breath, for Bob's reaction. He could suggest Matt go elsewhere, or threaten to sue if he tried to bypass the company to hire Dorinda. She was pleased to see him nod.

"Good," Bob said. "I could always hire Dorinda as a consultant for this job."

"I'd like it to be completely under her control. We'll be totally upgrading the computer lab. We'll need new equipment, software installation, memory transfer, the works."

Dorinda had an idea. She played around with it for a moment, while Bob answered Matt.

"That's no problem, I can have the quotes on the hardware within a couple of hours of receiving your requirements."

"In all fairness, there are people here who are better suited, I mean better qualified to fulfilling that kind of order than I am," Dorinda offered. Matt looked surprised, and not very pleased, by her honesty. "However, the rest of the assignment is really interesting to me." She paused. When she had their full attention, she continued. "What do you think of this? I'll hire Bob's company for the sale and setup of the hardware, and then I'll handle the programming and work out the rest of the details."

Bob considered it carefully, then nodded, satisfied.

Matt smiled. "It sounds like a plan," he said. "We're in business."

Bob reached over to shake his hand. Then he also offered his big paw to Dorinda. "Looks like we'll be working together for a while longer anyway," he said happily.

He walked away from the table well-satisfied. Dorinda was also pleased with the results of mediation, since she had only given up the part of the job that she had never liked doing. Anyone could figure out the hardware requirements. What she loved was programming and troubleshooting. And she could still do that, while leaving the more mundane details of this deal to Bob's well-trained staff.

"That went well," she said softly to Matt as she walked him to the front entrance. "Better than I expected."

"So I did good?" he asked.

"Yeah, yeah. What do you want? A medal?" Dorinda said flippantly, but she was feeling magnanimous so she didn't mention that this all could have been avoided if Matt had just not made his grand gesture in the first place. She was in too good a mood to harp about it. "It was fun," she confided in him.

"Do I get a second chance?" he asked.

"Don't beg. It's not attractive," Dorinda teased.

"Come to dinner with me tomorrow night," he urged.

"I have dinner plans with my folks tomorrow night," she said.

"Even better. Let me come. Your parents love me," he said.

"That's what I'm afraid of. But all right," Dorinda reluctantly agreed. She owed him one for starting out her business with a big juicy contract, and what could be safer than dinner at home? He couldn't very well talk about their indiscretion in front of her parents. "But I better not regret this."

"You won't. I promise," he said, with an odd intensity. For a moment she worried, but then she dismissed it. In less than an hour, she'd run through every emotion from panic to euphoria, and it had all ended well. Perhaps her luck had changed.

She took him to the celebratory dinner with her family. Gwen brought Herbie along as well. Dinner was a raucous affair, the meal peppered with the hilarity which tends to ensue when a major disaster has been averted. The scene reminded Drin of a movie she'd seen recently in which an airliner had nearly crashed. When the plane was safely down on the runway, the passengers cheered and laughed through their tears, the flight attendants hugged each other, and the crew gave each other numerous pats and hugs, and high fives.

Her parents' relief that Gwendolyn's marriage had survived its first real test was clearly evident. Earl kept squeezing Herbie's shoulder every time he came near enough to his son-in-law. Janine kept saying how happy she was. Gwen tried to play it down, but her joy was as obvious as Herbie's. If Dorinda was not mistaken, they played footsy under the table throughout the meal.

Her brothers weren't particularly gratified by the presence of their new brother-in-law. That, they just took in stride. The source of their barely contained excitement was nothing so unselfish as pleasure at their sister's good fortune. They were thrilled to be able to watch the basketball playoffs on their father's big screen.

Drin thought the semi-finals were going to go to the Bulls again, but she'd been getting the scores and the play-by-play from the sports section of the newspaper. It hadn't been a good year for her and basketball.

Matt wore a big grin through most of the evening.

"You look pleased with yourself," she finally commented.

"I'm just happy to be here," he said.

Dorinda enjoyed the lively conversation, and took part in the annual argument about whether the Knicks would finally get to the championship now that Phil Jackson had left the Bulls and come to New York. For the past two years the Bulls had reigned, but her father always rooted for the home team, right up to the final game. He could rehash the season for hours from his fanatical point of view, and it never ceased to start a debate. Drin liked the home team, of course, but her favorite players were not on it—so she rooted for them, despite the fact that they were playing for Los Angeles or Chicago. Her brothers were torn. A baseball player for the Mets himself, Rodney felt he should set an example like his father's and be loyal to New York, but Terrence loved the Bulls and he loved being on the side of the winning team.

This year her mother broke the tie. "New York is not

going to make it, despite the fact they finally hired Jackson. Maybe next year," she said soothingly to Earl.

"But they could. They've got everything in place this year. It's just like in '70 or '71. That was an amazing year."

"Don't get misty on us now, Earl," Rodney begged.

"This whole neighborhood would go crazy if they won."

"The whole city likes to celebrate. You were just a baby in '71, but remember when the Mets won the series."

"When they won, the entire neighborhood was out on the street, cheering and shouting," Dorinda said, smiling at him.

"Not this year, Earl." Her brother, the doctor, had predicted the winner of the championship, correctly, for five of the last six years. So had a lot of other people, but he still gave himself a lot of credit for his perspicacity.

"It's not over 'til it's over," Earl said, making a face at his eldest child.

"Give it up, honey," their mother said. "Terrence is right. They don't really have a shot. The Knicks don't have their game heads on. The Bulls have demoralized the other teams for years, playing the fastest, strongest game in the league. It will take any other team a while to feel like they've got a chance. I'd say the only possible teams are the Lakers, the Jazz, and maybe the Cavaliers. The psychological advantage Chicago has is enormous. They've won too many years in a row." Always the amateur psychologist, Janine liked to suss out the players' psyches in order to make her pick for the winners.

"Never count New York out," Rodney said.

"That's a motto to live by," Dorinda teased him. "For a player on the Mets." He shot a pea at her across the table.

"Your brother is right. The Knicks have come back before," her father admonished.

"They haven't had a bad season," Matt offered.

"Not at all, not at all," Earl agreed, smiling approvingly at him.

The whole family had welcomed Matt back to the table like a prodigal brother or son, and he basked in the attention. Willie was out for the evening with an old admirer of hers, but the reunion could scarcely have been made more joyful with her presence. Dorinda thought to herself, as she had so many times before, that Matt fit right in with her family—much better than she did herself. It had annoyed her when she was younger. But, as Matt said, his parents had always held her up to him as their shining example of what they expected from their only child, so they were even. Drin hadn't seen the Coopers in years, though her parents still saw them regularly. She wondered how it would be if the situation were reversed and she was sitting with him at his family's dining–room table.

Mrs. Cooper had always included her in the preparation of the meal. No men were allowed in her kitchen. Drin, a feminist from early on, hadn't exactly approved this strict separation, but it had made her feel special to share something with Matt's mother that he couldn't. She didn't feel comfortable cooking with her own mother, because Janine preferred to experiment when she cooked, and never used a recipe for anything. Her father had been the parent who'd made sure there was always something edible on the table. Her mother's offerings were more in the way of artistic arrangements. Matt, of course, could barely be coaxed out of the kitchen when he came over, no matter which of her parents was preparing the evening meal.

"This is great, Dad," Drin said as she finished her baked ziti. There was a chorus of compliments from around the table seconding her opinion.

"Thank you," her father bowed his head regally. At his imposing height, he might have looked like a warrior or a statesmen, but his bespectacled, scholarly expression suited his personality. Earl was a voracious reader, and had an amazingly high I.Q., almost as high as her mother's. They were both at the genius level, and, of course, both were interested in everything, and Matt reminded her of them in that way, as well as with his laid–back manner and easy–going smile. He could have been a Fay.

"I bought dessert," Janine called. All four of her children let out a cheer. "Smart–asses," she chided. "Why can't you be sweet like Matt here?"

"He was just being polite, Janine," Drin couldn't help pointing out.

"Not just that. He always ate everything I put in front of him. Especially desserts."

"He helped you make them; he'd look pretty stupid if even he wouldn't eat them," Rodney said.

"Wouldn't he though," Drin agreed. "Thank you, little brother. I take back what I said about New York teams."

"Good. And speaking of teams ... Mom, can we eat dessert in the living–room?"

"Sure," Janine granted her permission easily.

Everyone cleared their places at the table, and brought the dishes and silver into the kitchen to be washed. Rodney and Terrence were finished first, and claimed their places on the sofa before anyone else had even left the dining–room. Herbie and Gwen moved slowly, bringing up the rear, with much touching and bumping of hips involved in the procedure. When they wandered into the living–room, long after everyone else, they were holding hands.

No one but Dorinda seemed to notice. Everyone was engrossed in the game. Even Matt was watching the clock run down on the quarter while both teams put on a burst of speed and showed their agility as the ball went up and down the court, first into one basket, then the other— with barely any time–outs called. It was an amazing game, with both teams running and passing and sinking impossible shots and rebounds. The players were all in their best form, as if they couldn't do anything wrong.

"They're like machines," Terrence said in awe. He seemed to have recovered from his fanatical frenzy, and, like her, he was clinically admiring the beauty of the sport, all partisanship forgotten.

"They are at the top of their form tonight," Drin agreed.

"But it's like a war on that court," Janine chimed in. "They don't look like they're having any fun out there."

"This is for the championship, Janine," Rodney said impatiently.

"I know that, you ungrateful child. I'm just saying they should remember this is only a game."

"Not *a* game, *the* game," Rodney insisted.

"Just watch," Terrence ordered.

Dorinda did as ordered and watched the game go on, even staying in her seat for the half–time extravaganza. She watched the marching band and the baton twirlers with the usual degree of impatience, but she amused herself by watching the men's eyes glaze over as the skimpily clad Laker Girls took the floor. She had never understood the appeal of cheerleaders. That was probably a large part of the reason why she'd been so upset when Matt had fallen out of love with her, and into love with the head cheer-leader. The girl hadn't seemed, to Drin, to have anything to offer him, except perhaps sex. And Dorinda had been providing that.

It was hard to believe, though, that he was seduced by her sex appeal, because Matt had been so respectful, so protective, and so gentlemanly toward Joan. He barely seemed to notice her provocative behavior, or her reveal-ing clothing. Even after he started dating the most sought–after girl in their school, he didn't brag about it, or change anything about himself. It was Drin who cut him off, and closed down all the lines of communication between them, because she couldn't bear the pain she felt seeing them together.

Her mother's voice interrupted her thoughts. "Now those women look like they're having a ball."

Drin refocussed on her brothers. "They probably put petroleum jelly on their teeth, so they can smile all night long. Besides they're getting paid a lot of money to look like that," she said, more to them than to Janine.

"Their pay scale isn't even in the same league with the players'," Earl chimed in.

There were silly half smiles on Rodney and Terrence's faces as some of the cheerleaders did splits, smiling widely at the camera. "Just try to be a little open–minded, Drin," Rodney suggested. "Not all cheerleaders are empty headed fluffballs."

"The advertisers aren't paying a million dollars a minute for *their* performance," she shot back at him, but he was immersed in the sexy, energetic spectacle again, already.

Drin turned her attention to the television set. After a couple of minutes she, too, was entranced by the buxom beauties displaying thighs, taut stomachs, and breasts to the hordes in the bleachers. Their exuberance was appealing. Dorinda thought back to what her friends had said about her choosing "all work and no play." If she wanted to be happy, she was going to have to take a leaf from The Cheerleaders' Handbook and have a little fun. Without that, as her mother had just said, there would be something vital missing from her life—and she didn't mean only Matthew Cooper. He seemed to be interested in her, whether she changed or not. It was for her own well–being, with or without a man, that she needed a new attitude.

It was so simple. It was a revelation. She looked around the room at the family which usually made her feel so inadequate, and at Matt, whom she had once adored, and finally felt she could appreciate the people whom she loved. Maybe the angst she felt at the prospect of dating again could finally be resolved with a simple new philosophy, "Don't worry, be happy." It was one of Aunt Willie's favorite aphorisms.

Her unspoken vow of celibacy, the debates with her family and friends, all the turmoil of the last two years, had been leading up to this moment. It was as if a dam had burst somewhere inside her. It was a great relief to let it all go. She looked at Matt through new eyes, different eyes . . . open eyes. She didn't see him as the man who'd stolen her heart, never to found be found again. He was just her old friend, Matt. And the best lover she had ever had.

She wanted something to happen, anything: she did not know what.

Kate Chopin

17.

After the game, while her family was involved in the post–game review, she took Matt by the hand and led him up to her old bedroom, now the guest room, to speak to him in private.

"I do appreciate what you did, but you aren't doing anything wrong in giving me this job, are you? Misusing department funds or anything like that?" she asked.

"No, we really were going to upgrade the computer lab," he assured her. "I just put in a strong pitch for you to be the one to do it. The company that supplies our computer equipment is very expensive, and they've never given us the kind of attention we wanted."

"But mine is going to be a one–woman operation, at least at the start. Are you sure they'll be satisfied with that?"

"I'm sure you'll do a good job for us. As I told the administration, a hungry young entrepreneur will work harder for us than any big company. You need the account, and the good PR. It didn't hurt that you were a minority business owner. The government encourages institutions like New York Tech to use them. The school might even get a grant out of this."

"Oh?" She raised her eyebrows. "And what do you get?"

"My best friend back?"

"That's sweet, but I think Gerome won that one in the end," Drin said airily. He smiled wryly. "What?" she asked.

"Nothing. It's just that he was saying the same thing—when I spoke to him yesterday."

"What was he saying?" It would be just like Ger to gloat.

"It's ridiculous, but he's jealous of you."

"You're kidding!" she exclaimed, disbelieving.

"Really. He thinks you planned the whole thing: invited me to the wedding, or added my name to the guest list, came alone and then picked up Ronnie when you saw my date, enticed me into driving you back home, seduced me, and abandoned me."

"Why would I do all that?" Drin asked, open–mouthed.

"To get even for high school? To pique my interest? Don't ask me. Gerome is very conspiracy minded."

"He always was."

"The army really made him crazy, refusing to admit the Gulf War Syndrome existed for all those years. He sees traps and tricks everywhere, even in you."

"That's not exactly new either, honey. We always competed for your attention. His mother was never home, and my parents were always there—your room was our sanctuary. Remember how we used to fight over who got to sleep with you in the bed when we were seven or eight?"

"That's just because if you two got in the bed together, you'd fight all night."

"Yeah," she said. "Over you."

Matt looked embarrassed. "But I thought . . ."

"Yes?" Drin prompted.

"My parents said it was because you had a crush on each other. You know, he torments you, you tease him. You can see why they'd think that. That is how little girls and boys express affection."

"I love your parents, but they were way off–base with that one. I figured that out, later." He gave her a knowing look. Drin felt heat in her cheeks. She'd been brutally honest with him, when he'd finally admitted that he felt something more than friendship for her. She'd told him he was an idiot, and she'd been in love with him for years.

"And you didn't figure out that the antipathy between us was real at that point?"

"Well . . ." Now he really looked embarrassed.

"What?" Dorinda asked.

"It entered a whole new phase. I was busy, umm, defending your honor, as it were."

"That dog! What did he say about me?"

"Drin, it was a long time ago." He wasn't telling. It had to be pretty bad.

"That pig! Did he call me a stanky ho'?" Dorinda pressed. It had been a favorite phrase of his in high school. Drin had hated it, and he knew that and tormented her with it.

"He was just jealous, you said it yourself."

"That doesn't excuse—"

"I shouldn't have told you, but you can't be that upset about Ger's ravings from twelve years ago."

"That boy needs a smack upside his head. His brains are scrambled. What did you say he was saying about me the other day?"

"It wasn't that bad. And anyway, we both know he was wrong," he placated her.

Dorinda was still hot. "I can guess. That immature dirty-minded backstabbing weasel."

"I told him I was the one who initiated the . . . thing between us."

"But he didn't believe you, did he?"

"Not exactly, but Drin, we both know the truth. What does it matter?"

She had to think about that one for a second. "It matters. It matters because, because—" she spluttered. "Because you know damn well I wanted you as much as you wanted me. And the way Gerome looks at it, I feel like some desperate slut who couldn't keep her hands off you."

"You did?" He looked surprised. "I thought I was the only one who was desperate."

Drin tried to backtrack. "I didn't say I was *desperate*. I just said Gerome . . ." she faltered as she looked into his big brown eyes. "Gerome would think I took advantage of your, umm, weakness."

"Would you?"

"He would . . . I mean, I didn't. I thought we . . . We settled this, didn't we?"

"Not if it's true?" He stared into her eyes.

"What?" she asked, unable to look away, unable to move at all, or to think, as she waited for him to ask his question.

"You wanted *me?*"

"Matt," she said, trying, and failing, to break the eye contact between them. "We really should, probably, go back downstairs."

"Not until you tell me."

"Well, yes, but—"

"Yes, you'll tell me, or yes, you wanted to make love to me, too. Just as badly as I wanted you."

"I don't know," she played for time. "How much did you?"

"I have never wanted anything or anyone so badly in my life. I was aching for you. I was dying for you. When you touched me, I thought I was going to seriously injure myself or you, I kissed you so hard."

"Oh. Then I guess the answer is, yes," Dorinda said.

Drin was still poised to leave, but she had no desire to walk out of that room. She only wanted one thing, and that was for him to kiss her again. He came closer, leaned over, and gently slanted his lips over hers. Her hands came up to his waist and anchored there, as she was carried away by the sweetness of that kiss. It lasted for a long, long time; the two of them exploring each other's mouths. The kiss was pure heat, wet and flavored with coffee and sugar and the chocolate brownies they'd had for dessert.

"I didn't want to do this like this," Drin said softly.

"How did you want to do this?" he murmured against her mouth.

"I wanted it to be fun. Like you promised."

"It will be," he said, urging her hands up over his shoulders and wrapping his arms around her waist. He nuzzled her neck.

"This is my old bedroom," Drin said, her head falling back. "My parents are just down the hall. They could walk in here at any time."

"All part of the fun," Matt said, his hands slipping down to cup her buttocks.

She disagreed. "It could be very embarrassing."

"Let me go. I'll lock the door," he said, pulling away.

He smelled and felt so good. She held him close, kissed his neck. "They'll know what we're doing if we lock the door."

Gwen and Herbie chose that moment to barge in. "Oh! Uh . . ." they exclaimed.

Herbie said, "Sorry." They left.

"Now they'll know for sure," Matt said, but his hands were still moving on her backside.

"Gwen will keep them away, anyway." Drin felt very free. Her new attitude was already giving her more enjoyment than she ever could have had before. She pulled his head down to hers and kissed him, her tongue invading his hot mouth. "How do you like the new me?" she asked him.

"I like everything about you," Matt breathed against her forehead. "I always have." His hand slipped inside her blouse. She hadn't even felt him unbuttoning it. He covered one of her breasts with his large hand and squeezed it gently, then moved to the other. "Are you having fun yet?"

"Some," she replied, nipping his chin. "How about you?"

"I love playing with your nipples. They pucker up so tight and hard," he flicked his thumb over one and a shiver ran through her.

"You want to play?" Drin asked, unbuttoning his fly. She was determined to give as good as she got. He caught her hand and stopped her.

"Me, first," he said, and backed her against the bed, then bent her back over it, so her chest arched toward him. They landed in a tangle, but his mouth honed in unerringly on the taut nipples he'd teased into little buttons with his fingers. His mouth moved languorously from the tip of one breast to the other, his tongue playing in circles over them while his hand glided slowly downwards over her waist to the waistband of her slacks, which he quickly unfastened and pushed down over her thin cotton underwear and over her curls. Then he pressed his palm into her center, wet with desire for him, and she gasped. His fingers suddenly parted her flesh and his tongue flicked across her nipple at the same time and she cried out at the pleasure of it. His hands, his mouth, his whole body, gave her such pleasure. His tongue played in circles over her skin, echoing the rhythm of his fingers gliding back and forth, and Drin felt herself contract deep inside.

"This is the most fun I ever had," she panted. Her hands were free again and she hastily undid the rest of his buttons and pushed the last barrier from between them. Her hand curled over his silken smoothness and guided him to his care. He slid smoothly against her and then filled her. His nostrils flared, and his breathing grew harsh, as the pressure built in him as it had in her. He stroked into her and she rocked against him, arching her body up to his. All conscious thought was gone as her body took over and sought its own release. He began to stroke faster and she matched him, twisting as close as she could get and splaying her hands over his buttocks to urge him on until she felt a burst of joy so intense she laughed out loud.

Sated, she kept him within her while her blood cooled

and her breathing calmed. "I can't believe I waited so long to do that again," she said.

He looked at her curiously. "What did you mean by the new you?" he asked.

"In case you didn't know it, this isn't my usual style," Drin informed him. "I've changed."

"Changed how?" he asked.

"Well, for one thing, I don't think I'll be needing to release my pent–up aggression at the gym anymore." She sighed, happily.

"So you're not gonna run away this time, huh?" He smiled back at her.

"Run away? Not me. The boring seventy–hour work weeks are history. I've got a new hobby." She nudged him up and sat, and started rebuttoning her blouse. He watched her, bemused. She leaned over and gave him a kiss on the cheek. "This is a lot more fun than computer programming."

He nodded. "I think so."

"We'll have to do it again sometime," she said.

"Soon," he said.

Dorinda concurred, "Absolutely."

Work wasn't enough to satisfy all the empty space inside of her. Only love could do that. And if she couldn't have that, then this man was the perfect substitute.

We must take the good with the bad;
For the good when it's good, is so very good
That the bad when it's bad can't be bad.

Moliere

18.

Dorinda was feeling woozy, and she hadn't had a drop
of alcohol to drink. It had to be Matt. He was like a drug.
Now that she had let herself go, decided that dating was
back on her agenda, she had a lot of time to make up for.
She bade her parents good-bye, and followed Matt out to
his car. Once inside, she strapped herself in with her seat
belt. As he moved out of the driveway, she pressed the
button that released the lock. She felt compelled to be
closer to him. She wasn't sure she liked that feeling.

Drin leaned over and kissed his neck.

The car jerked to a stop halfway out into the street.

"Whoa!" he exclaimed. "I'm driving here."

"So pull over," she suggested, nibbling on his earlobe.

"Drinda, honey, we're a five-minute drive from your
place, or my place." He swallowed, deeply. She felt the
motion of his Adam's apple against her cheek, and gloried
in the surge of primitive satisfaction it made her feel. Sex
might have given him some power over her, but it was
mutual.

"Which do you want?" he asked.

"Huh?" Drin said, blankly.

"Your place or mine?"

"Can't you do better than that old line?" she asked.

"It didn't work out too well the last time we, uh, had, uh, sex in your bed, and I don't want you to wake up and freak out in the morning, again," he said.

"I don't care where we go." She was too busy exploring his neck.

"Your parents' place was . . . great, but I felt a little weird."

"You!" her indignation was muted when she mumbled the word against his cheek. "That was *my* childhood bedroom."

"Okay, so my place?" he asked.

"Absofuckin'lutely," she agreed, shamelessly eager to arrive at their destination and check out the limits of this newfound power.

"Okay." He put the car in gear and eased out into the street. Drin's ministrations did not cease. "You, umm, mind waiting to do that 'til we get to the stop sign," he started to ask, but the moment he turned his head slightly toward her, she took his cheeks between her palms and kissed him. She felt his body slacken. Then she felt the impact of another car as an SUV rear-ended them.

The screeching of brakes hadn't really registered in her brain as occurring directly behind them, but the crunching sound of metal buckling told her this was no simple fender–bender. They had only been moving at about twenty–five miles an hour, and would have been all right, if the impact hadn't caused Matt's foot to press down on the accelerator for an instant after the jolt.

Dorinda had read somewhere that when cars were initially designed, the interior could have been made much safer. Rounded, rather than squared edges, soft material on the dash and steering wheel rather than hard rubber, and buttons rather than sticks for the controls, would have made collisions much safer at higher speeds. However, the average car was a potential deathtrap, even going only twenty to thirty miles an hour. For the first time, as they rocketed toward a lamppost a few yards away, she understood the consumer advocate's point of view.

The car went up onto the curb as if it weren't there. At the last possible moment, as he finally found the brakes, Matt turned the steering wheel hard to the right. Dorinda, braced as she was for impact with the tall, fast approaching, steel lamppost, flew sideways into the door. Matt's chest hit the steering wheel just as the airbags inflated, blocking her view. It only took a few seconds, but Drin had experienced the crash as if in slow motion, her last view the agony on Matt's face. She couldn't see anything from behind the plastic air bag that had engulfed her, but she heard Matt groan.

"Are you all right?" she called out.

It sounded like he said, "Arrgh."

"You didn't break anything, did you?" Drin asked.

"What do I look like, a doctor?" came his muffled reply.

Dorinda started laughing. He had to be all right if he was making wisecracks. "I—" she tried to tell him that she'd gotten a hairline fracture to a rib during a karate tournament once, but she couldn't seem to stop laughing. "I—!" Or to catch her breath.

The door on her side of the car sprang open and she heard her father's deep voice. "Are you okay, Drinda?"

Her mother must have been on the other side of the car, because her shrill voice sounded like it came from half a mile away. "Matt!" she was shrieking.

"Calm down, Mom. I don't think it's as bad in the car as it looks from the outside," Rodney said. "The car is totaled, but Matt's talking and I don't see any blood."

Her father extricated Dorinda from the airbag, and helped her to stand. She leaned on him heavily, testing her legs, flexing her fingers, making sure she was still all in one piece. If she had had her seat belt on, she suspected she'd have been very bruised; as it was, the right side of her body throbbed a little because of that last daredevil move on Matt's part. But as she rounded the car, she realized he'd probably saved her life with that twist of the wheel. Her side of the Lexus looked completely normal, except for the fact that it was parked half on, half off the sidewalk at a strange angle. His side of the car had been destroyed. Terrence and Rodney and her mother had gotten Matt out of the car, and laid him on the ground.

"I don't think you're supposed to move an accident victim," he said.

"Don't worry, Matt. I'm a doctor, remember. It's safe." Terrence was shaking his head as he examined Matt. "You are one lucky son-of-a—"

"Ugh!" Matt said, just at that moment. "I'm not feeling too fortunate right at this moment, Terry," he bit out between clenched teeth. "Whatever you're doing isn't helping."

"I'm sorry, bro," Terrence said, continuing to probe his body. "I'm checking for breaks. You seem to have cracked at least one rib."

Dorinda barely restrained her "I told you so," and the rueful glance Matt shot at her over her brother's shoulder told her he knew it.

"How did this happen?" her mother kept asking. Drin realized the litany had begun before she'd even gotten out of the car, but only now was the question clear to her.

"I guess I got . . . distracted," Matt said.

"Hey, don't look at me," she told him. She pulled away from her father, but found her legs were too shaky to support her, so she slid to the ground, a few feet from where Matt lay.

"Honey, are you sure you're all right?" Earl asked, a concerned frown on his face.

"I'm fine. At least, I don't think anything's broken. I may have a few bruises, and a scrape here where I hit the door handle." She raised her shirt an inch and looked at her side. Small, angry–looking red welts a couple of inches

long were just faintly visible against her dark skin. Her
father squinted to see them, but turned his attention back
to Matt as Terrence stood.

"So, Doc, what's the verdict?" Matt joked. "Will I live?"

"Sure," Terrence said easily, but Dorinda knew her
brother, and she knew the look on his face meant he was
worried. So did the rest of the family, who moved in a little
closer, leaving her alone on the ground. She didn't blame
them. If she could have gotten up again, she'd have gone
to Matt's side, too.

"Where is that ambulance?" Janine said. As if on cue,
they heard the sirens. Down the street, Gwen and Herbie
were waving the red and white E.M.S. vehicle toward the
accident. They followed it at a quick trot.

Two young men in uniform got out of the car and moved
quickly and efficiently toward the car. "This way," Earl
directed. They didn't seem fazed by the damage, even to
the driver's side of the car, but they looked disapproving
anyway when they reached Dorinda, who was closest.

"Are you all right, Miss?" one asked, going down on
one knee beside her. "You should have stayed in the car."

"I'm fine. He's the one who needs you," she said, waving
toward the anxious circle around Matt. The other man
quickly moved on, but the first stayed with her, asking her
to move this way and that. She did as he asked, but her
attention was focussed on the man kneeling beside Matt.
He, too, was saying something about not moving injured
people.

Terrence introduced himself. "I'm a doctor, and I didn't
move him until I checked him over. There doesn't seem
to be any damage to the spine, but I think he may have
cracked a rib or two. I'm a little worried that a rib may
have punctured his lungs."

"Charlie?" the other emergency services man called.
"Bring the gurney."

Charlie gave her a pat on the shoulder and said he'd
be right back, and was gone in an instant. He brought the

stretcher in less than a minute, and while Gene, the other man, worked over Matt, wrapping his neck in a plastic collar and rolling him onto a hard-backed board, preparatory to lifting him onto the stretcher, they both soothed her parents, questioned Terrence, and took care of Matt. Dorinda felt comfortable with their capable, no-nonsense manner, and didn't bother them until they were lifting Matt into the ambulance. She hobbled over to the back door of the truck.

"Can I ride with him?" she asked.

"Why don't you ride up front," they said. "We'll need to check you out in the hospital, too."

Gene got in the back with Matt, and Charlie helped her into the high front seat. Her family called after them that they would meet her at the hospital, but Drin barely had time to acknowledge them before the ambulance was moving, fast, sirens blaring.

"He's going to be all right, isn't he?" she asked.

"We'll know better after the doctors see him," Charlie said noncommittally.

"Do you think his rib punctured a lung?" she asked, straight out, but quietly, aware that Matt could probably hear her in the back of the vehicle, since she could hear Gene speaking on the radio to the hospital.

"I can't really say. It seems likely," he answered, keeping his voice low as well. "They'll have to x-ray him and see what internal injuries he might have sustained."

She sat quietly after that, not sure what she was feeling, or even how she *should* be feeling at a time like this. She didn't know enough to panic, and it wouldn't have helped the situation, but Dorinda was scared. She'd just found Matt again, just gotten a vague inkling of what it might be like to have a future with him. She couldn't imagine him having a serious injury, let alone the possibility that she could ... lose him. Her mind skittered away from the thought. That couldn't happen. Not now.

She watched them take him out of the ambulance, and

then she went with him into the emergency entrance, but there they were separated. In the short time between her arrival and her family's descent on the scene, she had two interns circling her, clipboards in hand, asking for her vital statistics, relationship to Matt, and even for some information about him. She couldn't provide much on that score, and she felt terrible about that, too. Dorinda felt sick, and she didn't know how much of it was worry, or if it might be connected to the accident. There were no doctors in sight until her older brother arrived.

"How is he?" she asked first.

"I don't know, I came in to see you. I'll talk to his doctors in a minute. I didn't get a chance to take a look at you out there," he said, sweet big brother and clinical doctor at the same time.

"Yeah," she managed a smile. "You let Dad take me out of the car without checking for spinal injury or anything. But I didn't tell." Her voice sounded strange to her ears, but she couldn't make herself sound like a grownup. She hadn't felt so young and helpless since before she could remember.

"Hey, I checked you out. Remember?" he asked. She had a vague recollection of hands, squeezing in behind the airbag which was still too big for her to see around. Those same hands gently prodded and poked at her now. She was surprised to find they felt like the hands of a real doctor, competently placing a stethoscope to her chest, and examining the abrasion on her side. "That was you? I thought that was Daddy. Your hands are just like his." Again she heard an echo of her childhood in the tone of her voice.

"Huh," he snorted. "I've only got one baby sister, and I'm not taking any chances with her."

"Okay," she said. "But go help Matthew now. He needs you more than I do."

"Okay," he agreed, apparently satisfied that she was not seriously hurt. "I'll send Janine in."

Her mother's first words were, "What did you do to that boy?"

Her mother's baseless accusation left her spluttering. "Me? He was driving." Her reversion to childhood was complete.

"Yes, but he said he was distracted. So?"

"Why do you assume it was me?" Drin asked, stalling.

"Because I know you," Janine said. "You can talk the ear off a pig."

"Now that's one I've never even heard Aunt Willie say," Drin said.

"Dorinda Fay, I'm serious now. That boy's parents are going to be here any minute. I want to know what I'm going to be apologizing for before they get here."

"*If* there is any apologizing to do, I'll be the one to do it," Dorinda said, admitting nothing. "Terrence already checked me out, and he says I'm fine," she added, stretching the truth a bit. "Stop grilling me and make yourself useful. Help me get dressed." Janine didn't look too pleased at that, but she did help Drin to sit up.

Out in the hallway, Drin found the rest of her family shared Janine's point of view. They all assumed she was guilty of causing the accident and were nervous about facing Matt's parents. It made her determined to prove her innocence. When the Coopers walked in, their only interest was in finding out how Matt was doing.

They were proper parents. Dorinda loved the fact that her mother and father, sister and brothers had all come to their rescue, and she was glad they were there, but she couldn't help noticing that they seemed more concerned about Matt than about her. Janine was overwrought, but that didn't excuse the fact that she hadn't had one nice word to say to her daughter yet, whereas the Coopers were all concern.

"Dorinda, dear, we're so happy to see you're all right," Ted Cooper said, holding out his hands to her.

"The doctors say I'm fine. Just a few scrapes and bruises."

"Are you sure you should be walking around already?" Vivian asked. "You can never be too careful."

"I've got my personal physician watching over me," Drin said, nodding toward Terrence. "We're waiting for news about Matt. Did they tell you anything about his condition?"

"Yes, hmmm," Ted cleared his throat. "They were still examining him, but they seemed to think he'd be all right. I'm glad that you, at least, walked away from this terrible accident. I told him he shouldn't get a sportscar. At least he had those . . ." He looked at his wife, questioningly.

"Passenger side airbags." Vivian finished the sentence for him. "He's usually a very responsible driver. I don't think he's ever even been in a fender–bender before. It's a shame that he had to do this with you in the car," she continued.

"Oh, no," Drin protested. While her mother's assumption of her guilt had only made her defensive, the Cooper's apology for their son's supposed carelessness made her feel guilty as sin. "It wasn't, strictly speaking, Matthew's fault."

Mr. Cooper jumped on that. "Was it the other driver? In the old days, the person who rear ends the car was always assumed to be at fault, unless the driver in front was in reverse, but nowadays, with no-fault insurance, presumption of guilt isn't enough." Before Dorinda could object, he turned to his wife. "We should call Alfie, dear."

Earl immediately objected. "Alfred Hunter is nothing but a bottom feeder. He's been chasing ambulances since the sixties. I don't think we should bring him into this."

"We went to school with Alfie," Ted reminded him.

"And he cheated, remember?" Janine said. She'd been at Howard University with them.

Vivian Cooper had married Ted later. She'd been introduced to her husband's old school friend when he was a lawyer, not as a young rebellious student. "Who do you want us to call? 1-800-LAWYER?" she joked mildly.

"It would be better than calling Alfie Hunter," Earl insisted.

Vivian's smile faded, and she looked uncertainly from him to her husband. "Ted?"

"You've always held it against Alfie that he didn't use his degree to help the Civil Defense League or the NAACP, but that doesn't make him a bad lawyer. In fact, he's an expert in these cases. I don't want to see my son lose everything he's worked so hard for because of one little mistake. And if, as Dorinda said, the other driver was responsible, so much the better. Alfie will make sure they pay."

"I didn't say—" Drin started to correct him, but her mother and father were too busy stating their objections to his lawyer to let her get a word in edgewise.

"You weren't there. We spoke to the people in the other car, and there were no injuries. They were lovely, actually. I don't think we should talk about calling a lawyer until we know more about the circumstances," Janine said stubbornly.

"It wouldn't hurt just to call Alfie, and let him know that an accident occurred, would it?" Vivian suggested reasonably.

"You want to be careful about mentioning lawyers too quickly these days," Earl insisted. "If they get even a hint that we might have something to hide . . ." Earl looked at Dorinda.

"But we're not at fault," Ted argued, just as insistently.

"Why are you looking at her like that?" Vivian asked. "Is there something you haven't told us?" Now all eyes were on Drin.

"Get a lawyer, don't get a lawyer, I don't care. I'm going to find out what's happening with Matt." She walked away without looking back, but they followed her, and then Terrence dodged around her and walked past the nurse's station and into the emergency room. She watched him go, her feet faltering. He would be able to get them more detailed information than the nurse, so there didn't seem to be a point to bothering the beleaguered woman yet.

She turned to face the others. "I guess we'd better just wait for Terrence to come back," she said, hoping against hope that her parents could leave the subject of the lawyer alone and the argument wouldn't start again. It was typical that they believed her to be at fault, while the Coopers assumed that she was an innocent victim caught up in this situation through circumstance. She thought again, as she had before, that Matt and she probably should have switched families. He'd have loved a twin brother and two sisters, and her kooky, opinionated, free–spirited parents. She'd have loved to be the only child of this conventional couple, raised in their house of rules and high expectations. They would *never* move the injured victim of an accident. They wouldn't even talk to the driver of the other car, except, perhaps, to exchange insurance information. They would cling to the certainty that their progeny was not responsible for the car crash, no matter what anyone said. They wouldn't stand around badgering their daughter about what she might have said, or done, to cause the accident.

At the first niggling hint of remorse for her actions in the car, Dorinda promptly switched off this line of thought, and proceeded to worry about Matt. Terrence emerged from behind the swinging electronic doors in his white jacket, appearing so professional and adult that Drin was reassured, just looking at him. But the news he came to give them wasn't all good.

"His lung was punctured by one of his broken ribs, and he'll need surgery."

"He will be all right, though, won't he?" Vivian asked breathlessly.

"He should be fine," Terrence soothed. "He asked for you, Drin." She was at the emergency room door before he could add, "Talk fast." She hadn't realized he'd followed until he spoke from directly behind her. "The sedatives will be taking effect soon."

As if from a distance, she heard Matt's parents ask, "Does he know we're here?" She didn't hear her older brother's response. She hurried into the emergency room. She felt sorry for the Coopers, but she wasn't about to cede her time with Matt to his parents. She needed to see him for herself. It was selfish, but it was necessary.

The sight of his body draped in a sheet, ready for surgery, tubes and machines attached to him, wasn't a very reassuring one. He looked toward her and smiled. She moved to him, and stopped a foot and a half away. She could see the bruises, the bandages on his chest, the drawn look of pain on his face. All the emotions she'd just suffered through in the waiting room flooded over her again. In seconds she felt again the guilt, anger, sorrow, remorse, and even betrayal that her family and his parents had made her feel. She wanted to touch him, but she didn't dare.

"Hi, Drin. How ya doing?" he asked.

"I'm fine, you jerk." The words were out of her mouth before she'd even thought them. She wanted to rail at him for turning into that lamppost. They could have shared the brunt of the collision if he'd hit it head–on. Stupid, noble fool. "I give you one little kiss and look what happens. Do you think maybe someone's trying to tell us something?"

"Yeah. We're too old to make out in a car," he tried to joke.

She inched closer to him. "At least *you're* not trying to blame this entirely on me."

"Why would I?"

"My parents did. My mother is convinced my big mouth must have caused the accident. Your father, on the other hand, blames the other driver for rear–ending us."

"It figures. How long did it take him to call Alfie?"

"He hasn't yet. My mom and dad are trying to talk him

out of it," she informed him wryly. "Apparently they don't approve of your family lawyer."

He was smiling again. "I love your folks."

"Why? Because they'd rather wring a confession out of me than some stranger?"

"They're just trying to find out the truth, before they call in the barracudas."

"They didn't rule out the big guns, but they don't like Mr. Hunter." Matt was enjoying this too much, so she added, "They did suggest a television lawyer."

He chuckled, then groaned. "Please don't make me laugh."

"I didn't mean to."

"I can just picture Dad's face when they made that suggestion." Despite the pain he must have been in, Matt's smile was almost gleeful at the thought.

"Great," Drin said dryly. "I thought you were on my side."

"I am, Drin. Always," he said emphatically. She stepped closer. "That doesn't mean I can't love your family. In fact, I love them because of you, and vice versa." His words were starting to slur together, but she caught the gist of his statement.

"You've got to be joking. I'm nothing like them. I *want* a barracuda for a family lawyer. I think your dad was right on."

"That's just because you're feeling guilty," he mumbled. "Because you nearly killed me with that kiss."

"I didn't—" she spluttered. His eyes were drifting closed. "I'm never kissing you again, that's for sure," she said firmly, but she closed the distance between them and brushed her hand over his forehead. His long black eyelashes curved against his cheek, and she traced them with her fingertip.

"It was worth it," he said, so low she had to bend close to hear him. "And your family was great. They rescued us. Maybe saved my life."

"You're hallucinating."

"No," he whispered. His eyes flickered open "The doctor said it."

"Well, I love them, too, but—" His hand covered hers, on his shoulder.

"Shhh," he tried to shush her, but had trouble making the sound. The anaesthetic had a real grip on him now. "Drin? You didn't mean it when you shed 'ou woun't kish me, did you?"

"No," she said gently, soothingly.

He nodded, satisfied. "You will."

"Do you want your mother?" she asked softly. He didn't answer, but when she tried to move her hand, his grip tightened a little, which she took for a negative response to her question. She left her hand where it was and with her other hand, she stroked his forehead. "Everything will be just fine," she kept saying, but she didn't know if she was comforting him or herself.

He was asleep soon, but she couldn't face the people waiting outside of the room. As much as she appreciated his parents, they weren't the most sympathetic souls. She definitely didn't want her family to see her crying. She knew she could count on their comfort, and maybe Matt was right, and she was more one of them than she thought, but at the moment she didn't feel like she belonged with anyone but him. She leaned over and kissed him on the cheek. "You'll be okay," she whispered. "You'll be your old self in a couple of days, and then we'll really have fun. You'll see. I'm not going to hold the past against you anymore. You're back in my life, and I'm not going to let you go again."

A nurse came into the room, and Dorinda gently disengaged herself. She dried her cheeks and blinked her eyes, hoping they wouldn't be too red, and she went out to face their families.

It so often happens that others are measuring us by our past self while we are looking back on that self with a mixture of disgust and sorrow.

George Eliot

19.

Dorinda waited, with his parents and hers, for the operation to be completed. It was very late, and Rodney, Gwen and Herbie went home with Terrence, who wanted to get a few hours' sleep before he came in for his shift in the hospital in the morning.

The Coopers and the Fays were old friends, and no one seemed to feel the need to fill the silence with pointless chatter—a circumstance for which Dorinda was supremely grateful. She couldn't stop thinking about the kiss that had caused all this—and her eagerness to exert her new–found power over him. She couldn't believe what a fool she'd been, to be so afraid of the emotions he'd stirred in her. The simple love she'd felt when she'd kissed his cheek while he lay unconscious in his hospital bed had made her feel a thousand times more vulnerable than she had when they made love, and yet she wouldn't have given up an iota of the pain or fear she felt.

When the surgeon finally came out and told them that it had gone perfectly and Matt would be just fine, her knees threatened to buckle, the relief was so great. Matt was going to be in recovery for at least an hour, so the doctor advised that they go home, and return in the morning. Drin let herself be led out of the hospital and rode home with her parents, to sleep in the same twin bed where she'd so recently become her 'new' self—the fun, spontaneous, carefree Dorinda Fay who cast all her inhibitions to the wind to enjoy a forbidden tryst with her old lover.

She awakened early the next morning. The house was still quiet after their late night. Drin wandered into the kitchen and started the coffee maker, and sat at the chipped formica table her mother insisted on keeping because all of her children had grown up around it. She found comfort in these surroundings which had changed so little in the last twenty years. She had often shared raisin cookies and carrot sticks with Matt after school at this table. She had begged her father to let her hold the long safety matches to the gas grills that long ago ceased lighting when the knobs were turned. Her mother had kissed and then bandaged her and her brothers' skinned knees sitting on the counter next to the sink.

Later, Dorinda had taught her mother how to bake brownies in this room on a visit home from her freshman year of college. She'd argued with her parents about registering with the Libertarian party, here, less than a year ago—when they'd told her they'd decided to end their lifelong affiliation with the Democratic party. A feeling of peace enveloped her as, for the first time since she was a very young girl, Dorinda felt that this was truly her home. Her history was tied into this room, this house, this family. Matt had given her this, half-asleep, half-drunk on sedatives. His oft-repeated assurances that he loved her because of her family, and loved them because they were a part of her finally sank into her brain, her flesh and her bone.

When her mother wandered into the room half an hour later, dressed in her brightly colored sundress patterned after an ancient Egyptian mosaic, Drin stood and hugged her. Janine returned her embrace as if it were the most natural thing in the world, and, without a word, went to the refrigerator and pulled out a pitcher of orange juice. Dorinda couldn't remember ever feeling happier than she did at that moment.

"I'm glad I'm a part of this family." She had to say it aloud, share her revelation with someone.

"We are, too, honey," Willie replied from the doorway. "How is Matthew?"

"I called, and he's fine. Visiting hours start at eight. I'm going to the hospital now," Drin said.

"Can I come?" her aunt asked.

"Can you be ready in ten minutes?" Aunt Willie had been raised in the south, and she'd never gotten dressed in ten minutes in her life, but in her current glorious mood, Dorinda could ask the question without prejudice, and wait patiently for her reply.

"I'll go with your parents, later," Willie said, after mulling it over for a moment. "Pleasure delayed is a pleasure increased."

"Fine. I might see you there." Drin gave her a big hug on her way out of the room, and then flew to her old bedroom to get dressed as quickly as she could.

When she walked into Matt's room, Terrence was there. "Morning, Drin," he said.

"Morning, bro. How's your patient?"

"Technically, he's not mine. I'm just visiting," Terrence answered. "But he seems to be fine. Not too much pain, and—"

"I am still here in the room," Matt interrupted. "I can speak for myself."

"Just giving my sister the benefit of my medical expertise," Terrence excused himself. "Which she did ask for."

"But *I* didn't. And I have enough people poking and prodding me around here without you joining the party,"

Matt said. "Not that I don't appreciate that expertise, but I had planned to tell you I'm not paying for this."

"That's what you think," Terrence said ominously, but he walked to the door.

Dorinda gave him a hug when he would have gone past her. "What's that for?" he asked, surprised. He held her away by her upper arms and examined her face as if he were looking for signs of injury.

Dorinda didn't have any reasonable explanation for him. "For being such a good friend," she said. "And doctor," she hastily added as he shook his head.

"You didn't hit your head last night, did you?" he asked.

His bewilderment made her wonder when she had last told him how proud she was of him. "I'm glad you're my big brother," she said, but her attention wasn't really on Terrence any more. She was watching Matt. His smile grew wider with each passing moment.

"I wouldn't recommend it as a regular thing, but this car crash seems to have brought out a kinder, gentler you," Terrence commented. Then he gave her a quick kiss on the cheek, and strode out of the room.

"Hi, you," Matt said as she approached his bed. "I thought I was dreaming last night, but you meant it, didn't you?"

"What?" Drin asked, going to his bedside and giving him a quick kiss on the cheek.

"What you said last night, when I was drifting off to la la land?"

"What I said?" She hadn't intended for him to hear all that. She had thought he was unconscious. "About having fun?" she asked, trying to remember exactly what she had said when she thought he couldn't hear her.

"About having me back in your life, and not letting me go this time."

"Oh, that." She tried to laugh it off, but he reached out and took her hand and kissed it.

"I heard you," he said, staring into her eyes.

"I was . . . just—" She couldn't think of any excuse for her maudlin rambling. "I'm sorry."

"Why? I'm not," he said, kissing her hand again, and tugging her toward him. She sat on the side of his bed.

"You're not? But you said we never should have gone out. You didn't ever want to love me." These were not the words of a new, fun Dorinda Fay, she realized. She was going back on her promise to herself to leave the past where it belonged. In the past. She could have kicked herself. "Anyway, there's no point rehashing all that again. We're all grown up now, and all that is behind us."

"But . . ." his voice trailed off as he looked into her face. His eyes darkened at what he saw there. She kept her face blank. She was good at hiding her feelings. She'd gotten good at it in a hurry. After all those years of loving him, trusting him, she'd learned in a very short space of time that wearing your heart on your sleeve was not safe.

"You must have misunderstood. There is no way I could have said such a thing," he stated with conviction. "I loved you. I loved you so much it hurt. But I was sixteen years old. We weren't exactly going to get married. Not then. We were kids."

"We could have grown up, together. We could have stayed together. You never know what might have happened." She said it before she thought. Automatically. So much for her promises, to herself and to him. Drin had no intention of making the same mistake twice. Her relationship with Matt was not going to follow the same old pattern. "Whoa. Where'd that come from?" She hit her forehead with the palm of her free hand. "I didn't mean to imply that you need to explain . . . anything, to me. That's why I'm sorry. I think we've been through this already. You shouldn't, I mean, you don't have to justify anything you did." That sounded like an accusation. "Anything that happened," she quickly corrected herself. "I know you never meant to hurt me."

He interrupted. "Breaking up with you was the hardest thing I ever had to do. I never got over it," he said simply.

He sounded so sincere, she couldn't help thinking that maybe it was true. Maybe that was why he'd sought her out after the wedding. He suffered from their breakup, just as she did. Except in his case, since he was the dumper, rather than the dumpee, perhaps his problem was the opposite of hers. Maybe he couldn't walk away from anyone. With Francie, for example, he said he was just waiting for her to end it. Slowly, Dorinda became convinced she was right. She thought about his incredible devotion to Gerome. Theirs seemed to her to be a rather one-sided relationship, and this might explain why. What a pair that would make them. A woman who couldn't commit, and a man who couldn't leave.

"We have ten years to make up for," she said lightly.

"I'm looking forward to really getting to know you again, too," he said.

"Be careful what you wish for," she admonished.

"Starting with how to let go a little. Look at you. You're as stiff as a board. Come down here, where I can reach you," he coaxed

"Why?" Dorinda felt surprisingly nervous.

"I owe you a kiss." Matt smiled. He had bandages on his throat and chest, and a bruise over one eye. If he thought he was ready to pick up where she had left off, those drugs hadn't worn off completely.

"I think I'll wait until I can't do any more damage," she pronounced.

"You didn't do this. I did this. You just helped." She shook her head, but he pulled her toward him with the hand that still held hers. "Come on. Live dangerously," he urged.

"Who's stuck in that bed, full of tubes, and who can walk out of here whenever she wants? I'm not the one who's in danger."

"So what are you so afraid of?" he asked. "I thought you wanted to try something new and different."

"I don't want to hurt you," she said.

"I'll take my chances," he replied. "How about you?"

She felt herself slipping and pulled back. "I don't think so."

"I do," he said. "Just trust me."

"Let's get a doctor in here and see what he or she says about playing games in your present condition," she suggested.

He let go of her arm. "This can't work unless you stop worrying and just go with it."

"Stop worrying? Me?"

"You can do it, Drin. Believe me."

"I will." She kissed his cheek. "When you're better. You just came out of surgery six hours ago."

"If you can't do it now, you'll never be able to." He sounded so disappointed, Dorinda almost gave in. But she knew she was right about this. He wasn't thinking clearly.

"We have plenty of time, Matt," she said soothingly. "Be patient."

"Tell me again, Drin," he demanded. "I can wait if you can just say it."

"What?" she asked, confused.

"What you said last night."

"I don't remember, exactly," she stalled him.

"It doesn't have to be exact," he said wryly.

"I think I said we're going to have some fun."

"And . . ." he prompted.

"And . . ." she hesitated, then took a deep breath and spat out, ". . . and I want you back in my life."

"There, see, was that so hard?" he teased.

"Why do you do this to me?" she asked, plaintively. "Why do you always have to be the one in control?"

"You're a little mixed up, aren't you? You're the one who's always trying to control everything. Me. You. This thing we've got between us."

"You sound just like Gwen," Drin said, trying to smile, though she felt close to tears.

"Your sister knows you. Hell, everyone knows that about you. I only hope it doesn't take a near death–experience every time I want to get close to you."

"Don't be silly. I'm not that hard to get close to," she said.

"You have no idea," he said fervently.

The girls agreed with him. Drin spent most of Sunday with Matt, Monday organizing her new office space, and then that evening she went to her regular drinks date with her friends.

She gave them an update that shocked them, including her new philosophy—more fun, including male companionship, specifically Matt. She mentioned her baptism, by fire, in her own childhood bedroom, and while they were still gaping at her, she told them about the accident.

"You've been busy, girlfriend." Daria shook her head at her.

"I'm not saying I'm planning to marry him, or anything, but why not have some fun with him."

"Why indeed." Tamika snapped her fingers with a flourish, signifying her complete and total agreement.

"Ever since he woke up, though, I feel like I've . . . lost control of the situation."

"Why's that?" Claire stared at Drin consideringly.

"Maybe because I have?" she said. "When he was under anaesthesia I made myself a promise that we wouldn't let what happened before happen again, and he heard me."

"There's nothing wrong with that," Tamika said blithely. "Not much chance of that happening, is there?"

"I don't think so. Everything is different now. I'm not sixteen anymore, right?"

"Right," Daria said, but she didn't sound very confident.

"So what are you afraid of?" Claire asked, eager to cut to the heart of the matter as usual.

"I don't know that I'm afraid, exactly. I know what my

limitations are. And he's got some problems of his own. So I don't want this relationship to spiral into . . . something we—neither of us—can handle. But Matt says I'm just afraid to relinquish control. That I've become some kind of nut on the subject."

"You knew that," Daria said.

"You didn't know that?" Tamika said, surprised.

"What? That I'm a freak?" Dorinda asked.

"Not a freak, exactly. Well, maybe a bit of a control freak," Claire said with her usual honesty. "But more like a . . . well, I don't know. That's why your own mother calls you Worrywart, isn't it?"

"Those are two separate things. I'm a worrier, I always have been. The queen of angst. But that's not the same as wanting to . . . play God—as Gwennie says. You make it sound like I'm on some kind of power trip."

"Well . . ." Daria drew the word out until Dorinda was ready to take offense. Then she relented. "No, but . . . let me put it this way. You do have a tendency to try to keep a handle on things. You're a normal, red–blooded, healthy woman who has been celibate for almost two years. Why did you do that? Why fight mother nature?"

"I told you. I didn't need the hassles of being involved with a man. Sex isn't worth it. And *mother* nature didn't have anything to do with it. Abstinence didn't hurt me a bit."

"You seem to have changed your mind about that," Claire pointed out.

"Not really. I still think I was right to do what I did. But circumstances change. As someone said to me: all work and no play will make me a dull girl. I've got a new business, and I don't want to get swallowed up by it. Recently I've realized that I'm in danger of becoming out of touch, working on my own. I need outside interests. I've got karate, but that's not intellectually stimulating. And Matt was there."

"So it's his brain that interests you?" Tamika said, smirking.

The others chuckled, and Dorinda laughed, too. "You're one to talk," she said to Tamika. "You won't even date a guy who doesn't work out. Of course, I'm interested in . . . other things, but it is nice to be around a man who isn't threatened by my intellect. We can talk about everything—computers, for example."

"I thought you were going to use him to take your mind off work," Daria said sarcastically.

"That, too," Drin shot back at her, grinning, and they all laughed.

"Now who's talking smut?" Tamika asked.

"I am," Drin declared.

"I'm just saying that you don't have things as under control as you think," Daria said. "You can't. No one can. There are some things we just can't control. Hormones, for one."

"I think I've proven that my libido doesn't control me, during the last couple of years," Dorinda said arrogantly.

"I meant that we don't choose *who* we're attracted to," Daria finished. "You talk a good game, about not needing a man in your life—"

Claire interrupted. "Until now."

"But I think you were just scared to take a chance. You still are."

"We all are," Tamika added.

"Maybe I am. But I don't think so. You think I'm afraid of Matt?" Drin asked defiantly.

"Yeah," Claire said. They all nodded.

"I'm not going to fall in love with him again. I know better than that. I'm just going to . . ." Her voice trailed off as she looked into three pairs of skeptical brown eyes.

"We know, we know." Claire looked around at the others, who nodded, then back at Drin. "It's like the no-dating thing. You're going to prove another one of your theories. How does this one go? You can have lots of fun and games with this guy, without risking anything, because you already know what your limits are, or something like that, right?''

"You don't believe I can do it, do you?"

This time they all shook their heads and Daria spoke for them. "Circumstances are always changing. You can try to fool yourself if you want to, but you don't have any more control than anyone else, no matter how much logic you try to apply to the situation, things just don't go the way we plan." That was the kind of thing she would have expected Claire to say, not her rebellious best friend.

Drin stared at Daria in amazement. "So much for being a strong, progressive black woman." Daria was the one who came up with the theory that traditional relationships were no good for them, and therefore had a different man for each night of the week. She was supposed to be on Dorinda's side.

It took a moment for her to think of a reply. "I'm not trying to fool anybody. But I still believe in applying logic to solve problems. And this is the most logical solution I could think of."

Claire sighed. "I hope it works out."

"You'll have fun testing it, anyway." Tamika grinned.

Daria shrugged her shoulders. "Good luck, girlfriend," she said.

And ruin'd love when it is built anew
Grows fairer than at first, more strong
Far greater.

Shakespeare

20.

Drin went to the gym on Tuesday. She hadn't been working out with her usual regularity lately, and that combined with her slight injuries left her in a little pain after the session. She soaked in the tub that night, but her muscles were still sore when she woke up the next day.

She went to the hospital to find that Matt was being released, and she took him home in a taxi. His apartment was not far from hers, but the building had a lot more security, which was probably a good thing, as he had quite a little electronics collection in his living–room. On a large work table were some of the same computer components she owned, but his array also included quite a few devices in various stages of assembly, and the tools needed to build, test and modify them. She decided she'd explore later.

"Bedroom?" He pointed, and she led him straight through the living/dining–room area, passing a mismatched assortment of furniture he had been collecting that somehow looked right together. They both collapsed on the bed, groaning.

"We make quite a pair," she said.

"At least I didn't do this to myself," he said.

"How can you look so good without taking any exercise at all?" she asked.

"Sadist," he accused, then inhaled sharply as she eased his sneakers over his toes.

"Wimp," she shot back at him.

"Who, me? I'm not the one who's afraid to say I love you."

Drin was in the process of removing his socks and she stopped. Then she got back to it, joking, "You'll say anything to get me to take care of you, won't you?"

He sat up, slowly and carefully. She came around the bed and started to help him out of his shirt. He didn't move a muscle. "I love you, Drin. This is no joke." She unbuttoned his shirt, and eased it off his broad chocolate–brown shoulders. "So?" He waited.

"What am I supposed to say to that?" He had worn home the pants they gave him in the hospital; his had been cut off. "Lie down."

"What will you give me if I do?" His bandages were clean and white, and stood out against his dark chest. They didn't hide the muscles of his flat abdomen. Dorinda swallowed hard. She wanted to take care of him, feel tenderly toward him, like she had in the hospital, but it was difficult to think of him lying helpless and childlike in that hospital bed when he looked so enticingly masculine. She tried to push him gently backward, into his bed, but he wouldn't move.

"You should have stayed in the hospital a few more days. Your insurance would have covered it. Why did you have to come home so soon?"

"I had a feeling you might be willing to take care of me. And I wanted to be alone with you."

"Will you please lie down? I don't want your stitches to open up."

"You didn't answer my question," he said provocatively.

"What will I give you? How about whatever you want?"

"Good enough." He lay back down. "How about a private nurse for the next few days?"

"Sure," she agreed. Drin had been planning to try to take care of him anyway. "But why do I sense a game of doctor coming on?" She wanted to keep it light. She couldn't believe what he'd said to her.

"Not a bad idea," he said. "But I don't think I'm up to it right now. Maybe later." She stood over him, trying to figure out if there was anything more she could do to make him comfortable. He looked as if he were in pain. But his eyes kept searching her face.

"Would you like a codeine?" she asked in her best brisk nurse intonations.

"Sure. Especially if it'll get you to open up to me again."

She got the codeine from her purse. She'd called in the prescription to her pharmacy and it had been waiting when she'd stopped to get it on the way to his place. "Don't you think you're rushing things a little?"

"Rushing it? No. This is rushing it. Dorinda Fay, will you marry me?"

"Is this a new method for getting women into your bed?"

"What? Puncturing a lung?"

"Sleep with them a couple of times and propose?"

"Only if they're really great in bed." She could tell the codeine was starting to take effect. He wasn't looking so intently into her eyes anymore. He tried to keep the contact, but Drin evaded him. "Drinda, *will you marry me?*"

"What in the world would make you ask me that?" Dorinda couldn't understand where this was coming from. She didn't think she'd said or done anything to make Matt think she expected a proposal from him.

"You *said* you were never going to let me go again."

"When did I say that?"

"You know when," he said.

"I never said never," she said stubbornly.

"It was implied."

"It was inferred," she insisted. "And I just meant I

wanted to have you around. I didn't want to keep running away from you. I didn't mean you had to marry me.'' Her heart, her pride, and her dignity were all at stake. She could sleep with Matthew, even love him, but she couldn't marry him. It was too dangerous.

"I know I don't have to. You've made it abundantly clear that you're just tolerating my presence until you can think of some excuse to get rid of me. I want to make it as hard as possible for you, that's all.''

"Very romantic," she said sarcastically.

"It's hard to be romantic when you're flat on your back, aching, and your brain is sloshing around in your head. But if that's what you want . . .''

"No, no. I prefer you like this.''

"Helpless and at your mercy?''

"All sweet, and affectionate, and a little bit out of it. I can see the real you when you're like this.''

"And, of course, you get to remain completely in control.''

"Don't start that again," she warned.

"Okay, okay. I won't say it. But won't you trust me enough to at least try to take me seriously? Do you . . .'' He was interrupted by a big yawn. ". . . remember when you said you'd marry me. We were eight, I think.''

Drin remembered. "You wanted to share my ice cream cone at the time, I think, and argued that married people could put their mouths on each other's food. Twenty years later, you're still trying to convince me to do things that probably aren't healthy. I just can't figure out why. This isn't a Gerome thing, is it? You're not doing this because you feel guilty about . . . No.'' She answered her own question. He'd drifted off to sleep. "I doubt you'd offer yourself up in marriage just to appease your guilt at walking away.'' She puzzled over it for a while, but finally gave up and curled up next to him on the bed and took a nap.

* * *

He woke her up with a kiss. "This is nice. I could grow to like this."

"I was engaged once. I thought I loved him, but it just seemed the next logical step after moving in together. We moved in together because it was more convenient than living apart." She suddenly realized that Matt might have been motivated by a similar impulse. A man who couldn't walk away from people might well feel that; since the relationship would be pretty permanent anyway, he might as well legalize it.

He shook his head at her. "Convenient? You are the most inconvenient, stubborn, opinionated woman I know. This is passion. Pure and simple. Why can't you believe I love you and I want to marry you?"

"It's hard when you sweet talk me like that, but I guess I think that passion, as you call it, sprang up a little too fast."

"We've loved each other since we were kids. At least you said you did, and I know I did. We're adults now, and we're together again, and I happen to believe we're very compatible. Marriage is the next logical step."

"How do *you* define logic?" she asked, amazed at his reasoning. "Because jumping from exes, into reluctant lovers, and then—"

"I was never reluctant."

"Think back to that first morning after. You didn't look any happier than I did when you woke up."

"That's because I thought I'd blown it with you." She gave him a skeptical look. "All right, maybe I wasn't absolutely certain we'd done the right thing. We hadn't seen each other in years, and we'd barely exchanged ten words with each other," he admitted.

"That's all I'm saying. Then you try to buy my forgiveness

with that big contract for my new company. From there, you want to be married?"

"You skipped a step. We did have dinner, and in case I need to remind you, sex, at your parents' house."

"Oooh, yeah." She hit her forehead with the palm of her hand. "I forgot all about that. I guess you're right. Those are all the ingredients for a perfect marriage."

"Trust me. I know we can make this work."

"Oh God. Can't we just be friends again first? And maybe a little more." She reached up and grabbed his chin and gave him a hard, wet kiss. "I've already gone back on my promise to myself never to forgive you for what you did to me, and . . . and sacrificed my principles for you. What else do you want from me?"

"This." He leaned down and kissed her again, just as hard and as wet as she had, but slowly, with an intensity that sparked a fire in the pit of her stomach. "Forever," he said when he lifted his head. Dark fires glowed in his eyes.

"Mmmm," she made an appreciative noise. "That was nice. Let's do it again."

He obliged her, but after the kiss, he lifted his mouth from hers again. "You've got to admit, we're very compatible."

"We certainly are." Drin felt drunk. Again. His kisses always seemed to do that to her. But she was starting to get used to it. Again. And that was dangerous. She forgot about the danger as she turned into his heat and felt the hard length of his body against hers.

They made love, very slowly and carefully, and after the fire within her had consumed itself, she turned to him and looked into his glowing eyes. "Okay, you got me."

"What does that mean?" he asked.

She got out of bed, pulling his shirt on over her nakedness, and went into the kitchen for a glass of water. When she came back she'd had time to think about her answer to his question.

"I do trust you. It was me I didn't trust."

"And now you do?"

"I realized that I was always scared to let myself love anyone because after you left, I thought that meant I couldn't be loved again. Not like that. And, of course, I kept getting hurt, trying to protect myself. When it came to dating men, I chose very poorly and I got hurt. Which, again, I blamed on you. Because I chose them specifically so I wouldn't get hurt. I wasn't really loving. I was testing. And I don't want to do that anymore. You were right. I was afraid to be vulnerable. But I can't control you, and I can't control love."

"You love me," he said, a wide smile breaking across his face.

"I've always loved you. If you want to get married, I'll give it a try. It's crazy, but, let's do it."

"Why?" He sounded genuinely curious.

"I told you before. Remember? I'm going to do things differently now. I'm going to let my heart lead my head for a change. The logical approach just doesn't seem to be working for me."

The next month went by in a whirl of sex and wedding arrangements. Drin felt like a new woman. Work took a back seat to her relationship with Matt—something that had never happened during her adult life.

She was surprised at how easy it was to be spontaneous, loving, and just plain fun. She laughed a lot. When she went to buy her wedding dress with her mother and her sister, they joked and fooled around, and Dorinda forgot to be defensive or anxious and just enjoyed herself and her family.

She and Matt only had one real argument. He wanted Gerome to be his best man—but she'd seen Gerome on one of his alcoholic binges and she didn't trust him to show up sober, or at all. They went around and around the issue, sleeping apart for the first time since she'd agreed to marry Matt. Finally, she gave in.

"If you don't have a best man at your wedding, don't blame me," she admonished. When he would have continued arguing she said, "You won. Now let's make up. We've never done that before." It was fantastic.

When the big day came, despite the relaxed attitude she'd adopted concerning the preparations, everything was actually quite beautiful. Like her twin, it appeared she had a talent for arranging quicky weddings. Gerome showed up on time, and in his morning suit, and she conceded to her groom that he'd been right and she'd been wrong. She walked down the aisle, as Gwen had only a few months before, and this time she was smiling, and felt like she didn't have a worry in the world.

It was a great feeling. She recited the wedding vow she'd written with a heart full of joy. But when Matt started to avow himself to her, he modified the words they'd spent so much time working on together. It was a minor glitch, but the golden day seemed to dim a little. Her smile, as she walked back down the aisle, had slipped a notch.

Drin tried not to let it bother her. She really did try. But she couldn't help commenting on it again and again. Each time someone complimented them on the wedding, on the vows, on the marriage itself, she made a sarcastic remark about Matt's memory, his retention, his devotion. They were leaving on their honeymoon the next morning, and so she finished up the packing that night before they went to bed.

"Do you want to take your hiking boots?" she asked.

"Sure," he answered. "Whatever you think."

"You are very quiet."

"Mmm hmmm." He was lying in the bed, watching her, with a strange look in his eye.

"So what are you thinking about?" Drin prodded him.

"Today. The wedding. Us."

"Yeah," she smiled as she thought about it. "It was almost perfect."

"Almost?" He seemed to sit at attention suddenly, though she didn't see him move an inch.

"Well, there was that little mistake you made with the vows."

"I didn't make any mistake. I said what I wanted to say."

"But we agreed—"

"We agreed we would write vows for each other. I didn't realize that I was going to be graded on mine."

Drin was bewildered and hurt by his attack. "I thought you liked what we wrote."

"I did," he sighed. "Forget it."

"I don't want to forget it. This is our wedding night, and I want it to be perfect, don't you? Are you angry with me?"

"I'm not angry. I'm a little frustrated, but I'll get over it. Why don't you come to bed?"

"Let's talk about this," she said. "I didn't mean to make you feel like you were being graded."

"Maybe that was the wrong choice of words. I thought we were partners, equals, but this wedding was all yours. Everything had to be done a certain way. Perfect."

"Didn't you want it to be perfect? We're only going to get married once. I wanted it to be a day we would remember forever."

"How can it be? When you're so concerned with perfection, you can't enjoy yourself. It's the little things that don't go quite right that you remember."

"What do you mean?" she asked, truly puzzled.

"You know that story you were telling at the reception, about Gwen's wedding?"

"How Aunt Josephine embarrassed me when I walked down the aisle?"

"Right. You remember that moment, don't you?"

"Of course. I wanted the world to open up and swallow me.

"But that was the exact moment when I saw you again. Really saw *you*, my little Drinda from next door. The little sister I never had, who grew up to be the most beautiful girl I ever saw, and then the most amazing woman I ever knew. The way you held your head up a little higher when she said that, and kept on walking without missing a beat, *that* was my Drin, not the perfect girl in the white dress.''

"You didn't like that dress?'' She tried to tease him out of his serious mood.

"Don't make this into a joke, Drin.''

"All right,'' She tried to mollify him. "I'm sorry.'' She walked to the bed. "Whatever it is I did, I apologize. Okay?'' She leaned over to kiss him, but he turned his head so that her lips only grazed his cheek. "I guess it's not okay.''

"Listen to me, honey. I know you've been trying really hard to be this . . . other person. I love you for it, because I think you're doing it partly for me. But it's not going to work. You are who you are.''

"Who's that?'' she interrupted, offended.

He went on as though she hadn't spoken. "I love you, Drin. I love your illogical logic, and your worrying, and your vulnerability. You don't have to pretend you're so tough.''

"I'm not,'' she protested.

"I don't think you know what you're doing,'' he responded. "But you haven't changed. Not really. All these so—called changes are on the surface and they make you seem like a . . . caricature of yourself.''

"You chose an odd time to tell me this. Do you want to ruin our wedding night, too?'' she asked impatiently.

He pushed her out of the way and stood "Haven't you heard a word I said? *I didn't ruin our wedding.* You did that all by yourself, brooding about that one little thing that didn't go exactly like you planned. We chose to write those vows so that we could say how we felt, in front of everyone we love, in our own words. It wasn't a question of right or wrong. At least I didn't think it was. And how can telling you how I feel ruin our wedding night? Isn't that what married people are supposed to do? That's all I've been trying to do, all day."

"Calm down, Matt," Dorinda was on the verge of tears, but she held them in. She didn't want him to see how vulnerable she felt. "I'm trying to understand."

"Listen to me, it's not that difficult. What don't you get?"

"Why are you yelling at me?" Her voice was calm, in direct contrast to the turmoil inside her. It was how she always reacted to confrontation.

"I'm frustrated. I told you," he said.

"I heard you. I see that. I'm . . . I'm sorry." She didn't know how to end this argument, how to get back to where they'd been.

"What are you sorry for?" He loomed over her, tall and dark, and suddenly a stranger. "Huh? What?"

"I'm sorry I didn't understand. I'll try not to . . . not to . . . I don't know what I'll try. Not to be perfect? Is that what you want?" She was starting to grow angry herself. "Just tell me what you want and I'll do it."

"So you can have your perfect wedding night? Is that it?"

"What's wrong with that?" she asked. "I just want to drink some champagne with you, make love, wake up happy. Is that so terrible."

"Maybe champagne isn't what we need. Maybe this argument is the perfect aphrodisiac for our wedding night."

"Maybe for you," she accused.

"Drin, honey, I'm not doing this to ruin it for you. I have to say it. You asked me, and I think we can talk to each other, about anything. We used to be able to do that."

"When?" she asked suspiciously. "When were we able to do that?"

"Before," he said vaguely.

"When we were sixteen? Are you seriously comparing

our relationship now to the one we had then?" she asked in disbelief.

"No. Not comparing it. Trying to build on it."

"It's dead, Matt. Dead. We buried it." She, for one, didn't want it brought back to life. It was too painful.

"Maybe we should unbury it? Maybe that's what's wrong with us, now."

"What's wrong with me, you mean," she said defensively.

"With us, with you and me. There's something we're missing here, and maybe that's it. I don't know. That's what we're trying to figure out, isn't it?"

"You are. I'm happy letting the past stay buried, and I didn't think we had anything left to figure out. If you had doubts, why the hell didn't you say so before this? Why wait until after the wedding?" She couldn't keep the hurt tone from her voice, but she wouldn't let him see her cry.

He walked to the doorway and back again. "I wasn't waiting. It just happened, that's all."

"That's not good enough. How long have you been feeling this way? When were you planning to tell me?" she hammered away.

"I didn't plan anything."

"Well, that's good," Drin said, reverting to sarcasm. "I'm glad this wasn't part of some grand scheme you concocted, because if it was, I'd have to say your timing stinks."

With a groan of frustration, he walked back to the door. As he walked out he spoke, without turning back to her. "This is never going to work." Then he disappeared.

Drin went back to her packing. She didn't know what else to do. She wanted to scream, cry, run after him. But she couldn't. She didn't see how it would help the situation. It was when she was lying alone, in his bed, beneath her sheets, that she realized he was right. She had been behaving exactly like her old self—trying to maintain control. She had wanted to keep from getting hurt again. And it hadn't worked.

Forewarned, and forearmed, she still lay in the dark,

wishing for Matthew Cooper, who had left her again. Nothing had changed. Certainly not her. In fact, she'd regressed. She was in exactly the same position she'd been in twelve years ago. Except that this time, she couldn't blame Matt's fickle heart, or a cheerleader, or anyone, but Dorinda Fay. She had spent ten years directing her energies, and all her logic, and everything in her, striving to avoid this very situation.

He slipped into their bed, an hour later, and she was so happy that all she could do was turn and hug him close. He held her tight for a moment, then tried to look down at her. Drin realized he would see the tears on her face, and held on tighter, hoping they would dry, but they just kept coming. She looked up at him.

"Oh, baby, you're crying." He dried her tears. It was worth letting him see her weakness to have that thumb stroking her cheek.

"I love you," Drin said.

"Shhh, I love you, too," Matt's voice was so full of tenderness it brought even more tears, and a pain in her chest.

The fear was still with her. "But you'll leave me," she said.

"I'd never leave you," he vowed, raining kisses on her cheeks, her eyes, the corners of her mouth.

"But you did," she said, gasping for breath.

"I just went to take a walk. To think about us. I wasn't leaving. I wouldn't do that."

She pulled him close again and buried her face in his chest. The words were pulled out of her almost against her will. "But you did. You fell in love with someone else." She felt exposed, completely vulnerable. But she couldn't hold it in any longer. The fear.

"I'm so in love with you, I couldn't stay away if I wanted to. I didn't know what love was, then. I do now." He lifted her chin, gently but firmly, until she was looking into his eyes. "I will never leave you, Drin. Never. Ever. Again." Dorinda Fay Cooper suddenly understood the one fact that had eluded her all these years about love. There was nothing logical about it and no way to control it. She was just going to have to live with that. It was a little bit scary, but she thought she could learn to do it.

And, for once, Drin wasn't worried.

COMING IN JULY . . .

FIRE AND DESIRE,   (1-58314-024-7, $4.99/$6.50)
by Brenda Jackson
Geologist Corithians Avery, and head foreman of Madaris Explorations, Trevor Grant, are assigned the same business trip to South America. Each has bittersweet memories of a night two years ago when she walked in on him—Trevor half-naked and she wearing nothing more than a black negligee. The hot climate is sure to rouse suppressed desires.

HEART OF STONE,   (1-58314-025-5, $4.99/$6.50)
by Doris Johnson
Disillusioned with dating, wine shop manager Sydney Cox has settled for her a mundane life of work and lonely nights. Then unexpectedly, love knocks her down. Executive security manager Adam Stone enters the restaurant and literally runs into Sydney. The collision cracks the barriers surrounding their hearts . . . and allows love to creep in.

NIGHT HEAT,   (1-58314-026-3, $4.99/$6.50)
by Simona Taylor
When Trinidad tour guide Rhea De Silva is assigned a group of American tourists at the last minute, things don't go too well. Journalist Marcus Lucien is on tour to depict a true to life picture of the island, even if the truth isn't always pretty. Rhea fears his candid article may deflect tourism. But the night heat makes the attraction between the two grow harder to resist.

UNDER YOUR SPELL,   (1-58314-027-1, $4.99/$6.50)
by Marcia King-Gamble
Marley Greaves returns to San Simone for a job as research assistant to Dane Carmichael, anthropologist and author. Dane's reputation on the island has been clouded, but Marley is drawn to him entirely. So when strange things happen as they research Obeah practices, Marley sticks by him to help dispel the rumors . . . and the barrier around his heart.

Available wherever paperbacks are sold, or order direct from the Publisher. Send cover price plus 50¢ per copy for mailing and handling to BET Books, c/o Kensington Publishing Corp., Consumer Orders, or call (toll free) 888-345-BOOK, to place your order using Mastercard or Visa. Residents of New York, Washington D.C., and Tennessee must include sales tax. DO NOT SEND CASH.

ROMANCES THAT SIZZLE
FROM ARABESQUE

AFTER DARK, by Bette Ford   (0-7860-0442-8, \$4.99/\$6.50)
Taylor Hendricks' brother is the top NBA draft choice. She wants to protect
him from the lure of fame and wealth, but meets basketball superstar Donald
Williams in an exclusive Detroit restaurant. Donald is determined to prove
that she is wrong about him. In this game all is at stake . . . including Taylor's
heart.

BEGUILED, by Eboni Snoe   (0-7860-0046-5, \$4.99/\$6.50)
When Raquel Mason agrees to impersonate a missing heiress for just one
night and plans go awry, a daring abduction makes her the captive of seductive
Nate Bowman. Together on a journey across exotic Caribbean seas to the
perilous wilds of Central America, desire looms in their hearts. But when the
masquerade is over, will their love end?

CONSPIRACY, by Margie Walker   (0-7860-0385-5, \$4.99/\$6.50)
Pauline Sinclair and Marcellus Cavanaugh had the love of a lifetime. Until
Pauline had to leave everything behind. Now she's back and their love is as
strong as ever. But when the President of Marcellus's company turns up dead
and Pauline is the prime suspect, they must risk all to their love.

FIRE AND ICE, by Carla Fredd   (0-7860-0190-9, \$4.99/\$6.50)
Years of being in the spotlight and a recent scandal regarding her ex-fianceé
and a supermodel, the daughter of a Georgia politician, Holly Aimes has turned
cold. But when work takes her to the home of late-night talk show host Mi-
chael Williams, his relentless determination melts her cool.

HIDDEN AGENDA, by Rochelle Alers   (0-7860-0384-7, \$4.99/\$6.50)
To regain her son from a vengeful father, Eve Blackwell places her trust in
dangerous and irresistible Matt Sterling to rescue her abducted son. He accepts
this last job before he turns a new leaf and becomes an honest rancher. As
they journey from Virginia to Mexico they must enter a charade of marriage.
But temptation is too strong for this to remain a sham.

INTIMATE BETRAYAL, by Donna Hill   (0-7860-0396-0, \$4.99/\$6.50)
Investigative reporter, Reese Delaware, and millionaire computer wizard, Maxwell Knight are both running from their pasts. When Reese is assigned to
profile Maxwell, they enter a steamy love affair. But when Reese begins to
piece her memory, she stumbles upon secrets that link her and Maxwell, and
threaten to destroy their newfound love.

*Available wherever paperbacks are sold, or order direct from the
Publisher. Send cover price plus 50¢ per copy for mailing and
handling to Kensington Publishing Corp., Consumer Orders,
or call (toll free) 888-345-BOOK, to place your order using
Mastercard or Visa. Residents of New York and Tennessee
must include sales tax. DO NOT SEND CASH.*